"Think you'll ever take the plunge?"

Luke expanded on the question, though he had no idea why he was asking. "Picture life with four or five mean redheads running around your empty house?"

Jen snorted. "Can you even imagine me as a mother?" She crossed her arms over her chest. "I came down here to talk about Joseph and his math homework. You're tricky."

"Unless you're going to tell me whatever it is you and Joseph are hiding, I'll pick a new topic. Maybe kissing."

She blinked at him. "You think I can't handle a kiss without spilling the beans?" She leaned over the armrest of her chair. "Test me."

Before he'd decided he was going to do it, Luke had his lips pressed to hers. Instead of spice and heat, Jen's kiss was sweet and perfect. Nothing like he would have imagined.

But now he could picture starting each day with one like it... And, oh...that wasn't going to happen.

Dear Reader,

When I began this series about three friends who win the lottery, I spent some time imagining what I'd do with an unexpected windfall. It's fun to daydream, but my practical side kept getting in the way!

My no-nonsense heroine Jen dreams of a comfortable home with the space she's always wanted and the chance to buy new instead of making do with hand-me-downs. When the Hollisters move in across the street, she adds one more goal: chasing away the cop who tried to bully her friends. That cop turns out to be a good man doing his very best to keep his family, a collection of foster kids and the woman who brought them together, safe. Both Jen and Luke understand that "family" is a collection of the people who love you, and nothing matters more. I hope you enjoy spending time with them.

If you'd like to know more about my books and what's coming next, enter fun giveaways or meet my dog, Jack, please visit me at cherylharperbooks.com. I'm also on Facebook (CherylHarperRomance) and Twitter (@cherylharperbks). I'd love to chat!

Cheryl Harper

HEARTWARMING

A Home Come True

———

USA TODAY Bestselling Author

Cheryl Harper

H HARLEQUIN® HEARTWARMING™

Recycling programs
for this product may
not exist in your area.

ISBN-13: 978-0-373-36825-9

A Home Come True

Copyright © 2017 by Cheryl Harper

This edition published by arrangement with Harlequin Books S.A.

For questions and comments about the quality of this book, please contact us at CustomerService@Harlequin.com.

® and TM are trademarks of Harlequin Enterprises Limited or its corporate affiliates. Trademarks indicated with ® are registered in the United States Patent and Trademark Office, the Canadian Intellectual Property Office and in other countries.

Printed in U.S.A.

Cheryl Harper discovered her love for books and words as a little girl, thanks to a mother who made countless library trips and an introduction to Laura Ingalls Wilder's Little House stories. Whether stories are set in the prairie, the American West, Regency England or Earth a hundred years in the future, Cheryl enjoys strong characters who make her laugh. Now Cheryl spends her days searching for the right words while she stares out the window and her dog, Jack, snoozes beside her. And she considers herself very lucky to do so.

For more information about Cheryl's books, visit her online at cherylharperbooks.com or follow her on Twitter, @cherylharperbks.

Books by Cheryl Harper

Harlequin Heartwarming

Keeping Cole's Promise
Heart's Refuge
Winner Takes All
The Bluebird Bet
A Minute on the Lips

Visit the Author Profile page
at Harlequin.com for more titles.

This one's for my family—relatives, old friends, new friends and internet friends far, far away who encourage me when I need it.

CHAPTER ONE

DAYDREAMING ABOUT SHOVING a buttered dinner roll into Sarah Hillman's mouth to keep her from laughing again was a sign that it was time to leave the party. Almost everyone Jennifer Neil loved was there, but the noise of so many conversations, the heat of too many people in a cramped space and Sarah's joyful laugh had hit the overwhelming stage. Jen needed some quiet, some breathing room. Soon.

Food this good should mean no leftovers but three of Rebecca's perfect buttery-soft dinner rolls were left, and they would make excellent missiles to launch across the table. Sarah's best choice for return fire would be the grilled asparagus at her elbow. Jen hated asparagus. A food fight would not be the smartest way to maintain their peace.

Stephanie Yates was telling a story about a Peruvian lizard in her Peruvian shower that would have been hilarious except for two things. Jen had already heard this story half a dozen times, and Sarah Hillman had tipped her head back to laugh again. The throbbing pain in Jen's temple resumed.

When the walls started to close like this, Jen knew she needed to exit. She was suffocating. No matter how hard it would be, she had to save herself.

Unfortunately, she'd somehow landed as far away from the front door as possible in Rebecca Lincoln's cramped dining room. Rebecca had spent enough of the lottery winnings that she, Stephanie Yates and Jen had shared to fill a small bank vault redoing the kitchen, but nothing on the rest of her cozy house. With all of her new spare time and mad money, Jen had become a home-improvement show devotee so she knew any designer worth his or her paycheck should have insisted on knocking down a wall. Open plan was where it was at.

If the gathering had been made up of Jen, Rebecca and Stephanie only, Jen would have had zero trouble breathing. They'd spent so many Friday evenings here during high school that it was sort of Jen's home, too.

Even Sarah, her former nemesis, was growing on her. When Rebecca had informed Jen that the three of them would be giving away Rebecca's share of the winnings to worthy projects, Jen would never have imagined Sarah Hillman and her animal shelter would become so important to them and to Jen, in particular. If Sarah hadn't been such a spoiled mean girl in high school, she might have rounded out their group then.

Since Sarah and Jen's stepbrother, Will, the guy entrusted with Rebecca's funds, were now *together*, it just made sense to keep a close eye on her.

Honestly though, spending time with these women was easy. They accepted her rough edges.

But the other Musketeers had insisted on dragging along their beefcake, so the whole place was exceeding maximum occupancy. Rebecca's parents had been lucky. They'd bailed on this going-away dinner early, blaming a long day of flying. They'd taken a break from their Floridian retirement to be here to wish their son, Daniel, and his happy bride well.

There were still too many bodies crammed

in this space. It didn't take a math teacher to figure that equation out. Someone should call the fire marshal. She'd do it herself but her phone was in her purse by the door.

"I've got to get to the door," Jen muttered and craned her neck to check to see if she could maneuver between Rebecca's sparkling quartz-topped breakfast bar and the row of chairs.

The only person who'd managed to sit quietly through dinner, Cole Ferguson, was crammed in the corner next to her. While Rebecca had been buzzing back and forth from the kitchen, he hadn't taken his eyes off her. For most of the dinner, he'd managed to keep his eyes on his own plate, but it was impossible to miss how he turned toward Rebecca every time she spoke or her arm brushed his.

Sure, it's sweet now. But all the lovesickness in the room will be gross pretty soon.

Especially for the only single in the room of couples.

When Jen finally got his attention, Cole studied the room. "The door? Impossible." The big guy leaned back to carefully drape one arm over Rebecca's chair.

"Impossible, huh?" Jen twisted her chin to

crack the tense vertebrae in her neck. "When you say that, it's like waving a red cape and I'm the bull that's going to charge right out of here."

His rough laugh spurred her on, but no matter which direction she looked, there was someone blocking her. Fine. If she couldn't go high, she'd go low. Very low.

Thankful for her earlier decision to wear the designer jeans that had once belonged to Sarah, but had become Jen's favorite pair by way of the consignment shop, Jen tried to turn every bone in her body to mush. Slithering out of the chair with this little room wasn't easy, but once she was on her hands and knees under the table, it was a piece of cake to crawl right down the middle.

"These floors are spotless," Jen muttered with a shake of her head.

As soon as she reached the end of the table, Jen tapped Stephanie's knee and waited for her to check below the table. When it took a second tap, Jen started to wonder what sort of life Steph had lived in Peru.

The tablecloth lifted. Stephanie blinked twice at her.

"Scoot. I need out." Jen waved a hand and waited impatiently for Steph to move.

When an opening wide enough for her to wiggle through opened, Jen slowly stood and brushed off the knees of her jeans before stomping her feet to loosen her pant legs down into her boots. Then she held both arms out and stretched. This was going to work.

When she turned around, all the conversation had paused. Six pairs of eyes were locked on her.

Jen smoothed her hair behind one ear and smiled. Then she pointed at Cole. "He said it couldn't be done."

Every head swiveled to study Cole, the ex-convict who'd landed at Paws for Love in desperate need of a job to make good on his second chance. He held up both hands. "That's not how it went down, but…"

Rebecca grinned as she pressed a kiss against Cole's cheek. The pink that spread across his face would have been cute if he hadn't had a glare that could stop a train. That had to have come in handy in prison. Rebecca said, "Mistake. Nobody tells her what she can't do."

Cole opened his mouth to argue and

thought better of it. Jen was only doing what her friends expected of her. Being the first to bail on a party was her way.

"I guess this means you're leaving," Stephanie asked and opened her arms for a hug.

Saying goodbye was almost as hard as enduring one more minute of the noise and total sensory overload that came with crowds, even crowds of people she loved, but Jen hadn't come this far to quit now.

"Yeah," Jen said, surprised at the frog in her throat that accompanied the overwhelming emotion. She wasn't sure when Stephanie would be back in Texas, but June or the end of the school year would be the first chance she'd have to travel to Lima to visit. It was a long way away. "We'll always have Facebook." Facebook was filled with annoyances, too, but it was quiet and she did love seeing photos of the work Stephanie and Daniel did with HealthyAmericas.

"Sure." Stephanie squeezed her hard and fast and then stepped back. This was a tried-and-true goodbye, one that Jen appreciated. "I'm glad you came."

"Wouldn't have missed it." Jen offered Daniel a friendly wave. "Take good care of her."

Jen narrowed her eyes. "Or else." He was a doctor. It would be a shame to harm him, but she'd do it.

The fact that no one laughed at her threat was reassuring. She might have been the smallest and the poorest, but she'd also always been the one with the toughest attitude.

She'd cultivated that reputation. Years of being afraid had taught her to be fearless, even when she was afraid.

"We'll walk you out," Rebecca said quickly and the three men seated between her and the door stood in a gentlemanly fashion to let her pass by.

The heat that dusted Jen's cheeks was unwelcome. Sure, they would have done the same for her, but she hadn't needed the help. She'd managed like she always did.

Marching to the door as if she had zero concerns, Jen studied the pile of coats and bags on the floor. "In the next reno, add a coatrack, would ya?"

"If any of you ingrates would put your things in the closet like I've asked a million times, we wouldn't have this problem," Rebecca answered.

Before Jen could come up with a retort that

would make it easier to deal with the sadness of saying goodbye to a friend, someone rang the doorbell.

The sudden peal of bells would have been startling in normal circumstances, but with her nerves rattled, and having been standing so close to the door, Jen clapped a hand over her racing heart before she yanked the door open. "What?"

Then she realized who was standing on the porch. Luke Hollister, Holly Heights' newest policeman, enemy number one to her friend Sarah, and the topic of at least fifteen minutes of the evening's conversation. Sarah and Will, Jen's stepbrother, had recounted how Hollister had harassed them both in the hunt for Sarah's father, Big Bobby Hillman, causing Jen to file away a long list of grievances against her neighbor.

Until that evening, Jen hadn't known she had such a good reason to dislike him. Now that she did, it was sweet. There was no need to try to make friends with him and his relatives when she'd been watching from her windows. She'd gotten some of his mail and had sneaked across the road to put it in his mailbox. If she'd known he was so good-looking at close range, she'd… Well, she'd have done the same thing.

"What are you doing here?" Jen asked and tapped her cowboy boot. "Did someone call the cops?" Unless she'd somehow done it with the power of wishful thinking, Jen knew the answer to that. As loud as it was inside, it was that peaceful and quiet in the cool September night.

"I thought small towns were supposed to be welcoming," Hollister muttered. At least he had the good sense to appear uneasy. "I need to talk to Sarah. Miss Hillman."

Before she could turn and yell over her shoulder, Sarah, Rebecca and Stephanie stepped up behind her. At this point, she was all too aware of how vertically challenged she was and that was doubly irritating.

"What do you want?" Sarah demanded. "Unless you have something to tell me about my father, I'm busy." She'd been waiting for answers from Hollister or the Austin Police Department for weeks. Her father, Big Bobby Hillman, had embezzled funds from his car dealerships and disappeared.

Hollister had been certain she was helping Bobby or biding her time until she could disappear and had hounded her for information. Passing on the single clue she had to his whereabouts had been Sarah's only choice. She deserved to know what was happening.

"Bobby will be in Austin, at the main station, tonight." Hollister's arms hung loose at his sides, almost like he could reach for his weapon at any minute. But he wasn't armed. Maybe he was always on guard. "Radio silence has been in effect while the department worked with Miami police and the Marshals to bring Bobby into custody and transport him home. Thanks to you, they were able to track him from Tampa."

Jen turned to wrap her hand around Sarah's. Whatever their history, Jen hated to see someone as suddenly pale as Sarah was.

"Is he…okay?" Sarah cleared her throat. "I want to see my father."

"I thought you would say that. This is not protocol, but I got permission for you to visit Bobby in Austin tomorrow." Hollister's grim face was lit by the soft glow of the porch light. Jen wasn't sure what she'd expected from a jerk who'd threatened her stepbrother, Will, in an effort to get Sarah to turn in her father.

Hollister seemed to be waiting for something. The grim set of his lips matched the tilt of his chin. He was determined. "I'll have to go, too."

Sarah's fingernails were sharp needles in Jen's hand; she said, "I'll go but without you, Hollister."

He shook his head. "That's not the deal. It's either both of us or no one. You can talk to Bobby, get a lawyer hired. He's going to need one."

Sarah was committed to helping the police right her father's wrongs, but she'd do her best to protect him at the same time. Jen could understand the conflicting urges, the need to see justice done and the desire to protect someone she loved.

At least Sarah no longer had to worry about where her father might be. This close, she could check on him every chance she got.

Hollister sighed as he pulled out his wallet. Sarah clenched Jen's hand tighter and refused to take whatever he offered, so Jen held out her free, unbroken hand. The business card was hard to read in that light.

Sarah snorted. "You and those cards. I'm surprised you have any left." She shook her head. "I'm surprised I don't have those details committed to memory."

Hollister put his wallet back in his pocket. "Last one. I guess I was holding on to a souvenir. I'll introduce you to the detective who took over the investigation and my part in this is done."

"We'll all be so relieved. I still expect you to be lurking in the bushes when I step outside in the morning." Sarah glared at him. "That's what you like to do, right? Take advantage of the element of surprise, sleepless nights and a lone woman all by herself."

Hollister's lips tightened into a firm line. "I like to catch criminals. I do what it takes. I didn't have to do this for you, you know." He held up a hand to stem whatever angry retort Sarah was building. "I've got a new lead on the B&E at the shelter that I'll pursue next week. When we tie up these loose ends with Bobby, I'm hoping you and I will have no reason to see each other in the future."

"At the grocery store, you better go the other way," Sarah muttered. "I'm dangerous with a cart."

Jen tilted her head as she considered that threat. What it lacked in violence, it made up for in creativity. Sarah Hillman had always been the most stylish of her bullies at Holly Heights High School.

Since she still hated a bully, Jen waded into the choppy waters to add, "And she's got a lot of friends in this town." Not strictly true but more than Hollister had. Besides, he needed to know she was watching him…if not from across the street.

"Two o'clock. I'll meet you at the station." He had nothing else to say, so he walked to his car. Turning his back on four angry women was either brave or foolish. Maybe both. When he opened the car door to slide into some vintage-y Mustang, he met her stare for an instant. It was hard to see his eyes in the darkness, but it was also impossible to ignore how that stare felt as it was locked on her.

Before she could respond with insolence, Sarah reached around Jen and slammed the door shut.

Instead of being too loud and too much fun, for Jen at least, the silence that filled Rebecca's foyer vibrated with tension.

Eventually, Sarah wilted and Rebecca wrapped her arms around her in a tight hug.

"He's okay." Sarah rested her chin on Rebecca's shoulder and closed her eyes. "My father's okay. Ever since Hollister suggested he wasn't calling because he was dead in a ditch somewhere, I haven't been able to get that picture out of my head."

Jen had to contain a low growl of disgust. Using a woman's fears against her might be standard operating procedure, but he wouldn't get away with it again, not with any of her friends.

"Do you want to sit down?" Jen asked and then pointed at the table. The whole group moved together to watch Sarah collapse into a chair.

Sarah took the glass Rebecca offered her and drank it down in one gulp. "How will I afford a lawyer? I didn't win any lottery." She closed her eyes and waved off all the offers filling the air. "It was rhetorical. I will find a lawyer. Not Cece Grant's husband, either." She squeezed her eyes tightly. "Can you even imagine the storm in the paper *next* week?"

Jen smiled at Rebecca who chuckled. They were still weathering the rough waters that came from Rebecca's—Holly Heights' favorite citizen—arrest and the hubbub over their defense of Cole, the town's latest black sheep.

"I'll get some recommendations from my accounts in Austin," Will murmured. "We'll find the best."

Sarah nodded firmly to Will. "Yes. Together we can do anything." The color returned to her cheeks. "This is going to be fine." She met Jen's gaze and added, "Thanks for throwing your weight to my threat. That should have him shaking in his shoes."

Jen narrowed her eyes, certain Sarah was teasing her.

"What can I say? You've grown on me." Jen grunted as Sarah wrapped her arms tightly around her neck. An awkward pat of her shoulder provoked a watery sniff from Sarah.

"I hate pretty criers."

Everyone laughed and Jen decided it was safe to resume her escape. Hit the door. Find some peace and quiet. Settle her nerves.

She added a step. Annoy the neighbor. If things were uncomfortable enough, they could send him back to Austin. Permanently.

"If you need me to go with you tomorrow, let me know. I'll pack my brass knuckles." Jen didn't own any brass knuckles, but if she needed some, she could leave early, pick some up.

"Will's going with me." Sarah didn't even glance over her shoulder to make sure he agreed. It must be nice to have someone to depend on like that.

"Okay. Call me. Let me know how it went." Everyone called out their goodbyes as Jen grabbed her purse and stepped out into the peaceful night. Hollister was gone. That was a good thing.

She might as well be the only person on the planet at this point. Rebecca lived in the oldest part of Holly Heights where the houses were close together, but there was not a person moving. Jen headed for her car as a burst of laughter came from Sarah's place.

All the couples were happy again. That was nice.

And the only single person in the group had left the building.

CHAPTER TWO

LUKE HOLLISTER TOOK a deep breath as he started up the Mustang and backed out of Rebecca Lincoln's driveway. When he'd stopped by both Sarah Hillman's apartment and Will Barnes's and neither turned up his target, he'd decided to do a drive-by of known accomplices. That kind of persistence had always worked in his favor and tonight was no exception.

If he'd been able to look into a crystal ball to see a vision of facing off against four angry women, he might have tried to call first. However she'd done it, no one could deny that Sarah Hillman, formerly the pariah of Holly Heights, thanks in no small part to his best efforts, had built a formidable posse.

Sarah was tough enough. In all the times he'd tried to break her in order to find her father, she'd never once fallen apart. Even at her worst, when she'd been one step from homeless, he'd seen fear, but not the weakness he'd been searching for. The fact that she'd converted pillars of Holly Heights, the town's newest millionaires, to friends suggested she had more going for her than he'd ever expected from a spoiled princess.

He'd been in Holly Heights less than a month and already he'd heard the praises of the Yates and Lincoln families sung. He'd met Rebecca Lincoln at the shelter. By process of elimination, the other angry woman flanking Sarah had been Stephanie Yates.

And down in front, his neighbor, Jennifer Neil. Red hair like hers, cut in some cool way he couldn't name, caught a man's attention. He'd never once managed to stop her outside to introduce himself when he made it a priority to know his neighbors. Now that he had a family to protect, that knowledge mattered more than ever.

All four of those women knew how to murder a man with their eyes.

And the men behind them would have finished him off with pleasure if there'd been anything left after the battle. Cole Ferguson, the ex-con he'd met at the shelter, and Will Barnes, the guy he'd tried to strong-arm into informing on Sarah, were familiar. The third guy he'd never met, but the expression had been "die" to match the rest.

He refused to feel guilty about any of the tactics he'd used in the Bobby Hillman case. It had taken longer than he'd liked, but his way had worked. Sarah had given them the tip they'd needed. So he'd been wrong about her involvement. He wouldn't start doubting his gut now.

"At least I won't have to see them again after next week," he muttered as he made a slow turn in front of Sue Lynn's diner. The place was already closed. Of course. Holly Heights was one of those places that rolled up the sidewalk at sundown. At this time of night, Austin and Houston both were nearly as bright as day. Before he'd come here, he'd imagined places like Holly Heights were myths. Wasn't convenience a twenty-four hour thing these days?

Or at least it was in the only two cities he'd called home before leaving them behind for the "comforts" of country life.

As soon as he found one of those comforts, he might feel better about his move.

He missed the city, the noise, the *conve-*

nience. Most of all he missed the work he'd done in Austin as the department's best detective, work that had mattered.

Luke swung the Mustang into the parking lot of the only store open at this time of night. Because of its proximity to the highway, this neon one-stop shop stayed open until midnight. "Chicken it is." Luke scanned the empty parking lot as he got out and carefully locked the car door.

Nothing moved. He didn't feel the prickle of eyes watching him. That took some getting used to.

"Howdy, what can I get you?" the young girl behind the cash register asked. Luke studied the store. Was she here by herself? That wasn't safe.

"Gimme the four-piece and a large drink." Luke slid cash across the counter and took his change and the big cup she handed him. By the time she had his order ready, he'd filled his cup and studied all the security features. Cameras in all four corners of the store offered good coverage. As long as they were taping instead of placed there for show. When the store was robbed, the police would have something to work with.

He hoped there was a panic button behind the counter and thought about asking the girl. If she hadn't been scared before, a random guy asking about her security measures ought to do it. Instead, he raised his bag in a wave and headed out to the car.

With a quick turn of the key, he opened the car door and slid inside.

Then he considered his options.

If he went home, he'd never taste one greasy bite of this chicken. The bag would be snatched out of his hand before he shut the front door behind him. "Scavengers. Every single one of them."

He'd made the move to help his foster brother, who needed a new start and his mother was struggling to find her way, too. Still, that didn't mean it was easy sharing this space.

Parking in front of the empty gas station to have his dinner might answer his question about whether the station had a panic button. He'd have the awkward job of explaining to his new coworkers why he was there instead of home.

Or he could drive. Luke reversed out of the parking spot and eased out onto the road that went past Paws for Love animal shelter. He was in no hurry. Luke turned up the radio so that classic rock filled his ears, cracked his window to let the sweet smell of autumn in Texas flow in and took the first piece of chicken out of the bag.

As an officer of the law, he understood that any distraction while driving was a bad idea. As a hungry man with nowhere to go but home, he knew he needed the time by himself and the chicken, so he meandered the roads around Holly Heights until the food was gone and he could no longer postpone the inevitable.

The first uptick in his blood pressure came as he tried to park in his own driveway. He'd chosen this house because it had four bedrooms, the yard his mother had been dying to have her whole life and a peekaboo view of Holly Creek. He'd thought the water would be relaxing, but keeping his four-year-old niece away from it was a constant job.

Dodging three different bicycles, all left to fall where they were abandoned, made it impossible to get the Mustang anywhere on the pavement that belonged to him. Since the house he'd chosen was at the dead end of a quiet subdivision, there was plenty of space in the street.

It was a good thing comfort in Holly Heights cost about half of what making do did in Austin. Even after selling the house he'd called home, getting enough space for his family had been a stretch.

He'd bought the car at sixteen and then taken ten years to restore it—he hated parking it in the street.

Luke stretched as he got out of the car in order to make sure whatever tension he could chase away was gone before he stepped inside.

His mother didn't need to hear the irritation in his voice. He could pretend to be easygoing.

When the door swung open before he had a chance to use his key, Luke nearly tumbled inside, but caught himself on the doorjamb. His sister's little girl, Mari, was staring at him, one finger in her mouth. Since she was wearing a tutu and carrying a lightsaber, he had a feeling she'd had a good day.

"Hola, Mari," Luke said as he scooped her up. She was usually one of his favorite people in the house.

Mari didn't answer. She rarely did, but she pressed both hands to his cheeks and leaned forward to kiss his nose. Her usual, sweet greeting.

Luke squeezed her tightly and then set her down. "Where is your *abuela*?" In the Hollister family, everyone spoke English and Spanish, usually at the same time. Mari's mother, Camila, had spoken nothing but Spanish when the Hollisters had agreed to foster her twelve years ago. Everyone had learned Spanish that summer.

Since it came in handy on a nearly daily basis working law enforcement in southeast Texas, Luke counted that education as one more thing he owed his adoptive parents.

Mari smoothed her long ponytail over one slim shoulder, straightened her tiara and pointed like the princess she might be. Or the Jedi. Or both, really.

He didn't need the clue. The noise would have told him.

Connie Hollister, his mother, was lecturing again. And Joseph Martinez, the newest foster kid lucky enough to land with the Hollister clan, had not yet learned to keep his mouth shut.

"Homework comes before video games, not after," she said and tried to point imperiously at the hallway so that Joseph would go to his room. Before she finished the motion, her arm fell limply in her lap.

A bad day, then. Grief had robbed his mother of some of her fire. Every day he wondered how to discuss the depression; understandable though it was, it scared him. The family needed Connie Hollister. *He* needed her.

Luke leaned a shoulder against the arched opening to the living room as Mari ran to her mother, tugged her hand and pointed in his direction.

"Ah, now you've done it. Luke is here." Camila's satisfaction at this rubbed him the wrong way. He wasn't the father. They had no father anymore, not since Walter Hollister had died six months ago, but he seemed to be filling in more and more.

"What's the problem?" he asked as he bent to press a kiss on his mother's cheek. She was pale but her eyes were snapping with irritation, looking not unlike the four women he'd left across town.

"Joey hasn't been doing his homework. One of his teachers called me today," his mother explained.

"Joseph," the boy said slowly. "My name is Joseph."

Whatever his life had been before, it hadn't broken Joseph Martinez. At fourteen, he was as annoying as any teenager could be.

Logic and reasoning were long-term strategies but they were all he had to work with.

"Go put away the bikes, Joseph." Luke braced his hands on his hips, prepared for an argument. "The next time I find them like that, I'll lock them away." He pointed at Mari, who ducked her head and pursed her lips, as certain of her safety in this case as she was every other time he'd made the threat.

"Why am I the only one?" Joseph muttered as he reluctantly paused his game and then turned it off. He had to step over piles of Mari's toys to slump next to the door. "I know my bike's not the only one out there."

"Nope, but you're on your way to do your homework." Luke leaned closer. "And Mari's a baby who needs to get ready for bed."

Joseph rolled his eyes and stepped outside.

Satisfied that the trick his older brother had used on him more than once still had power, Luke followed Joseph. The kid had picked up his own bike and slid into the seat to ride slow circles on the driveway. Luke bit his tongue and grabbed Mari's bike and Renita's.

"Where's Renita?" At seventeen, his sister was doing her best to take control of her life. She would go to college on a scholarship and be anything she wanted to be.

"Babysitting. You need to go get her at ten." Joseph rode in front of Luke. "I'll be glad when I get a job. Then I can get a car, and get out of this hole. Go home."

Luke opened the door to the garage and set both bikes inside before he tried to answer Joseph. At some point, the kid would settle down. They all did.

"It's hard to change schools," Luke said in his most patient voice. "Everybody's got to adjust to a new town, but this is going to be good for you. Your old home was not."

Joseph silently shoved his bike in the door and then slammed it shut. "Yeah. Sure. Good for me."

Luke tilted his head back to study the sky. In the country, he could see the bright white lights instead of dull tiny pinpoints against a sky that never went completely dark. Amazing.

"You know at your old home it was only a

matter of time, J." As a police detective, Luke had learned to keep his mouth shut and his ears open at all times. Every little scrap of information he picked up might have value. Listening to the guys on the gang task force discuss troubles at Joseph's middle school had been enough information for Luke. His mother wouldn't make it through losing another kid to violence like that.

"Nah, I'm too smart to get caught in a mess," Joseph said as he scraped a tennis shoe against the driveway.

"The wrong place at the wrong time is all it takes. Bullets don't care how smart you are." He'd seen that proven time and time again. Coming to Holly Heights, where he'd investigated the theft of bake sale money from an animal shelter, where not a single person was injured should be living the dream. Except this was so boring he was sleeping through it.

"They got bullets here, too, Luke. This is Texas." Joseph's grin was contagious. "Come on. That was a sweet one." He held up his hand and Luke slapped it in a reluctant high five.

"If you ever wanted a fresh start, here's your chance, kid." Luke caught Joseph's hand

and held on. "Hear me. One way or another, you're going to do your homework. Upsetting Mama right now? I won't allow that. She needs peace and quiet."

"Quiet? Around here? With so many of us? I want to see that." Joseph tugged his hand. "I hate math. The rest is okay."

Since he'd hated math, too, Luke found it hard to argue. "Do your best. That's all she expects." Joseph nodded and disappeared inside the house, which was closing in on Luke.

Luke walked slowly to his car and started it up. Instead of doing a U-turn and heading for freedom, he eased into the driveway and turned off the engine.

What would it be like to be living in Austin all by himself again?

He'd barely appreciated it for the time he'd had. Now he'd bask in every single second he had alone.

When his mother got stronger, he could reconsider what he wanted. Life in Austin had been too hectic to help her out with the family, and more than anything he wanted to give back. Whatever Connie Hollister needed, wanted or didn't even know to ask for, he would do. She and Walt had saved him. For now, she thought small-town life would give her and her family what she dreamed of.

Luke missed his father. Walter Hollister would have talked her out of a move like this.

These nights, he wished he could turn to his older brother Alex for advice or to complain, but Alex was gone, too.

Luke had to keep it together.

And he was already exhausted. A trip into Austin to see his old desk, his old partner, his old chief and the case he'd dogged for months closed by someone else wasn't high on his list of favorite day-off activities.

At this point, it didn't matter. All he could do was what had to be done.

CHAPTER THREE

"WHAT DO YOU THINK?" Jen asked as she held up the drawing Cole had put together with suggestions for the landscaping outside her new house. "With the wrought iron fence. This place will be nice, right?" For their first day of work, the fencing guys seemed to be making good progress. They'd started as soon as the sun came up, so she'd missed out on her extra Saturday sleep, but it would be worth it. Posts would be finished along one side of her property by the end of the day.

Her mother snorted. "How much will that fence *cost*? There's so much of it."

Since she'd asked that about every single improvement Jen planned to the house, which was already almost three times larger than the home she'd grown up in, Jen snapped, "Forget that. Decorative fencing will add prestige to this place. How does it *look*?"

"Pretentious," her mother drawled, standing

in the driveway, scanning the area. "Like you don't want anyone to visit. I mean, a fence like that with a gate? Who do you think you are? Royalty?" her mother scoffed. Working split shifts as a waitress had always kept her mom humble. "Do you think a fence with spikes at the top is necessary?"

"Most mothers would be happy their daughters were improving the security of their homes." For a woman who could still remember the panic of being chased all the way home from the bus stop by a pack of kids who thought it was funny to watch a skinny redhead cry, this fence was a dream come true. Then, she'd wanted something else between her and the world besides a single flimsy door. Anyone who thought about coming over the top would be discouraged before even trying.

Once she was inside her fence and her house, she would have no worries anymore.

Jen waved the piece of paper at her mother. "It will mean you're safer, too, after you move in. That's important to me. Think of all the space we'll have, and nothing but the best of the best. Just what you *deserve*."

Brenda Barnes shook her head slowly. "How many times are you going to bring this

up? I'm not moving in with you. One of us
would murder the other in the first week and
then what would happen with all your pre-
cious lottery money?"

"Well, you could take it and run off to Mex-
ico. We aren't that far." Jen fluttered her eyelashes at her mother. There was no doubt in
her mind who would kill whom. The Great
Cake Baking Assignment of 2016 had proven
beyond any doubt that her mother was tough
as nails. They'd managed to make dozens of
cakes for the Paws for Love bake sale, and
only extreme love and true devotion had pre-
vented Jen from telling her mother where
she could put her measuring spoons. "If I'm
dead, I won't be slowing you down, will I?"
That had been her mother's number one complaint—Jen worked too slowly in the kitchen.

Since Brenda had been waiting tables at
Sue Lynn's for as long as Jen could remember,
she was an Olympic-level star in the kitchen.
Jen might as well have wandered in off the
street. Between Brenda and Rebecca, she
spent zero time cooking and liked it that way.

Jen had worked every job she could find
for years to pay off all the debt she'd picked

up in college, yet having to cook had never been one of them.

After she'd hit the lottery, Jen had concentrated on the job she *was* good at, teaching math to surly teenagers. The baking thing had been a moment of insanity that turned into a two-week long sentence and dishpan hands.

"You need to get a hobby." Her mother slid into the Honda Civic that had been missing the back bumper ever since she bought it.

Jen wandered over to the driver's window and motioned for her mother to roll it down. "I have a hobby. Spending money completes me, Mom."

A reluctant laugh escaped her mom's lips. "Lie to everyone else, but your mother knows." She narrowed her eyes. "We are never going to live together again, Jenny. My house is perfectly spacious now."

"Can I buy you a new car, then?" Jen motioned at the back. "I know bumpers are extravagant and all..."

"Have you talked to your brother about your investments lately?" Brenda asked as she always did when she was ready to end a conversation.

Jen and Will, her stepbrother, were closer

now than they ever had been. Since they'd mixed like orange juice and toothpaste when they were kids, that wasn't saying much. This time Will brought with him the world's coolest daughter, a niece Jen wished lived in Holly Heights instead of Austin. If Chloe were here, she'd have opinions on every bit of the landscape drawing.

"I saw him just last night. Besides, you know we meet every week to talk about investments and charities and Paws for Love. Don't worry. Will's got his eye on me." Since he was the golden boy who always reassured her mother. The fact that Brenda was only his stepmother had never convinced her to take Jen's side over Will's.

And the guy *was* smart, even if he had fallen like a rock for Sarah Hillman.

"Get a hobby." Her mother pointed to punctuate every word. "Or a date. And if you put up razor wire or hire men with dogs to patrol this compound, I will ask Bobby Hillman how to steal every penny you have for your own good."

Brenda tilted her head. "You understand? Now give me a hug. I'm going to be late for the dinner shift."

Jen awkwardly stuck her head in the window and wrapped her arm around her mother's neck. For so much of her life, Brenda had raised her all alone. When she'd married Will's father, they'd had a hard time working two new people into their lives and her mother's tiny house. After her divorce, her mother had done her best to make sure Jen and Will stayed connected. Her mother's smell of fresh laundry and lavender was expected and reinforced Jen's decision to convince her mother to move.

Brenda worked too hard. Now that Jen was a woman of luxury, she could spoil her mom. She felt so guilty as she watched her mother pull out of the driveway.

Jen refused to accept a *no*. That's who she was.

Her mother didn't want a roommate. Fine. Maybe a house next door? Jen crossed her arms as she walked the large expanse of yard to the empty lot beside her property.

How long would it take to build another home?

Jen bent down to pat Hope, the pit bull mix she'd adopted from the Paws for Love shelter. All the noise had rattled Hope, but she was sprawled out in a sunny spot next to the lead

Jen had put in the yard. When the fence was finished, Hope would have total control of a truly spacious kingdom. "Getting what we both deserve, right, Hopey?"

Hope turned her head to give Jen's hand a lazy lick and she stretched her legs out behind her. The spot of fur that had been cut out where she'd been wearing the collar when they rescued her was growing in nicely, but she seemed to like the pink bandannas Chloe had insisted were the perfect accessory.

This dog. Jen blinked away tears as she considered what Hope's life had once been. Everything was so good right now. With Hope snoozing peacefully in the sunshine it was difficult to remember all the hard times.

Which made her think of Sarah.

Since she'd been clutching her phone like a lifeline ever since two o'clock had rolled around, she knew she had no messages. Surely Sarah would let them all know about how the visit with Bobby went.

Maybe her friends had made plans to get together after she'd left the dinner party.

The old familiar feeling that everyone was having fun without her rolled across Jen.

"Don't be an idiot. They care for you.

There's no news yet." Jen shoved the phone in her pocket as Luke Hollister's car came down the street.

She didn't return his wave but started for the driveway.

Then she realized Luke would have the news she was so anxious for.

Suddenly wishing she'd done a bit more than pull on a faded orange University of Texas sweatshirt and gray sweatpants with a hole in the knee, Jen marched across the street in order to catch her prey before he disappeared inside. No way was she knocking on the door.

Instead of hustling to avoid her, Luke Hollister slowly pushed down the lock on his car door down and closed it. He didn't lean against the vehicle, but waited; his careful stare seemed to be cataloging details as she approached.

"What's the news?" Jen asked. She would not run her hands through her hair in an effort to make it look less Saturday stay-at-home matted to her head. She *would* control the conversation.

"Hi, I'm Luke Hollister. We didn't introduce ourselves last night but I like to observe the usual pleasantries." He offered her his hand which she studied carefully before slipping hers inside. Luke Hollister was sharply dressed with dark pants, a white button-down and a beautiful gold tie. Last night, his vibe had been more undercover cop with a scruffy beard. Today, he could be the department's chief spokesperson. "And you are?" He didn't squeeze in a manly move to dominate, but there was no mistaking his power when he shook her hand.

Remember what you're doing. Staring in wonder at his very nice hand should not be it.

"Jennifer Neil, but you knew that." She brushed her hand through her hair because she couldn't help it. "Last night. Anyone who's hounded Sarah the way you have has a roster of her friends."

"And enemies. And people like you who've been both at one time or another. That is one long list." He shrugged. "I'm a thorough cop."

Jen rolled her eyes. "So I've heard. All I wanted to know was whether Sarah got in to see Bobby. Then I'll return to my side of the street."

"Yes, Sarah was still with him when I left. Will had a list of lawyers they were contacting." Hollister closed his eyes for a minute. "And that's all I know. Once you're out, they don't tell you much. Sarah will have to give you any updates about a court date and what happens next."

If she didn't know Hollister's methods, Jen would have guessed that was a sign of regret on his face. The corners of his mouth turned down, but she had the feeling he didn't spend much time with regret.

"Fine." She took one step back. "Thank you."

Before she could turn around, Hollister said, "I wanted to mention, that work crew that start at dawn on Saturday could be construed as an act of war in some places." He rubbed a finger over the frown wrinkling his forehead. "A house with a four-year-old who manages to sleep in is one of those places. Could you make sure they wait until a reasonable hour?"

She was paying them extra to work as fast as they could. No way was she going to alter their schedule. Annoying Luke Hollister would be the cherry on top.

Jen wondered what the story was. Besides his wife and daughter, how many people lived in that house? At least one of them liked loud guitar solos and open car windows, no matter what time of day it was.

Then she realized she didn't have much to lose. They weren't going to be friends. "Funny you should mention the noise. Exactly how many people live in your house anyway?"

"There are six of us." Hollister braced his hands on his lean hips. "And you? What with the fence going up, I'm guessing that number is going to be low."

Jen glanced over her shoulder. What was wrong with her fence? She'd seen similar on all kinds of nice houses. A cop should appreciate security measures. "Just me. And a few frequent visitors, none of whom will disturb your peace."

"Great. They'll be the only ones," Hollister muttered.

"If my renovations are bothering you, feel free to look for someplace new to live, someplace not in Holly Heights." Jen turned and retreated to her own driveway. "They'll be here early again on Monday, before I go in to work. If you have students, we'll be on the same schedule."

"So, you're a teacher? What school?" Hollister asked. He didn't have a notepad in hand, but she had the feeling he was filing away every detail. No doubt, he could remember this picture of her as a fashion disaster any time he wanted to.

She'd done her best to always put her best foot forward with respect to how she looked, ever since she'd learned she had a knack for making secondhand and vintage fabulous. Not that he'd know that. He'd have to have seen her years ago to understand how far she'd come.

"The high school." She thought his eyes widened a bit but it was hard to be sure at this distance and she wasn't going to get any closer. Not today. For their next skirmish, she'd be dressed for battle.

"Interesting." The small smile that curved his lips was easier to see and made her twice as nervous. Before she could escape, the front door of his house opened and a little girl in a tutu came running around the car.

Jen expected a shriek or a giggle. That was what all little girls did when they were excited.

Instead, Hollister picked the little girl up and settled her on his hip. Watching such a sweet face press close to his for a kiss made her simultaneously make an inward *aw* sound that she would deny ever happened and wonder how this guy, who obviously loved his daughter, could be the same jerk who'd made Sarah miserable.

Her confusion froze in place for too long. Before she could move, the little girl was on the ground and charging her direction, swinging what appeared to be a plastic sword.

Jen had no other choice but to brace for impact.

CHAPTER FOUR

"MARI, WAIT," LUKE YELLED as he watched his niece race across the road, tutu bouncing with each step. She was small but she was fast. Being so quiet tricked people who didn't know her well. They mistakenly thought she was shy. Instead, she had no fear of anything except being forced to speak.

And dogs? Mari couldn't resist them.

He watched Jen hold out both hands as if she was ready to catch the little girl, but before he could warn her that she was not the ultimate destination, the pit bull on the bright blue lead in the yard jumped up and issued a warning growl. Now everyone froze.

"I've never heard her do that," Jen said as she stared at the dog.

In his experience, dogs had one of two reactions when confronted with Mari. Either her exuberance sent them running for cover or they were putty in her hands. This dog was still a huge question mark.

But the brindle tail was wagging cautiously.

His neighbor squatted next to the dog and immediately dodged a long pink tongue.

"I think she was afraid I was in danger," Jen said slowly.

Mari immediately clutched her lightsaber closer and took a slow step forward.

"You shouldn't have a dog like that out where it can hurt someone," Luke snapped as he caught up to Mari and picked her up. Her wrinkled brow reminded him so much of his sister Camila that he did a double take. "Your dog scared her."

Jen ran a hand down the dog's back and immediately the animal flopped down to offer up a bright pink belly. It almost matched her bandanna.

In an instant, Luke cataloged that detail about his neighbor. She was the kind of woman who dressed her man-killer dog in pink.

"A dog like that," she said carefully, as if every word leaked out around the grim line of her lips. "What do you mean by that? She was a dog who was dozing in the sunshine in her own yard before she was awakened by a kamikaze in purple high-tops." Jen scratched her hand over the dog's belly and got the immediate feedback that it was good by a quickly dancing right foot.

Mari's silent laugh next to his ear turned down his adrenaline a notch.

"You know those dogs are dangerous," Luke insisted. He was supposed to watch out for Mari. The fact that she'd find trouble if he blinked was no excuse.

Jen slowly straightened and tugged her sweatshirt down. No matter how tall she stretched, she'd come no higher than his collarbone. Still, she didn't back down. With one jab, she pointed at him. "My dog. My yard. If you'd teach children to approach all dogs slowly, cautiously and after she's asked permission, neither one of us would be pulling gray hairs tonight." She ran a hand through the hairdo that had definitely seen better days and huffed out a sigh. "I don't think most dogs react well to being attacked in their sleep."

Mari hung her head in the way she always did when she was pretending she was so sorry but making sure that everyone knew how cute she was. One quick look from her through her batting eyelashes was usually all it took to convince Luke to fold like a weak hand.

"If you want to pet her, let's give it another try," Jen said softly. Apparently she was no more immune to Mari's charm than anyone in the Hollister household.

Against his better judgment, Luke let Mari slide from his arms. When Mari smacked his leg with the lightsaber, he grunted and managed to catch it before she got her second swing in. Jen didn't laugh at his wince but some of the tension around her lips eased.

Luke crossed his arms tightly over his chest. "This is Mari," he said as his niece inched closer to the dog. Jen offered Mari her hand and they both squatted next to the animal.

"And this is Hope. She's pretty special." Jen scratched under the dog's chin before she loosened the bandanna. "She's adopted from an animal shelter. We had to do some surgery to take out a pinch collar so she has a funny haircut."

Mari traced the faint line around the dog's neck and was too distracted to dodge the welcoming lick.

Luke would have grimaced, but he knew Mari would enjoy every second. His mother would have had a minor fit about dogs and dirt and germs and whatever the current scare in the kindergarten was. Years as a school nurse in Austin had given her a justified concern.

But she wasn't here and another of Mari's silent laughs made everything better.

The long, sad day of saying goodbye to the life he'd been building was forgotten.

"Adopted." Mari looked back at Luke and then fiddled with the dog's ears and scratched under her arms. "That's the best."

Hearing Mari repeat his mother's comfortable saying, which she used at every holiday gathering, was enough to tug the heartstrings of even the angriest jerk in the world.

"You are so right, Miss Mari," Jen said. "And Hope seems to agree with you." She stood and watched Mari kneel to run her hand over the dog's side.

The little girl and the dog got to know each other quickly. Hope, determined to get the best scratching of her life, rolled in one direction first and then wiggled and squirmed so that Mari could reach the other side, too.

"She hardly ever talks." Luke stared hard at the child he'd grown so attached to.

"Why?" Jen asked quietly.

"She doesn't waste any breath with words when a thwack with a lightsaber will do," Luke said with a sigh.

"I like her style," Jen said as Mari smoothed out the hem of her tutu. Hope had shifted to rest her chin on Mari's leg. They seemed to fit together perfectly now. They were peacefully communicating without words. "Where did you find those shoes?"

Luke raised an eyebrow at her and noticed a wash of pink sweep over her cheeks. "You don't really expect me to answer that, do you?"

"I appreciate bold clothing choices," Jen said with a shrug. "I figured you were a clothes guy. I mean, those pants have to have some kind of designer label in them." He couldn't miss her cut a glance at his dark suit pants and wondered what it meant that she'd noticed what he was wearing.

Luke rubbed the ache in the center of his forehead. "Probably some no-name brand. Got them at the department store after my mother shoved them in my hands and told me they were good value. She likes value." Luke glanced over his shoulder to his house and considered why someone wasn't watching where Mari was. If it was supposed to be his mother, maybe she was resting? The fencing company had rousted them all out of bed earlier than necessary. "Mari, we should go. *Abuela* will be worried."

He watched Mari hug the dog with all the dramatic sorrow of a little girl who was used to getting what she wanted without having to raise her voice. At some point, he was going to have to put a fence up. The Holly Heights Hollisters could have a dog where the Austin Hollisters had never been able to. That was a nice change.

But his fence would be a normal wood privacy fence, not this wrought iron monstrosity.

"So, I guess you aren't building this to keep your dangerous dog locked up," Luke said as he gently petted Hope. "That must mean you need to keep someone out."

Jen's scoff clearly communicated her disgust at his suggestion. "Why can't I like nice things? Why does everyone want to make this into some paranoid statement of my fears?" She wrapped her arms tightly over her chest but quickly extended a hand as soon as Mari began a reluctant walk back to Luke, dragging the toes of her shoes on the concrete with each step. She picked up her lightsaber with a delicate sigh. When the little girl slapped Jen's hand for a low five, Jen gave a curt nod. Then she caught Luke's eye and mouthed, "Impressive."

Mari's shoulders were slumping but she couldn't help stealing one last glance at Hope as she crossed the street.

Luke straightened his tie and then met Jen's eyes. Both of them had twitching lips.

"You seem pretty good with kids." Luke shook his head. "Want to take a budding actress under your wing?"

"Nah, I like them older. Mouthier. With graduation and the end in sight." Jen sighed. "Little kids are too…fragile."

Mari violently thrust her lightsaber at the bushes lining the small porch. "Right. So delicate." Luke wondered if his mother had seen the torn leaves and missing branches yet. When she did, she would not be happy.

"I don't think she's got what you'd call 'natural landscaping ability' but she's got something." Jen smiled up at him and then, almost as if she realized she was doing it, the smile slipped away to be replaced by a serious frown. "Sarah's a friend. You get her the answers she needs and we don't have a problem."

Luke tipped his head back and studied the clouds drifting lazily overhead. Even the blue sky seemed bluer here. "I'm out of options on her dad's case. A hearing will be set. If the judge determines there's enough evidence to proceed with a criminal trial, and he will, Bobby will get jail time. Then there will be civil cases, too, on behalf of his employees." He stared at Jen. "She's going to have a long, hard time with him. Might've been better if he'd stayed gone."

"Then why did you hound her the way you did?" Jen challenged, her shoulders square. She was ready for a fight. Under normal circumstances, he could take a petite female with one hand tied behind his back. In her case, he wasn't so sure. She almost vibrated with the power of her conviction. She'd battle until she was out of breath. For the right thing, she'd battle until she was spent, or worse.

In this case, the right thing was friendship. That was attractive, even if she appeared to be considering his jugular in a worrisome fashion.

So, he answered slowly, "It. Was. My job."

He held both hands out. "I'm going to do my best to get the answers I need. I have to. Justice is what's important." He stared hard at her. "And sometimes justice means doing the tough things to get those answers I need. The people I serve depend on me to do that. She had the answers. That's all."

Jen narrowed her eyes. He expected her to hit him with angry words. Instead, she tightened her lips. "Use that focus for her now. Get some answers on the shelter break-in and we might let you live."

Luke snorted. "Threatening an officer of the law?"

"I'm rich. I'll hire a very good lawyer and make sure he can get in behind my fancy fence while you're stuck on the outside looking in." Then she slipped the leash she had hanging off the mailbox onto Hope. With one last glare, she turned and marched down the long driveway that led to her nice house.

"If I'm looking in, does that mean I'm *not* dead after all?" he muttered. Luke tried to calculate the square feet of calm and silence that a house like that would hold and then sighed as he crossed the street.

Back in the Hollister house, Mari had

wisely taken her weapon with her and disappeared. Joseph was sprawled in front of the television playing some space game, keeping up a running commentary through his microphone with whoever he was competing against. His sister Renita's head was bopping along with the pop song she had blasting through her headphones as she studied. Renita was all boy bands while Camila preferred hair bands, but both of his sisters liked the volume turned up. How his mother could stand it so calmly was a mystery he was going to investigate one day for his own sanity.

Luke bent over Renita's shoulder to read the title. "British poets of the twentieth century." The idea of having to wade through that sent a shiver down Luke's spine. He'd scraped by in school, but his sister was going to graduate at the top of her class or die trying. When she brushed her braids over one shoulder and pulled her headphones away to ask, "Did you need me?"

Luke squeezed her shoulder. "A little light reading?"

She rolled her dark brown eyes. "Paper due next week. Since I plan to be babysitting for the Monroes every night and their twins prefer to talk to me, rather than sleep, I need to get a head start." She tapped her pen on the paper in front of her. "Notes for the organization of my soon-to-be brilliant exploration of the effect of war on poets." She waggled her eyebrows. "Even Mrs. Jones was impressed with my topic and she's heard them all."

Luke bet she had. "And how's math?"

Renita tipped her chin down. "You mean, how is trigonometry?" She wrinkled her nose. "I'm pretty sure Mr. Wilson thinks girls should be learning how to cook or something." This time she didn't roll her eyes. Luke knew she'd heard worse.

"Must eat him up that you aced his test."

She raised both hands and clapped. "Yes. It does." Her eyes sparkled as she brushed each shoulder defiantly. "So I'ma keep doing it."

Luke motioned toward Joseph who was now shouting into the microphone attached to his headphones. "Think you could help the runt with whatever he's got?"

"I tried." Renita shrugged a shoulder. "Couldn't hear me over the chip on his shoulder." She stared up at Luke, her genuine concern easy to read. Renita had been with the Hollisters for almost five years, long enough to understand the difference between fosters and family. "Kid's mad about the move."

That was his diagnosis, too. They'd all been through it. He, Camila and Renita had all learned what real family could be. Joseph would, too. "Know anything about a Ms. Neil? A teacher at your school?"

When Renita straightened in her seat, he knew he'd made an error. "Why? Is she hot stuff?"

A big error. "Only if you count her temper. She's our neighbor."

Renita tapped her pen on the table. "She must teach geometry, maybe algebra. Only Wilson teaches trig. Too bad. I could have put in a good word for you." She waggled her eyebrows at him again.

"There are no good words strong enough to sway her, I'm sure." Based on his few encounters with Jen Neil, Luke would say she had backbone and enough loyalty for a dozen people. "Still, it's helpful to know the neighbors." Luke pointed at his sister's headphones. "No rest for the brilliant. Back at it."

She winked. "Sorry about leaving my bike out on the driveway. Won't happen again, bro." She pulled his hand until he leaned down

so that she could hug his neck. "I forget sometimes."

If there was any sign that Renita had
crossed over, become a full Hollister, that
was it. Forgetting as if she truly were Connie's baby.

Luke patted her back, awkward with the
hugs as always, and tapped her book. When
she stuck her nose in between the pages in an
exaggerated move, he wagged his finger at her
and then followed the quiet sound of running
water into the kitchen.

His mother was bent over the sink, wash-
ing dishes. "We have a dishwasher for that."

"I'm better at it than any machine." His
mother handed him a dripping plate. "And
now I have you to dry. We'll be done in no
time."

Since he'd been heading to the peaceful
deck that lined the house, Luke was less than
thrilled, but he refused to sound like Joseph.

"Have you missed Mari?" he asked casually.

"She was with you. Said very clearly *Luke*
before she hit the door at a dead run. Now
she's under the table." Connie motioned with
her chin. "I assume she's waiting to defend

herself against whatever you're going to tell me she did."

Luke bent his knees to stare at his niece. She was pretending not to listen but not well.

"Introduced herself to the neighbor at a dead run." Luke opened the cabinet to stack the dried plates inside.

They both turned to look at Mari, who said very clearly, "Dog."

His mother sighed. "Of course. I should have known that she'd be unable to resist for much longer. Every day when the crazy rich lady comes out to get her mail, Mari watches the window like her favorite cartoon. Kid's dog crazy."

Luke continued to dry and stack as he thought about how to bring up the subject. With Mari listening, the whole conversation could be dangerous.

"I guess it's time to think about adopting a c-a-n-i-n-e," his mother said, spelling out the last word. They both glanced down at Mari. She was watching them suspiciously but she hadn't learned to spell that well. Dog would have been too easy.

"Your father always wanted one. I told him no, no, no." She didn't tear up as she'd been doing every time she'd mentioned her husband, a sign of progress, but the grief was still so close to the surface.

"The house in Austin wasn't good for *canines*, Mama. You were right about that." Luke tossed the towel over the dish drainer and leaned against the counter. "This place? Perfect."

She glanced down at the little girl, who was intently listening. "You are right. And this family could use a new member, one who doesn't have homework to fight over."

Luke smiled. "We'll figure that out. He'll figure it out. You know that."

She smiled back. "I do. I've fought harder battles than this." She poked his arm. They'd had some legendary shouting matches when he'd first arrived at the Hollisters' house.

Until his brother, a brawny kid named Alex, had taken him outside, hung him up by his jacket and made some very creative threats. That was all it had taken for Luke to get the picture. From that day until his brother had been shot by a stray bullet during a street fight, he'd done his best to follow in what had been his cooler older brother's footsteps.

August 14, 2000. That was the day everything had changed.

Luke had become the older brother. And he'd decided then and there that he'd spend the rest of his life doing his best to make sure criminals ended up behind bars.

No matter what it took.

Did that make him popular? Not always.

But it was satisfying at the end of the day.

"What did the crazy rich lady have to say?" his mother asked absentmindedly. She washed and rinsed in a comfortable rhythm. Maybe she was better at this than the dishwasher.

"She wanted to know about Sarah Hillman. They're friends." Unless he concentrated, he'd fall behind in his drying duties and his mother would frown. Luke quickly opened cabinets and put things away.

His mother hummed.

"She didn't seem all that crazy." Luke wasn't exactly sure when his mother had started calling Jen crazy. It had been before the fence people showed up at the crack of dawn, though, and that was the only real sign of psychosis he'd seen. "Turns out, she's a teacher. She might have a suggestion to help Joseph. Renita thinks she teaches math." The unease he'd felt ever since he'd moved back in and been cast in the role as head of the family lightened a bit. Having something to do instead of a list of worries was good. He waited for his mother to say it was a good idea, a bad idea, or…something. She was the real head of this crew. He wanted her to be in charge.

"Pretty. If you like that sort of thing." His mother cut a sly glance at him out of the corner of her eye.

"Angry redheads aren't my type," Luke answered, although in Jen Neil's case, that wasn't strictly true. Something about her was impossible to ignore.

His mother's forlorn huff was the first warning that he'd strayed into dangerous territory. "You need to find someone nice, Luke. A woman who might distract you from your *job.*"

Jen Neil wasn't nice. Nice made him think of puppies and daisies.

Jen had a rescued pit bull and plans for a spiked fence. In the garden of life, that woman was a cactus.

Nice? No. Interesting? Yes. Maybe even exciting. She had personality to spare.

"Holly Heights is an excellent place to raise

a family. You told me that yourself, remember?" she sang in a teasing tone.

While it was good to have a touch of the old Connie Hollister back, this wasn't the subject he wanted to stick with for long. If he told her he wasn't sure he wanted a family, she would wilt completely, and lying to her was next to impossible.

"I remember." Luke took the last dripping plate from her and listened with relief as the water drained. He could make it out of there.

"Being a police officer is a wonderful thing, son," she said as she cupped his cheek, "but you were meant to be a father, too. You wait and see. She's close, whoever she is. I can feel it."

Luke didn't have the right words so he smiled at his mother and watched her bend to speak to Mari. "Come with me, young lady. We have some bushes to trim the right way."

After they left the kitchen, Luke stepped out on the deck that had sold him on the house. Here, all there was, was the faint sound of birds chirping and the breeze rustling through the trees. He took a deep breath as he braced his hands on the railing. "One year. You do this for one year and everything will be fine."

A boring job. A cluttered, cramped house. All the problems that came along with angry teenagers.

He could do anything for a year.

CHAPTER FIVE

"THE FIRST WEEKLY MEETING of not talking about Paws for Love can come to order. All discussion is postponed until our next board meeting or else," Sarah said as she banged the salt shaker on the table for emphasis. Rebecca had gotten to the diner early and claimed the best table in Sue Lynn's. The rest of the Wednesday dinner crowd flowed around them, but the three of them were tucked away in a corner booth with a good view of the sidewalk.

Which was helpful. Without the shelter to talk about, conversation might be sparse. They could do a running commentary of everyone who walked down the street if worse came to worst.

Jen patted the purse she'd settled carefully next to her in the booth. Her whole life, she'd lived with second or thirdhand things from her mother and thrift store finds. She'd gotten good at that. Having money was taking some adjustment. This brand new purse? It cost four student loan payments.

As soon as she'd collected her lottery winnings, she'd paid off every cent of debt she'd been carrying for years, but it was difficult to get out of the habit of measuring everything in terms of those payments.

She'd only bought it on her solo shopping trip to Austin for two reasons. First, she'd had a *Pretty Woman* moment in the department store with a snooty saleswoman and Jen had wanted her to regret her big mistake. And second...okay, it was possible that there was only one reason. She'd been thinking about making the drive back to Austin to return it ever since she'd pulled in to her driveway.

"Want to tell us what you found out about Bobby's trial?" Rebecca asked as she studied the menu. Jen was surprised Rebecca had been able to wait this long. She'd always been the caretaker in their little group, the one who encouraged Steph to go for what she wanted and Jen to trust people. Without Rebecca, there was no way Sarah would be sitting at this diner table across from Jen.

Rebecca's new mentoring program must be

taking up every spare minute. That and free-falling straight into love.

Jen kept one hand on the straps of her newest purchase and forced her attention back to her friends. Why was Rebecca studying the menu anyway? No idea. The thing hadn't changed in ten years. There was no need to mess with perfection.

"What can I get y'all?" Sue Lynn asked. She brushed one loose curl back over her ear as she studied the modest crowd and waited.

"Burger. All the fixin's." Jen handed over her menu and tried not to roll her eyes as the other two dittoed her order. Sure, salads were on the menu, but Sue Lynn had the best burger in town.

After Sue Lynn walked away, Sarah covered her eyes with both hands. "The lawyer says, with Daddy's cooperation, they might be able to keep him close to home. Nobody seems to think there's any other option than the minimum sentence."

"Even though he ran away," Jen asked and immediately realized her mistake when Rebecca wrapped her arm around Sarah's shoulders and glared at her. "I mean, of course not. He was a real pillar of this community before he…" What? Lost his mind? What would cause a man to steal from his own business? It made no sense to Jen. Hard work was what paid off. He was already doing very well for himself. Greed was the only answer. He deserved jail time. His fancy lawyer, the one Sarah would be paying for forever, would protect him.

But Sarah… His daughter loved him. Jen might see it mostly black and white, but his daughter would be all caught up in the gray area.

"Yeah, and he's remorseful," Sarah said with a twist of her lips. "Or pretending to be, anyway." She shook her head. "Never mind. I don't want to talk about him, either. I've spent enough time worrying about Big Bobby, the man who left me here to stew in his mess. Let's talk about something else."

Jen glanced at Rebecca, who seemed just as stumped for good conversation. Eventually, Rebecca waved her phone. "Did you guys see the updates on the HealthyAmericas Facebook page? The welcome-home banner those kids in Alto made for Steph and Daniel? It was sweet, right?"

Jen squinted at the tiny picture on Rebecca's

phone. If she recalled, Alto was one of the villages that Steph and Daniel and their medical team had to hike into because there was no road. That sounded awful, but the kids in this photo had beautiful grins. So did Steph. She was in exactly the right place.

"Cute." Jen slid the phone back across the table and checked on her new purse again.

When she looked up, Sarah and Rebecca were watching her. Embarrassed to be caught staring, as if she was admiring her stupidly expensive purchase, Jen ran a hand through her hair.

"Are those tags? On your dress?" Sarah asked slowly. "Did you forget to remove them?"

Jen fidgeted and tried to shove the tags back inside. "I might want to take it back." She'd been a little nervous all day because she couldn't decide whether the long-sleeved knit dress with the cute, funky belt worked for her. Ripping the tags off equaled true love.

"And the purse? Should we ask Sue Lynn for a lighted display case?" Sarah drawled. "I mean, it's pretty, but you're watching it like you think it will get up and dance."

"For the price I paid, it should." Jen cleared her throat. "Not that I'm bragging."

"This? Still?" Sarah asked. "You have millions. You could buy one of those for every day of the week and not feel the pinch. Instead, you're dressed like the world's worst shoplifter and guarding your purse like it's a treasure chest." There was no bitterness in Sarah's voice, but it had to be hard to be in her position. Before her father's fall from grace, she might have had money to burn, but now, she was struggling to afford a lawyer and keep a roof over her head.

"I should have left it at home," Jen said. But it was a purse. How did other women do it, carry something that cost more than rent as if it was no big deal?

Watching Sarah and Rebecca exchange a worried frown reminded Jen she had a reputation.

No weakness.

"I could have reunited you with your hobo bag, the one with all the fringe, the one I picked up for almost nothing after you sold it." Jen tried a smirk but it was clear neither woman across from her was buying it. Only after bluffing failed would she try the whole truth.

"Handbags by designers whose name I can't even pronounce might be too advanced spending for me at this point," Jen muttered.

"What I could do with that money," Sarah said with a pout and all three of them laughed, but Jen wondered if there might be some honesty behind Sarah's words. Did she think she was more deserving than Jen?

"This is stupid. We can talk about something other than the shelter or shopping," Rebecca said. "We're all there all the time, but there's a real world happening, as well."

In about two seconds, conversation would turn to Will or Cole. There would be loveydovey gushing, and Jen would have to take her chances on jumping out the window.

"Had a chat with the enemy on Saturday." Jen raised her eyebrows as both Sarah and Rebecca leaned forward.

"Are we talking about…" Rebecca craned her neck to make sure no one was listening "Cece?" All three of them studied the crowd as if whispering her name could conjure her up.

Then Jen shook her head. "No, Hollister.

The one true enemy." Cece had been another bully in high school but she was no match for Sarah Hillman. Sarah was twice as smart and nearly as vicious, even if she only sharpened her wit now on Cece.

Sarah and Rebecca leaned back.

"Oh, that guy," Sarah said with a curl of her lip. "What was he doing? Lurking somewhere, I bet. He's a lurker."

Rebecca tipped her head to the side, her nose wrinkled, but she didn't argue.

"He was going home. He's my neighbor." Jen sipped her Coke and watched their jaws drop. Having a chance to surprise either one of them was so satisfying. In this group, she was often outsmarted and outniced, but she'd hardly ever been surprised.

"Your neighbor," Sarah squeaked as if she couldn't believe the horror. "There goes the property value! Do you hear screams at night from whatever innocent bats he manages to catch and torture?" She jabbed her straw into her glass and sniffed.

"What are you babbling about? Innocent bats? I…" Jen held out both hands and frowned at Rebecca.

"Tell us more." Rebecca nodded. "We can do this conversation justice."

Jen studied Sarah to make sure she wasn't going to lose it completely. "He lives across the street. A lot of people live there, actually. I think it's his mother, his wife, his daughter and…a sister? A brother? I'm not sure how they can all be related."

"Someone married him?" Sarah was horrified. That much was clear. She was shaking her head so hard that Jen was afraid something would rattle loose.

"Someone very pretty. And the little girl? A-dore-a-ble. She had the cutest shoes. I'd steal them if I didn't have feet the size of small boats." Jen held her leg out to Sarah to show off the boots she was wearing. "Remember these beauts?"

Sarah stopped shaking immediately and narrowed her eyes at Jen. "Rubbing my nose in my consignment shop sacrifices never gets old, does it, you redheaded meanie?"

Jen laughed. "Redheaded meanie. You are getting soft in your old age. And no, it does not. I liked your old style, when you had more money than sense. Nowadays, you're all jeans and T-shirts."

"Wash and wear. It's practical." Sarah tossed her hair. "And I can find you one man who will swear I make it look good."

Since that man was her stepbrother, Jen was already feeling a little queasy at the direction of the conversation.

She turned to Rebecca, who was the only one who could pull it back at this point.

"I've met a Hollister, too. Renita. She came in to my office to talk college planning. A high school student planning her future? She's a guidance counselor's dream." Rebecca pursed her lips. "His sister? If so, there's more to this family than you imagined, Sarah. She's so smart she's giving her trig teacher flat-out fits and since he's a chauvinist windbag, I'm a huge fan of hers."

"You weren't going to tell us this?" Sarah asked.

Rebecca shrugged. "You don't react well when Hollister's name comes up. For good reason." Rebecca made a face to stall Sarah's angry response. "We won't argue he's a troll. Okay? It's just… Well, his sister seems great. She has no interest in animals—" Rebecca waved one hand at Sarah and Jen as they immediately stiffened "—not that she dislikes them, because I asked whether she might like to volunteer at the shelter, but she's more into business, taking over the world, that kind of thing."

Jen knew Sarah would share her disbelief at hearing that anyone wasn't head over heels about animals. They exchanged a pitying look and Sarah said, "So where are you sending her to work? The hospital? Because I can tell already she's one of your kids."

Rebecca sipped her drink. So innocent looking with her blond curls and guidance counselor's uniform of khakis and shirt with the school mascot on the pocket. Jen knew better. The girl had tricked Stephanie into taking a flight to Peru, where she fell in love with Rebecca's brother all over again. She was devious. That was why they got along.

"I hear Dinah's been looking for good help lately." She smiled sweetly.

"Since you hired Debbie Jordan right out from under her nose? Yeah, we know." Jen snorted. Devious.

"Debbie was necessary for my mentoring program's expansion. I did Holly Heights a favor. Again." Rebecca's smug smile was contagious. For a half a second, she'd stumbled when the town turned on her and Cole, the ex-convict who'd stolen her heart, but now she was gaining new ground. "Moving the program out of the high school is going to be the best thing to happen to my volunteers since I started the thing. And Renita? She wants a business degree and to be an entrepreneur. The girl is already working as a babysitter, saving money for college. I'm going to get her a scholarship that will let her pick the school. And in the meantime, she's going to be running Dinah's Shop-on-in three nights a week. Maybe she can do something about the weird collection of clown dolls Dinah's got in the window right now." Rebecca wagged her head. Like she thought she was hot stuff.

"Poor Renita." Sarah wrinkled her nose. "You did warn her about the proximity to Cece, didn't you?" Dinah was Cece's mother and they were tight. She'd run the Shop-on-in, the Holly Heights version of the weird little-bit-of-everything store, ever since Jen could remember.

"I did. Renita's smart. She can handle it." Rebecca straightened in her seat. "Hey, there she is." She pointed at a thin girl with awesome braids who was walking…

"And there's Hollister." The three of them watched the couple out on the sidewalk. They couldn't hear the conversation through the glass but it was easy enough to see the second Hollister realized they had an audience. His flat stare wasn't friendly. It wasn't exactly hostile, either, but Jen could appreciate his caution.

"No monster should look that good in a uniform," Rebecca said softly.

Jen whipped her head around so fast a sharp pain caught her off guard.

Sarah yelped, "What did you say?"

Rebecca shushed them. "Settle down. He's good-looking. Only a fool would argue with that."

Doing her best not to let the relief show that someone else had gone first and said what she'd been thinking, Jen narrowed her eyes as if she had to study him to come up with an answer. "Tolerable. He's tolerable."

Rebecca held up a hand and waved. Jen smacked it. Then all three of them leaned back so that Sue Lynn could slide their plates in front of them.

"I can't believe you'd admit something like

that," Sarah muttered. "The personality of a junkyard dog. You like that?"

Rebecca shrugged. "I'm falling for a guy who's been in prison and resembles a large green superhero. It's not like anyone would hold my judgement up as a fine example." Then both Rebecca and Sarah turned to Jen.

Sarah's glare was ferocious. "What do you think?"

Jen thought he was handsome enough to give an A-list movie star a run for his money. But she normally didn't go for that sort of thing. "Doesn't matter. Only his wife's opinion counts. Got it?"

Sarah slumped back and repeated, "Someone actually married him?"

All three of them turned to look out at the man on the sidewalk. He was watching them so closely that Jen had the feeling he knew exactly what their conversation was about and he disapproved. Mightily.

Of course, he was a cop. He had experience with confessions.

She could feel the heat of embarrassment creeping up over her cheeks.

The guy was good at his job, clearly.

"I think he's coming in," Rebecca whispered before she took a huge bite of her hamburger. All three of them tried to pretend they were engrossed with the food in front of them when he paused at their table.

"Ladies, I wanted to let you know that, thanks to the tip I received," he glanced at Rebecca, and Jen had to wonder if she knew what Hollister was talking about, "the Austin police department has tracked down a kid who visited the trailer park where Eric Jordan and Mike Hefflin live. Goes by the name of Red. They were able to tie him to a pawnshop outside of town where your laptop was found. They don't have him in custody and there's not much chance we'll be able to do much to recover the cash he took from the shelter break-in, but I thought you'd like to know."

With the new developments in her father's case, Sarah must have been distracted from the break-in at the animal shelter. The thief had stolen the money they'd raised with their big event, as well as all the small electronics he could carry.

At least Hollister was still working that case.

One point in his favor was that he'd ruled out Rebecca's new love, Cole, as a suspect almost immediately, even with his record. Unfortunately, he'd focused a little too much time on Eric Jordan, who was thriving as an assistant to the shelter's veterinarian. Since Rebecca had also hired his sister, Debbie, to help her expand her mentoring program, they were all invested in the outcome of this investigation.

Sarah frowned. "A phone call next time. The fewer minutes I have to spend with you in person, the better."

Hollister patiently tipped his head. "I'll let you know when they track Red down. He's often here in Holly Heights so you might be on the lookout for a kid about twenty, bright orange crew cut."

"Fine. And you'll leave Eric alone?" Sarah snapped. "The kid's doing well at the shelter. I don't want him distracted."

"Eric's still our best connection." Hollister braced his hands on his hips. "We'll question him, roll through the trailer park to make sure Red doesn't turn up, but at this point, I don't think Eric's involved. The other kid, Mike, might be a different question."

The silence at the table was immediately uncomfortable.

"I'll ask Cole to be watching the basketball hoop in the trailer park. If Red shows up, he can give you a call," Rebecca said with a cautious glance at Sarah and a quick smile.

Jen didn't say a thing. Yep, this close, there was no way to argue about how handsome Hollister was. And his devil horns didn't show.

"Guess I'll let you get back to your dinner," Hollister said. He studied Jen's face and then leaned down. "When you have a minute, I'd like to talk to you about…something else."

Shocked, Jen immediately choked on the French fry she'd been nonchalantly nibbling. The feeling of his hand resting gently between her shoulder blades was reassuring. This officer of the law would not let her die from junk food inhalation if he could help it. When she could breathe without coughing, she picked up her drink and sipped. "About what? Talk about what?"

"Math." He tapped the table. "But I don't want to take up any more of your time. I'll see you in the neighborhood."

He turned to go before she could tell him that she was entirely too busy for whatever he had in mind. Then she saw Cece Grant barreling toward them and knew she had bigger problems than whatever Hollister wanted. Her pulse started pounding, the immediate fight-or-flight response to the former bully hard to ignore even after all these years.

You aren't a kid anymore. No weakness. The fast beat of Jen's heart was distracting, but she'd learned to control the flush of pink that came along with the burst of adrenaline.

Instead of beginning with polite conversation like any normal human being, Cece immediately gave a tiger growl as she stopped in front of their table. "That is one prime bit of man right there." She narrowed her eyes as she studied them. "Let's see. Sarah's managed to snag the most eligible normal bachelor in town already, and Rebecca has tumbled for the *least* eligible bachelor in town." Cece tsked her amusement. "That must mean it's Jen's turn." She laughed as if she was telling the most amusing joke.

She can't hurt you anymore. Act like you have no fear.

Jen waited for her to quiet down. "Did you want something?" Sarah and Cece would trade insults like cocktail party chatter. Rebecca would bend over backward to make sure everyone got along.

If she was still sixteen, Jen would have grabbed her plate and sped for the door. There was no way she'd get cornered like this.

But now, she was a grown woman. She had more money than anyone else in this town, even compared to Rebecca because she wasn't determined to give it all away. She didn't have to be nice to avoid Cece and she didn't have to put up with her either.

Learning to tolerate Sarah instead of trembling in fear had required squaring off against her as many times as it took to conquer the fear. Acting like a frightened little girl was no longer an option, even if she still felt like one inside sometimes.

Cece sighed. "Oh, I forgot. You didn't have all the training in the social niceties the three of us had, did you?" She patted Jen's arm. "I guess your mom was slinging hash those days."

If her mother had been behind the counter of Sue Lynn's that evening, Cece would be wearing a full bottle of ketchup at this point. Fighting for family was easy.

Jen retaliated and said, "I guess I'm fortunate to have that explanation to offer. What's your excuse for bad manners?"

Cece stepped back. Had she managed to catch her by surprise? Nice. The boost to her confidence made it easier to enjoy her French fries.

"You guys are so much fun. I don't know what I'd do without our joking banter." She slipped a pamphlet on the table. "Guess what? Halloween is coming!" She did a cutesy kind of bounce and Jen could feel the snarl forming on her lips. "We'll be doing our usual trick-or-treat with the businesses around the square, but you all must enter the best-decorated house contest." She flipped open the map and tapped the smiling jack o'lantern at the corner, right over her home. "Not that you'll win. This little guy has marked my place for the past three years, but it's nice to have new blood in the competition. However, there is an entry fee and since you, Sarah, don't have a house per se, that knocks you right out of the running. Sorry." She made a moue as if she was so sad about that. "But Rebecca, you've always been a popular stop on the tour. Kids go crazy over your pumpkin cookies. I'm sure I would, too…if I ate sugar." She winked at

Sarah and Jen felt the hamburger take a dangerous turn in her stomach.

"You've never had a shot at this, have you, Jen? It's an expensive competition, but the kids love it so." Cece pursed her lips. "You would make an excellent witch. You should work that into your theme." She flipped her sleek bob. "The red hair, you know."

"You've got that covered, Cece," Rebecca said. "Maybe two witches is one too many."

Everyone turned to her in surprise. Usually, Sarah did the talking for them. Rebecca's pleasure at coming up with a good one was easy to see. When Sarah held up her hand for a high five, all three of them celebrated.

Even Cece seemed impressed. "I can't tell you my theme, of course. That would give you an unfair advantage."

Jen nodded. "Sure, and I've already got one of those. Millions in the bank is such an unfair advantage." Her breathy sigh was so satisfying.

Then she blinked innocently around the table and held up her hand for her own high five. Rebecca and Sarah were grinning as they answered.

Cece rolled her eyes. "Oh, sure, dumb luck can compare to hard work."

"About as much as marrying rich does," Sarah said slowly. Then she held up her hand. The high fives were raining down as Cece stepped back from the table.

"Fine. The entry form is on the back. As you know, Rebecca, all the money we raise goes to help the fire and police departments buy gifts and food at Christmas for our town's less fortunate families." Cece slyly smiled. "I will refrain from mentioning who at this table could have qualified for that in the past or… even right now."

Then she turned on one expensive heel and sauntered from the diner.

"Why was she even here? She doesn't eat anything except the souls of the innocent," Sarah asked as she took a deep breath.

"That's the first time I've ever been able to do that, insult from the hip like that." Rebecca nodded. "I am getting good at this trouble thing."

Jen winced. "Poor Cole."

Idly, Jen flipped open the contest info and studied the map of Holly Heights. Here, in one easy picture, was an illustrated representation of her life to date. The house she grew up in didn't even register on this map. That made sense. The kids from her neighborhood would have been anxious to find better candy. While her neighbors had celebrated every holiday, because no family with kids could skip one and certainly not Halloween, this over-the-top decorating contest had been something they observed, not participated in.

But Cece was right. This year was going to be different.

Jen was studying the rules when she felt the weight of two heavy stares.

"You're going to do it?" Sarah said eagerly as she leaned forward. "Enter the contest?"

Jen crossed her arms over her chest as she considered the question. "My mother says I need to get a hobby, other than spending money. This could combine both." She fiddled with the contest info. "But if we do this, we better win. Second place is not an option, not with Cece in first."

It would be nice to dethrone Cece Grant, a very small piece of payback for the misery she had perpetuated during their high school years.

"I got a shiver down my spine," Rebecca

said, her eyes wide. "If you could see your face right now, you would, too."

"You do have this evil glint in your eye," Sarah added, "almost like your intergalactic death ray is nearly complete. Boy, am I glad that's not aimed at me any longer." She leaned forward. "It's not, is it?"

Letting Sarah get too comfortable would be a bad idea, so Jen smiled. "A witch. That could work. I'll call Chloe as soon as we pay the check. She's my secret weapon." Will's daughter had a flair for the dramatic that dovetailed with Jen's big ideas so neatly that she made the perfect partner in crime.

"Are you going to be a good witch or a bad witch?" Rebecca asked.

"That is the question, isn't it." Jen tucked the contest rules into her too-expensive purse. "Good or bad. Which direction will I go?"

This was going to be fun. The interior designer she'd hired might be able to give her some inspiration, and Chloe would pick up this ball and run with it.

Rebecca reached across the table to push the pamphlet down. "Are you sure about this? Think of all the people? The noise? The party atmosphere? It's just not you, Jen." Sarah wrinkled her face and then nodded.

They didn't think she could pull this off? "I'll hire actors. Put it all outside the fence. Keep an eye on everything from my windows."

"Says the creepy eccentric with too much money," Sarah muttered.

"Or I could put in security cameras." Jen straightened in her seat. She'd been trying to come up with a plausible reason for doing that, that wouldn't make her friends and family worry. This could be it. "We could have our own party, monitoring the feed from inside the house." As soon as she heard the words, she realized that sort of sounded like the plot of a horror movie she'd seen.

While that wasn't enough to convince her to abandon the plan altogether, her friends' concerned faces changed her mind.

"Or not," she said with a shrug. "It was an idea."

"Cece knocks it out of the park every year because her displays are interactive. Last year she was a witch who handed out treats disguised as tricks. Her hubby had a hunchback. There might have even been screaming bats."

Rebecca stared off into space. "Although, they might hang out at her house *every* day."

Jen blew out a frustrated breath. "I want to do this. We have so few occasions to rehash our high school feuds. This time we could win." She smiled as Rebecca laughed.

"We're in, however we can help," Sarah said. "What should we do…" They were quiet for a minute, the wheels turning as they tried to come up with a great theme.

"Good thing we have Chloe," Jen finally said. "She's our ace." Her coconspirators attacked their hamburgers, as happy to have a new plot as Jen was. All the people and noise and mess aside, this could be a blast.

Then Jen realized this could be something else to annoy her neighbors. Even better. If Luke Hollister decided life in Holly Heights was too noisy for his little girl, then he'd leave. Would this be a huge waste of money that hurt her penny-pinching heart? Yes, but the potential payoff was too big not to roll the dice. She could beat Cece. With unlimited resources, she'd deserve the shame a loss would bring. She'd have a great reason to talk Chloe into staying a weekend or two with her. The house that she'd bought because it was large enough to spread out was still too empty to be comfortable, but the chatter and mess of her favorite teenager would fill up some of the corners.

And the Hollisters were unprepared for the hubbub of the Halloween tour of decorated homes. She'd be perfect behind her tall fence, but the neighbors would have to deal with the loud, bustling traffic.

It was like some evil genius had dropped this plan in her lap.

This was going to be unforgettable.

CHAPTER SIX

"ALL RIGHT, LUKE," his new partner, Davy Adams, said with a tired sigh as he turned into the trailer park, "how do you plan to handle this?" As soon as the two kids under the basketball goal saw the cruiser, they stood tall.

Almost like they expected the cops to make a visit and had formulated a plan on how to act when it happened.

Annoyed at the sarcastic tone the older cop used anytime Luke wanted to take the lead, he bit his tongue and waited for the car to come to a stop. "I plan to ask questions. All we need to know is Red's schedule. Shouldn't be too difficult." Never mind that asking politely had gotten them nowhere with Mike. A kid like Eric, one who might see a future on the horizon thanks to his work at Paws for Love, he'd have more weak spots. Soon as Luke found one, he'd press hard enough to hurt.

They'd get what they needed. This case

would be closed and he'd never have to see Sarah Hillman again.

That should garner enough positive feeling from his neighbor to ask for a favor.

Before they even closed the car doors, Mike called out, "You smell bacon, E?" His confused frown changed to a grin as he passed the basketball to Eric with force.

Typical kid. Thought calling a police officer a pig was brave.

As if they didn't hear worse every single day.

Or at least they did in the city. Maybe that was unusual in Holly Heights.

If Eric Jordan was as smart as the vet at the animal shelter insisted, the kid would find new friends and quickly.

Davy Adams's patient expression was slowly morphing into a look of irritation. "Okay, Mike, no need for disrespect. We've come to ask you for help with a case." He braced his hands on his utility belt and spent a long second giving each boy a stern stare.

This was Adams's best bad cop. It was a joke.

"How many times you gonna ask before you get it? We ain't got nothing for you." Mike held out both hands and turned in a slow circle. "No evidence here."

Luke crossed his arms over his chest and studied Eric Jordan's face. The kid kept his focus on the ground as he bounced the ball. Weak spots. This kid could be pushed.

"Tell us what you know about Red, when he likes to drop by." Davy was trying for reasonable negotiation. What a waste.

"We haven't seen him since Cole chased him away." Eric clutched the ball hard and met Luke's stare head-on. "That's the truth." Luke considered him, evaluating whether or not Eric was believable.

There was some truth to it, but something else made it a challenge for the kid to hold his ground. "I've got homework." He tossed Mike the ball and turned to go.

Resigned, Davy had pulled out his notebook. "What about your neighbor? Red's girl. She hasn't been home lately, either."

Mike's snort was loud and clear when Luke went to follow Eric down the road to a very neat trailer. He memorized the license plate on the Subaru parked in front before he wrapped a hand around Eric's arm to pull him to a halt at the bottom of the steps leading up to a nice deck.

"Whoa," Eric snapped and yanked his arm out of Luke's grasp. "Hands, Officer."

Luke moved to block the kid's escape inside. "Tell me."

Eric shook his head. "I have no idea what you're referring to, *Officer*."

"Whatever it is you know, tell me." Luke gripped the stair railing hard. Letting a kid like this get under his skin would be a mistake.

Eric scrubbed a hand over his face and grunted. "I've already told you everything. We didn't break in. I wouldn't do that. That shelter? It means a lot to me. It should be very clear I don't have a sudden flashy sports car or a private basketball court of my own. What is your malfunction?"

Hit the weak spot.

"What happens if you don't show up for school, Eric? The shelter keep you on? And those community service hours? What happens to them if the shelter cancels your volunteer time?" Luke asked. He and Eric had talked once already about the shelter break-in, so Luke was up to speed on the kid's record and the current community service sentence he was fulfilling at Paws for Love.

"I have been going to school, so it doesn't matter. Getting good grades. Miss Lincoln is determined I'm going to be a vet tech, so I gotta do well." Eric waved a hand. "Check my records. You'll see."

"If we pick you up at school and bring you down to the station to ask you what you know, you're going to miss tests," Luke told him. "A few days of that and your grades will take a downturn."

"Harassing a kid? Think people will let you get away with that?" Eric wasn't so sure, but it was a good tack.

"We'll have to see. Won't do much for the shelter's reputation if they keep you on. Of course, they aren't on solid ground there right now anyway so…" Luke shrugged.

Davy Adams walked up, a ferocious frown on his face. Luke's time had run out.

"Hate to see you lose your hours at the shelter, Eric." Luke leaned close enough to see the glint of fear in the kid's eyes. He was close. If they could get one tip on the next time Red would be in town, they'd pick him up and this case of the break-in at the animal shelter could be closed.

"Hate to see you lose your job because you were illegally threatening a minor, Officer," someone said in an icy voice from behind Luke. He turned to see a petite woman standing on the deck behind him, her cell phone in her hand, taping their conversation. There might be several inches of difference in their heights, but it was easy to see the family resemblance between this woman and Eric Jordan. Eric's sister was ready to go to battle. "Unless you have a warrant or something that gives you permission to step onto my property, you move out of that child's way and go on about your business."

"Miss Jordan, we were trying to get some information on the habits of a robbery suspect," Davy Adams said in his calmest, most pleasing voice. "Anything Eric knows might be a help to close this case. He can be the hero here. If we can do anything to return Paws for Love's stolen property, we want to do that." Davy turned to Luke. "Isn't that right, Luke? We need Eric's help."

Luke eased back, unfamiliar with playing "good cop, good cop." Eric's relaxed posture was progress, though. "That's right. Solving this case is my goal." That was easy to say because it was the pure truth.

"Uh-huh." Debbie Jordan stomped down the stairs and made a beeline for Eric. "Tell them."

If he hadn't been watching so closely, Luke would have missed the quick blink of Eric's eyelids. "What? What are you talking about?"

"Whatever it is about your heathen friends that's been keeping you up at night, tossing and turning, you tell them." She pointed a finger at the kid and Luke was pretty sure she could convince anyone to tell the truth about anything.

And Eric was a smart kid. His shoulders slumped. "Red is dangerous, sis. We don't need his trouble."

"A very good reason to get that criminal behind bars. You help these men do their jobs. That's what I pay my taxes for." She shot a narrow-eyed glare over her shoulder at Luke.

Eric sighed long and loud. "Fine. All I know is…" He checked to his left and then to his right. Was he looking for Mike? The area under the hoop was empty.

"Mike went home," Davy said in a low voice. "It's just us."

Eric nodded once. "All I know is that Mike said he had plans on Friday night. That's the night Red used to roll into town. We'd play hoops sometimes, but Red's girl has Saturday and Sunday off at the day care where she works." He held up both hands. "You say she ain't been home. I can't say yes or no to that. I'm spending lots of time working at the shelter, but that was their normal. Before the break-in."

Luke watched Eric drop his hands. The shadow in his eyes was gone. Luke was certain the kid had nothing left to hide.

"Check back Friday night, then," Luke said easily. "Will do." Then he stepped away from Debbie Jordan. "Thank you for your help."

This time Debbie Jordan's hand whipped out and she caught his sleeve. "No. Not that easy. You ever come at Eric like that again, and I will complain so loudly to the Holly Heights police that they will hear me in Austin or wherever you came from and wherever you're going next. He's had some trouble. He's done with that. You treat him with respect."

The "or else" didn't escape her lips but Luke could read it crystal clear.

Before he could cut through her bravado with a reminder that he had a badge, and a duty to protect the other citizens of Holly Heights, something he took very seriously, Davy Adams smiled brightly, tipped his imaginary hat and offered her his hand. "We do appreciate your understanding and assistance, Miss Jordan. Eric, you keep up the good work, okay?"

His smile slipped as Luke passed him on the way to the car. Great. Another lecture about how to handle small-town people better.

It was as though Adams had forgotten he already had years of experience. So what if Holly Heights didn't give him much to work with. He wasn't going to let go of all that he'd picked up on Austin streets.

"How many times do I have to tell you to go easy?" Adams muttered as he slammed the car door closed. "You could do it with Cole Ferguson, a guy who's spent time in prison. Why was it easier to give him the benefit of the doubt than it was to treat this kid like a *kid*?"

That was a good question. The fact that he didn't have an easy answer bothered Luke.

"Jordan isn't much of a kid," Luke said as he fastened his seat belt. Besides that, he'd seen enough trouble in high school to know that nothing about a person's date of birth had much to do with what he or she was capable of. "It's not like the kid's an exemplary citizen, Adams. And we needed that info."

Easygoing Davy Adams was deadly serious as he said, "Try again."

Luke rubbed his forehead as he tried to come up with a better answer. "With Ferguson, I guess… Listen, I follow my instincts. That's what cops do. You know that. When we questioned Cole Ferguson about the break-in, the guy was clueless as only an innocent person can be. He's got nothing, no money and slim prospects at getting another job if the shelter fires him. Also, he's rebounded from his past mistakes."

"One of which was trying to rob a gas station." Davy started the car.

"As a kid. Kids do dumb things that they don't think through. That's what this break-in feels like, too. Cole Ferguson is not a kid anymore." One look in the guy's eyes had been enough to see that Ferguson had learned some hard lessons. He was better off for it.

"Fine. Instinct. Judgment. I'll buy that and even agree it was easy to see Eric and Mike were the keys." Adams reversed quickly down the road and turned out onto the highway. "But here's the thing you don't seem to grasp, former city police detective. This isn't one case. These kids? I've been a cop here for more than three decades. We watch them grow up. We know their stories. We know their parents' stories, because we went to school with them or we're related or something. Eric's had it rough, and by all accounts, he's making a change, going the right way. Running into an authority figure determined to throw his weight around won't help that. Could hurt him."

Luke felt the muscle in his jaw twitch as he stared hard out the window. "I have a kid brother. We're here because he was surrounded by a bunch of kids sitting on the edge of disaster. Drugs. Gangs, maybe. If Jordan is stepping away from that ledge, good for him, but I have a duty to make sure this town is safe. For my family. For everyone's family, even Eric's."

Adams grunted. "That's the job, Hollister. It's always the job. What you're forgetting is that you're a part of this town, too, not on the outside, patrolling the perimeter. You want to live here, you learn to work with the people who live here with you. Austin? Yeah, okay, that's different. Big city like that, you can be a jerk and you're one in a sea of people. Here, if you're a jerk and the wrong people pick up the cause, you're gone. And I'll tell you this. That family of yours that you want to fit in here in Holly Heights? They'll never live down your dumb choices. Even if they are for the good of the town."

Luke shook his head. "So don't rock the boat, is that it? Not even to solve this case. That's what you're telling me? Sarah Hillman will dog my steps until I get her an answer." He'd seen her persistence. More than once, he'd been shocked at whatever core of strength she had inside that kept her from folding. When it put him in the crosshairs, he wished he'd managed to find her weakness.

Maybe she didn't have any.

Luke rolled his eyes at that. Everyone had a spot that brought them to their knees. His? His family. And he'd do what it took to make sure none of the trouble that had driven Joseph and his new family, the one that had saved Luke, from Austin took root here.

"I'm saying, rocking the boat looks different here. If you could make friends, the co-operation you're looking for wouldn't make you enemy number one on at least four different women's lists now." Adams whistled. "You definitely need to work on your public persona, son. Life in a small town is nothing like you've ever seen before, obviously."

Luke didn't have a thing to say to that. He couldn't be any more a fish out of water than if he'd landed gasping on a beach somewhere. Adams had a point.

"Got a suggestion? Other than ease up on interrogation? That one, I've made note of." Luke pretended to jot down the advice.

Adams raised an eyebrow. "Why would I waste my breath? Hot shot like you's already sure you know everything."

For half a second, Luke could see Walter Hollister's face. He'd heard that more than once from his father.

"I do. I want to know." Luke sighed. He had to make it here. He'd be able to keep a close eye on Joseph. He'd solve this break-in. Eventually, he'd find a new job somewhere close that made it possible to check on his family but didn't make him feel like he was being smothered.

Easy.

"Community. Look up the word. Try to build it. I'd say making friends would be a good start, but I'm not sure you're ready for that." Adams parked in front of the small station where they shared desks with the other shifts. "Work your way up to friendly. Maybe try not to smash people under your heel for a week."

Smash people under his heel? The anger at that accusation made it hard to bite his tongue.

Adams was making him out to be a bully, the worst kind of cop there was.

He was trying to get answers.

"I'll give your contact in Austin a call, see if they want to come down to be a part of our visit on Friday night or if they want to keep up with their beauty sleep." Adams slid out of the car and shoved open the glass door to the modest block-shaped building that served as the police department.

Adams didn't mention the fact that it was Luke's contact with the Austin gang unit that had connected him with the pawnshop or provided all the new info they had on Red.

Of course not. That might mean acknowledging that Luke knew how to do his job.

Luke paced in a tight line in front of the station and tried to dump some of his irritation before he stepped inside. Nothing would come of antagonizing his coworkers. Defending his actions further or demanding credit for the progress in the case might feel good in the short term, but acting like a know-it-all would earn him no points.

He could do this, play nicer with his new coworkers and the people he protected. His biggest case was a robbery with no injuries. Treating it like a murder case could be a mistake.

And he needed this place to work for his family.

Maybe it was time to see what he could learn about small-town police work. Luke yanked the door open and followed his partner inside.

CHAPTER SEVEN

DID EVERYONE WHO WAS ABOUT to meet the expensive interior designer they'd hired feel completely unworthy? Jen was overdressed and terrified her likes and dislikes would send the man running for the hills.

She brushed damp palms over the other purchase she'd made in Austin, a turquoise silk jumpsuit that had no good function in her world but seemed the right kind of outfit to wear to meet with her interior designer.

When the doorbell rang, she checked to make sure the tags were well hidden, fussed with the weird belt that didn't want to stay tied and then took a deep breath.

Why was she so nervous? It made no sense. He was her employee, not her judge. The hard racing of her heart reminded her of old times and every day before she'd gotten on the school bus, home of the worst bullies in town.

"Don't be an idiot. You can handle this. If

you don't like what he brings, toss him out on his ear and hire the second-best designer in Austin. Simple." They'd already met once in his funky offices that resembled a boutique art gallery in a long line of train boxcars. Tripp Bromley had been perfectly friendly when she'd handed over a lot of money to put him on retainer.

Retainer. Like he was a lawyer, one who'd taken the vision binder she'd struggled over and tossed it on a pile before giving her the grand tour of his space, complete with a gander at all his design awards.

But now, he was in her house. Or would be if she ever managed to open the door.

"This isn't the first day of school and he isn't a kid waiting to point and laugh." Jen put one hand on the doorknob. "If he does, you can give him a hard chop across the throat and shove him off the porch. Easy." But only if she stopped acting like a mouse. Jen tried her best firm smile as she opened the door.

There, on her bare porch, stood Tripp Bromley, designer to southeast Texas's rich and even semifamous. He had his own decorating show where money was no object. When she'd asked Sarah to name the best, she hadn't been a bit surprised when he was the answer.

"Tripp, welcome to my home," Jen said as she reached down to wrap a finger inside Hope's collar. "No need to worry. She's a big marshmallow."

Tripp took a large step over the threshold, the silver on his boots glinting in the light, and patted Hope twice on the head before he swept past them both to turn in a slow circle. "Good. You followed directions. I prefer a blank canvas when I work."

Jen nodded and closed the door. "Blank canvas is easy for me." She shook her head. "You should have seen the place when I bought it. The previous owner—"

"Doesn't matter what was before. We are only interested in the future." He tapped his portfolio and laptop. "Where should I set up? Oh, the couch. Yes, I'd forgotten I sent the test piece along."

Before Jen could offer him something to drink or suggest her barstools might be more comfortable, Tripp was perched on the cushions and setting up. "You have your vision board." He swept a glance around the room. "Somewhere?"

"It's more of a notebook. I gave it to you?" Jen hated the question in her voice, but it matched her uncertainty. The urge to apologize was hard to stifle. "I didn't have a suitable board."

Tripp studied her face as if he suspected she wasn't taking the assignment seriously. "Boards make the vision come into focus, but I'll soldier on without it. You'll remember it until I wipe all that away with my inspiration."

She would remember the hours she'd spent cutting up magazines that seemed to be a waste of time.

Tripp pursed his lips and then clicked open a file on his laptop. A three-dimensional rendering of her living area opened and spun around. Tripp tapped the screen and then glanced at her. Jen took that as a sign she should move closer, so she bent to study the room.

Hope climbed up between them and Tripp's only reaction was a wrinkled brow.

"Let me show you my preliminary, but keep in mind that colors can easily change." Tripp tapped the living room and it opened to show a monochromatic room that appeared to be based on the colors and lines of the couch she hated. "I like to call my style Texas modern. If you've seen the show, you know that." And he'd gone full speed ahead with the modern. The fixtures were shiny metal. Every line was square and symmetrical, and when Jen looked at it, all she could imagine was being forced to sit on this couch for the rest of her life.

Tripp's eyes were narrow as he turned to her. "Do you love it?"

There were some moments when she realized she was going to have to tell the truth even though it was hard. Everyone thought Jen spoke her mind without hesitation but she spent a lot of time thinking things through. And the fact was, even if he was the best and he'd pick up his plans in a huff, she could not live with this couch for the rest of her life.

"You don't think this couch…" She patted the cushions that were so hard she might as well have been knocking. "I mean, it itches." She squirmed and tried to complete the list of all that was wrong with that piece of furniture without using a lot of breath.

Tripp tipped his chin up. "Interesting." Interesting like she'd passed with flying colors? Or interesting like she was hopeless and didn't deserve nice things? His tone could mean either. "I make it a policy not to work with clients who aren't able to work with me."

"Because I don't like the couch? That's what you're getting from a preference for a cushy seat." Jen heard her angry tone and tried to moderate it. She wanted this to work. She needed to hire the best. "Here's the thing. I'll be sitting on this couch to grade homework and tests. I spend a lot of time grading. I need a good, comfortable place to spend a lot of time. Do you get that?"

Tripp pointed at the room. "Right. And I asked you to pull pictures of things you liked. What you did, instead, was pull pictures of rooms I've already designed." He bent to dig around in the large bag he'd dumped on the floor. "The binder is here, after all, and here's the couch you hate, front and center in one of your inspiration pages." Then he raised an eyebrow.

If this had been a murder mystery, Tripp would have announced the killer complete with a dramatic *Aha!* of accusation. Her binder was the candlestick in the library that had resulted in this killing couch.

"I like the color. It's nice." She tried to

smile confidently. "I don't want my leg to go to sleep because it's dangling over a hard edge. See?" She kicked one of her feet, flashy in her favorite pair of gold flats, to draw his attention to the fact that her feet didn't touch the floor. That was a problem she was familiar with, but if there'd ever been a piece of furniture that discouraged folding her legs under her and snuggling down more than this couch, she'd never seen it.

"You're not ready to work with me, dear." He patted Hope on the head again and folded everything up. "I warned Sarah when she called to beg me to take you on that I'd moved beyond a certain kind of client. At this point, I'm much more interested in people who are going for an artistic statement."

Jen knew her mouth was hanging open. "You're here as a favor to Sarah?"

Tripp's sad face was dramatic but unconvincing. "I don't take anyone on without a referral, not anymore. But Sarah gave me my start years ago when her father was furnishing a penthouse downtown." Tripp sighed. "That was the first time I'd ever worked with funds equal to my talent. When she refused to take my first or second no to help you as an answer, I gave in gracefully. Tell her I consider us even. It's clear you'll be happier with someone else."

If Jen had known she was asking for favors to be called in, she might have made a different choice. She and Sarah were friends, but it was important not to take advantage of that friendship. Why hadn't Sarah told her how hard she'd had to push?

One quick glance around the cavernous rooms snapped Jen out of her confusion. If she didn't get someone hired fast, she'd be stuck with this couch through semester tests and she'd lose all function in her lower extremities. "Who would you recommend? What designer fits my style?"

"Hard to say," Tripp drawled. Jen forced herself to sit very still as he examined her from head to toe with a detour over Hope and her pink bandanna. "Let me think on it."

He stood so abruptly Hope scrambled to follow. Her confused grumble reminded Jen of the growl Mari had surprised out of her. She might not mind a little growl at superior Tripp Bromley. Watching him pack his laptop away with precise jerks was annoying enough to strengthen her backbone. "What about the retainer? How soon can I expect that to be returned?"

Jen crossed her arms over her chest, certain her scowl would fill in any missing blanks. His answer better be polite and *Soon*.

He wrinkled his nose. "Oh, no. You should have read the contract. That retainer covered this consultation, but we won't be moving forward, so it's forfeited."

Jen blinked slowly. "By you, not me. How does that make any sense? You did no work. You collect no pay. That's the real world."

Tripp pivoted to stare her down. "No work? You saw those renderings my poor assistant slaved over." He motioned vaguely at the couch. "Plus, I'll cover the cost of this. And I'll send you a name for someone who will give you comfortable instead of a statement." He waved one hand. "The end."

She was going to kill Sarah. The end.

"Fine." Jen yanked open the door. "I hope you get lost on the way back to civilization."

Tripp shuddered. "Mean." He paused at his car and called, "No hard feelings, sweets."

Jen squinted at the luxury sedan as it reversed down the driveway. Did he actually have a driver? That would have been evidence enough of his inability to connect with the real world.

That was where she lived.

Before she turned away, she caught a glimpse of Luke Hollister riding a pink ten-speed down the street, Mari pedaling her own purple bike with training wheels right behind. Her sword was in the air. Was Luke part of her biker gang or the target?

When she realized she was smiling at the picture, Jen shook her head. The guy was head over heels for his little girl. That just made him twice as handsome.

When he glanced in her direction, Jen realized she was frozen in her doorway. He lifted a hand to wave, snapping her out of her daze, and Jen stepped back in a hurry.

As soon as she closed the door, Jen remembered her lack of furniture and having to kiss her retainer money goodbye. She marched over to the kitchen island and snatched up her phone. Now that the shock was wearing off, it was time to rant.

"Did he bring a truck filled with wonders?" Sarah said instead of wasting time with a boring hello. "When can I come see?"

"Three weeks from never, that's when,"

Jen snapped. "Was this your idea of a joke? This reminds me of old times." Jen inched down on the couch to arrange herself around a sprawled Hope. Every brush of her silky fur made it easier to breathe. The disappointment was bad enough. The fear that she was going to mess this up, her chance to have a space to be proud of for the first time in her life, made her angry.

"What are you talking about?" Sarah asked in a patient tone.

"I can only imagine you had some ulterior motive for sending someone who was so clearly unwilling to stoop to my level. Just like the old days, when every single one of your smiles was a distraction for whatever joke you were about to make at my expense." Jen closed her eyes and tried to ignore the memories.

Silence on the other end made her even angrier. "Nothing to say?"

A sniff was her only answer at first, but Sarah eventually cleared her throat. "I don't know what's going on, Jen." Her quiet, serious tone caught Jen's attention.

"Tripp made sure to mention that he couldn't help me, not even as a favor to you.

Why didn't you warn me that he was a jerk? Is it because you all stick together?" Jen kicked one of her flats off, and was immediately satisfied at how far it flew across the empty room.

"Warn you?" Sarah said, irritation seeping through. "I tried to give you a list of five other decorators." She huffed out a laugh. "Forget that. I tried to tell you more than once that you should do it yourself. Nobody will be able to build the home you want but you. Remember that?"

The last part of her speech ended with a hard snap. Things were heating up.

Jen immediately felt better.

"Because you think I don't belong in the richy rich club, right?" Jen kicked the other shoe off and tried not to be disappointed that it didn't fly as far.

"No, you ingrate, because you have the best style of anyone I've ever met. There's no one I know who could put together the outfits you do on their own. Why in the world would you trust someone else to do what you would love so much?" Sarah drew in a deep breath. "But you insisted. You demanded. You even tried asking nicely that one time. That's when I knew nothing but your plan would make you happy, so I did whatever I could do to get you what you wanted. Because I'm your *friend*."

Righteous indignation. If Jen had to label Sarah's tone, it would be righteous indignation.

That was pretty convincing.

"Say I believed you," Jen said slowly, mainly to irritate Sarah further, "what would you say to a friendly request for that other list of names at this point?"

A long string of curse words made Jen laugh.

"That's what I thought you'd say." Jen stared at the ornate ceiling that had made her think of Italian villas and cash money the first time she'd seen it. "Then how about a friendly shopping trip this weekend? It's time this felt like home."

"One minute you accuse me of playing a dirty trick on you, and now you want to go shopping," Sarah said. "Without even a hint of apology, I'd add. You've lost your mind. Call another friend. With your gentle and loving personality, I'm sure you have hundreds to choose from."

The thing that Jen liked most about Sarah

was that she hit back. With Rebecca, there would be muffled tears and then a determined cheerful attitude and Jen would end up feeling like a garbage can for weeks because she'd hurt her. With Sarah, she'd watch her back, but there was no doubting where she stood.

"I have as many friends as you do, and she's terrible at buying things. Rebecca hasn't bought anything but kitchen appliances in years." Jen wiggled her toes and focused on the pretty gold flats she'd snagged at the consignment store. There was very little doubt in her mind who they'd originally belonged to. "And the only person whose taste I trust enough to haunt the consignment store in town, even when I was pretty sure you were the devil's minion, is you. I need your help."

"A compliment is not an apology, Jen Neil." Sarah's huffy voice was good. She'd had a lot of occasion to practice it.

"Yes. Something else I learned from you." Jen smiled at Sarah's grunt. It was the truth, even though Sarah had apologized more than once for being a terror in high school. Jen had thought she'd let all that go. This episode was enough to convince her she might still have some work to do. "Come with me. I'll apologize in the car."

"Clever. The one sure way to get me on board," Sarah said with a sniff. "Fine. Let's go on Saturday, and make this apology count." Then she ended the call before Jen could agree.

Which was perfect. Things would get too mushy if they went any further.

As she listened to Hope snore, the terrible feeling that Tripp had seen through her shell to the unworthy person underneath faded. She lived with the certainty that someone would eventually call her a fraud. Surviving an episode made it seem a little less scary. Dressing carefully was important. Buying the right things, now that she could, mattered. Sarah would steer her in the right direction, and between the two of them, they'd have this place look great in no time.

Relieved and anxious to move on to something else, Jen picked up her phone again.

Watcha doing? Texting Chloe had gotten easier. Her niece was one of the few people on the planet whom Jen would rather talk with, but she was also a teenager who typed faster than her mouth formed actual words.

Homework. Spanish. The long line of Zs emoji conveyed her feelings brilliantly. You?

Plotting world domination. The usual. I need an OTT idea for Halloween decoration. Jen was slowly learning how to work the abbreviations into her text, mainly by researching them as Chloe used them. OTT meant over the top, the only way to go in this competition.

When her phone immediately rang, Jen laughed out loud. "I wasn't sure you knew your texting machine also made phone calls."

"This is going to be so much fun!" Chloe squealed. "But I can't come this weekend." Her excitement turned into a long, drawn-out wail. "Dad's traveling, won't be home until late Saturday night." The breathy way she said it suggested it was the cruelest turn of events ever and Jen understood in a flash why Sarah was happy enough to agree to the shopping trip. No Will, so Sarah was free. Ugh.

"Sarah and I are going to do some shopping in Austin. We could pick you up Saturday. You could stay with me if your mother's okay with it." Jen didn't even get the words out of her mouth before Chloe was shouting to her mother to get permission.

"She said yes. Shopping for what?" Chloe's

voice was nearing decibels that only dogs could hear.

"Furniture. We can brainstorm ideas for Halloween, too, if you want to come along." Jen had zero doubt Chloe would be ecstatic.

"Yes! Yes! Yes. I'll get all my homework done on Friday night. I'll shop. I can see Dad on Sunday when he drives me home. This is awesome." Chloe's enthusiasm was what she needed. Sarah would be thrilled to spend time with the girl who was going to be her stepdaughter someday and she'd easily forgive Jen's misstep.

Maybe she was the evil genius, after all.

"I want to win this competition. We need big. Interactive. We need help." Jen sat up and rubbed the ache in her neck. Stupid couch. She had things to do and no time for sitting around feeling sorry for herself.

"Hmm. Do you want to go kid friendly? Or gory…" Chloe was already plotting.

"I'm not sure, but I want sound effects. Lighting. Big." Jen paced through the empty rooms and tried to imagine what she'd choose to put inside them. If she had to guess, after Saturday, she and her team would have enough furniture to fill the place up.

"We're going to need a fog machine," Chloe added so matter-of-factly that Jen had a shiver of delight.

"Start a list. We have until the week before Halloween to put everything in place. The judging and awards are handed out on Halloween." Jen had already memorized the rules.

"That's not a lot of time, but we can do this." Chloe was quiet for a minute. "Hansel and Gretel? The house would sort of work for that. Or maybe we do a twisted fairy tale thing. Or a cemetery with vampires rising up from graves…"

Jen could hear scribbling. Chloe was on the case.

"I love all those ideas. We'll brainstorm on Saturday. I'll pick you up then. Love you, kid." Whenever her mother's insistence on Will's hero status set her teeth on edge, it was easy to let the irritation go. All she had to do was think about this awesome young woman he'd brought with him.

"Can't wait, Jen. This is so exciting," Chloe said. "I love you, too. Hope your credit cards are ready."

"Do your homework. I'll go warn the credit

cards about what is coming." Chloe's giggles were sweet as Jen ended the call.

Most days, Jen was okay that having children didn't seem to be in her future. She spent enough time trying to force-feed them education, and she'd learned early how dangerous this world could be. Besides, she loved the peace of being on her own.

Then she talked to her niece. Will and his ex Olivia had done an outstanding job of raising a girl more than equal to the challenges of life. Chloe was going to be happy, brave and strong.

And little Mari from across the street seemed prepared to take the world by storm.

These kids were all right, but that didn't mean she had to rethink her own plans. "What's your opinion, Hope? Twisted fairy tales could be fun. I could still be a witch, too." Her dog was completely unconcerned as she padded over to sit patiently next to the counter where the treat box lived.

Life was good. It was comfortable. And after Saturday, she might have the couch to match.

CHAPTER EIGHT

AFTER A LONG DAY of patrolling Holly Heights and the highway in and out of town, Luke was glad to be away from the patrol car. He and Davy had written a few speeding tickets and answered a domestic call to break up a fight over too many late nights out, but all that was left now was paperwork.

He hated paperwork. Marcus, his old partner, would have filled out forms in his spare time if he'd had the chance because he'd loved it so much. They'd made a good team. Luke had the hunches; Marcus dotted every *I*, crossed all the *T*'s and grinned like a maniac over a properly filled out incident report. After years of handing over all his reports to Marcus, being forced to sit and painstakingly weigh his words and spelling was the worst.

And judging by Davy's grumbling under his breath, Luke was going to be looking at a fair distribution of all paperwork while he was with Holly Heights. Since every glance Davy had given him that day seemed to be an evaluation—like a disappointed father hoping for better behavior—Luke was pretty sure he'd get zero help from his partner.

Great. If the excitement got to be too much for him, he could look forward to dying slowly, one paper cut at a time.

When his cell phone rang, Luke nearly sighed with relief, but his mother was only supposed to use it in emergencies while he was at work. Luke yanked the phone off his utility belt. "What's wrong?"

"It's Joey. He's in trouble at school." His mother's voice was weak. "Principal held him off the bus and gave him detention, so he needs a ride home but I don't feel...well. Camila got the job waiting tables in Austin, so she went to work today and didn't answer her phone. The principal called again because she would like to go home now. Can you..."

She didn't finish the request, so Luke said, "Sure, Mom, I'll pick him up. Don't worry."

"Thank you, baby," she said before she hung up the phone. He'd expected her to be a little low. This would have been his parents' anniversary. They should be celebrating forty-one years together today.

At some point, she'd be strong enough to handle these calls again. Wouldn't she?

Wishing he was on better terms with Davy, Luke stood. "Okay with you if I take a quick break?"

The older man pinched the bridge of his reading glasses and dropped them on his desk. "More info, please."

Luke tilted his head back to study the ugly ceiling. "My brother's had some trouble at school, needs a ride home. I'll be back in twenty." Probably. Maybe. If Joseph was hurt or sick or whatever, it could take longer. And then there was his mother, whatever shape she was in.

Adams studied the clock. "You go. There's only an hour left, I'll cover the rest of the shift. Like a friend might do." Then he waggled his eyebrows, slid his glasses back on, and stuck his nose into the tiny notebook from which he'd been transcribing notes.

Relieved, Luke dug in his pocket for his car keys, trotted through the small parking lot and slid into his car. Conscious of that urge to hurry that would make him do something stupid unless he controlled it, Luke drove cautiously by the town square and turned off at the middle school. All the buses were gone, the long pickup line had receded and there were only two cars left in the large parking lot. He pulled in to the nearest open spot and turned the ignition off. Whatever this was, his mother would handle it. He was only transportation. He wasn't the parent.

No matter how many times he told himself that, that he wasn't the parent, every single day he felt the weight of responsibility tighten around his shoulders one more notch. Maybe it was time that he finally talked to his mother about the topic he'd been avoiding, explain how worried he was about her and the depression that was dragging her away from them.

If only she'd get a little stronger or look a little more like the feisty Connie Hollister who'd picked him up from child protective services all those years ago.

She'd seemed formidable then.

When he'd told her she'd be sorry if she took him away from his parents, she'd bent as low as she could so that there was no way he could avoid her stare and said, "Not as sorry as they will be." Her sweet smile had confused him, but she'd never once shown him anything other than patience.

Some people were meant to be parents. Connie and Walt had been those people.

Him? He was meant to keep those people safe. And he wasn't accomplishing much of that here in Holly Heights.

As he yanked open the door, the school's safety officer met him, one hand up. "Sir, the school is closed."

"Yeah, I'm here to pick up the kid who's keeping everyone from going home for the day," Luke said as he tapped his name badge. "Kid's name's Martinez, but I'm here on behalf of his mother, Connie Hollister. She's under the weather."

The guy studied the badge. "We'll have to check to make sure you're on the list." He waved vaguely at the front desk as if that was the general area where the list was kept.

Of course they would. They better.

If there was any doubt that he and Joseph were connected, though, the kid's reaction should have cleared that right up. "No way! Brought out the big guns." His sneer was normal. The spooked look in his eyes was not.

Neither was the red mark on his cheek, right under his eye.

"You been fighting?" Luke asked as he stepped closer to Joseph.

The safety officer and the tall gray-haired woman who stepped out of an office both joined him, the three of them pinning Joseph in.

"Not that he'll tell us," the woman said with a sigh. "Principal McKelvy. I expected Joseph's mother." She studied his face and uniform very closely. "We'll have to check the list."

Luke nodded. "Fine. One of you do that while the other tells me what's going on."

She raised an eyebrow and stepped behind the desk. Luke couldn't quite make out what she was muttering as she shifted through stacks of files, but it wasn't complimentary. "We're a bit shorthanded, so things are…" She gripped a file and yanked. "Jumbled." She handed the safety officer a file. Then she crossed her arms tightly over her chest. "Joseph here decided to skip his last two periods. Officer Huertas was checking the bathrooms to be sure we were clear to lock up when he spotted his backpack."

"Mom said you got detention," Luke said as he tried to make sense of the different stories. "Is that what you told her? How were you planning to get home?"

Joseph didn't meet his stare. One lazy shrug was his only answer.

"Why are you lying to Mom?" Luke wanted immediate answers.

Adams's advice about trying another way than applying pressure was still fresh enough that it was easy to remember.

"Name's here, Principal," the safety officer said and plopped the file down on the counter. "He's got permission to pick up."

She smiled and offered him her hand. "I hope we won't be meeting like this often, Officer Hollister."

That was all she had to say?

He motioned with his head to get her to follow him out into the hallway.

Before he could get a word out, she shrugged. "He's not talking. I don't know what happened, how often he's been skipping class or what he planned to do to get home. Believe me, I've been asking."

"Can't you threaten him with… I don't know, a real detention?" Luke ran a hand down his nape and turned to stare back at the doors that led to freedom. If this turned into one of those Afterschool Specials where he had to be all understanding and wise, he and Joseph were both in trouble.

"I'm not big on threats. I'm not very good at them and they don't seem to work consistently." She patted his shoulder. "He gets a warning for this first offense. That's to give *you* the opportunity to straighten this out. If it continues, he'll get proper detention. Eventually, we'll go to the next step, which will be on his record. The record that will follow him to high school. I don't want that."

Luke wanted to be grateful for her understanding, but more than that, he wanted her to fix the problem.

"Kids who move to new schools often take time to adjust. Did you have any trouble like this in his old school?" the principal asked. If he lied, she'd know. Those were the kind of eyes she had, like she could see the truth way deep down inside.

"A little. We moved here to avoid trouble." Luke would never be comfortable with school authority figures. As a kid, he'd always been on the wrong side, never the honor roll or special awards. He'd done his share of skipping class.

Until Walter Hollister found out and threatened to take his car keys away. Since they spent nearly every weekend tinkering on the Mustang, Luke had been in deep solid love with that car. That made it easier to turn his back on his wild ways. Then Alex had been shot and nothing but the safety of home made sense for the longest time. Until he'd met the policeman who arrested his brother's killer and decided to become a detective.

The decision had kept the grief and guilt away for years.

Knowing what he was meant to do had made all the difference to Luke's future. They had to help Joseph make it there.

"Moving was a big step. It's clear you're committed to Joseph, but you're going to have to do something else. Geography didn't magically solve your problem. It hardly ever does."

Luke realized that was true for both Joseph and his mother. He'd thought new scenery would lift her spirits, restore her to her old self. Apparently, he was going to have to do more on both fronts.

Principal McKelvy wrinkled her nose.

"From what I understand, you're going to need to look into some tutors. In English, Joseph is a solid C student, but math… He needs some help."

Luke rubbed the ache in his temple. "Yeah. Got a list of people my mother should contact?"

She tilted her head to the side. "If you can convince her to take on another student, the high school geometry and algebra teacher, Jennifer Neil, works with younger kids. Or she did. Now that she's rich, I don't know if the satisfaction is worth the extra time with surly kids."

Hearing Jen's name reminded him of catching her watching him from the safety of her front door, framed like a beautiful, expensive picture by her house. He should have seized his chance that day, asked for her help, but there was something about her that made him hesitate.

Almost as if he knew getting too close to her was dangerous. To what? If he knew the answer, he'd feel so much better. Sometimes a man just understood he'd met the fork in the road that could change everything.

Uneasy again, Luke asked, "Surly. Has he

given you a lot of attitude?" His mother would not go for that. She'd worked in schools for so long that disrespect to teachers and staff was a hard line her kids learned not to cross.

The principal shook her head. "Any kid forced to do extra work with anyone is a surly kid, no offense to Joseph. He's been perfectly well behaved this afternoon. I gave him some filing to do. Other than the rhythmic kicking of one sneaker against his chair, he did it without complaint."

Luke tried to imagine that, his brother elbows deep in manila folders but the picture wouldn't come. Instead, he could see Joseph riding his bike in circles before finally putting it away, like he'd been asked to do.

The kid had a good heart. They had to figure out what was going on before that good heart was twisted or injured in a way that he'd never recover from.

"Don't guess you'd like to tell me about any drug or gang problems you have here." Luke waited for her to deny in a huff that lovely Holly Heights had such a thing.

Every cop knew better.

And this principal was in no mood to pretend. She sighed. "Well, they're both isolated and connected. We don't see much of either but we have had dealers picked up near the school grounds. Low-level players from Austin." She smiled grimly. "We rely on our friends on the police force to warn us to be on the lookout."

Luke nodded. He tried not to think too much about Eric, Mike and the Red guy who was clearly connected to something else. His contact on the Austin Gang Task Force hadn't hesitated when he'd given him the nickname.

"Please tell me Joseph hasn't had that kind of trouble." Principal McKelvy's voice was soft but firm. If he said yes, the way she looked at Joseph would change.

"No, but there was some activity in his old school and one of his buddies from the neighborhood got picked up on possession of marijuana." Not a big fish, but each tiny step could add up and take a kid to a cliff he had no choice but to jump off.

"I guess we can count on you to keep an eye out. For the school and for Joseph, then." Principal McKelvy checked her watch and gasped. "Oh, man, I am so late. I wanted to get everything refiled but... It'll have to wait. Let's get this place shut down." She bustled into the office. "Tomorrow. The ad for a new secretary goes in the paper or else."

The safety officer was handing Joseph his backpack when Luke stuck his head around the corner. "Let's go, J." He didn't wait to see if the kid followed him. The principal and the safety officer would sweep him out in their wake if he didn't make tracks fast enough. When they were both settled in the car and buckled in, Luke glanced over at Joseph and shook his head.

"They were worried you were there to kidnap me, right?" Joseph said in a fake, happy voice. "Good to know the security is topnotch at Holly Heights Middle School."

Luke tightened his grip on the steering wheel before he backed calmly out of the parking space. When they were on the road that would lead them directly home, Luke said, "What happened?" He was trying for patient. That would be his first tactic. If that failed, he'd go for hostile witness.

"I hate math. I've said that, remember?" Joseph didn't look his way but picked at a small hole in his jeans that would no doubt grow.

"That doesn't mean you can skip it." Luke was so unprepared for this kind of conversation. He tried to imagine what Walt would have said in the same situation but the voice wouldn't come. "What's with the red mark on your cheek?"

If someone had hit the kid, they were going to have to get to the bottom of this fast. Skipping class was one thing. Violence was something that would keep Connie Hollister awake at night. And Luke was determined to get rid of all those things as fast as possible.

"Bumped the stall. I was in a hurry when I heard the door open." If he'd had a chance to watch Joseph's face when he talked, Luke might have a better feeling about whether or not that was the truth. The kid's voice sounded right, but they'd all had a lot of practice making lies sound like truth before they were lucky enough to find the right foster parents.

Luke stared hard at the empty lots at the front of the subdivision as the car rolled slowly down the street. "What are we going to tell Mom? The truth or the handy lie you've already passed her?" He wasn't sure the right way to go.

Joseph shrugged. "Not much difference, is there?"

"Why do you think it's the same to let her

believe you got in trouble instead of… I don't even know what you were doing." Luke grimaced. "Were you going to walk home?"

"I could. I walked that far…before. When I lived at home. I could do it here. There I had to watch for traffic and stuff. Here, what's going to get me? A runaway cow or something?" Joseph snorted at his own joke.

"Bad people drive cars, you little jerk. They can go anywhere. Get on the school bus. Ride to the end of the street. Get off the school bus. It's that simple. Or am I going to need to set up some door-to-door service to guarantee you make it home." Luke squeezed his eyes shut. "And why wouldn't I have to make sure you actually go to school?"

As soon as Joseph straightened in his seat as if a bright idea had hit him, Luke muttered, "Never mind. The school will call us to let us know you didn't make it to homeroom. Don't you even think about it."

Joseph collapsed against the seat and picked up his backpack, half a second from sprinting from the car as soon as it rolled to a stop.

"We'll stick with your story. You've been tardy too many times but you're going to straighten up your act and if I have to come pick you up again because you missed the school bus, the ride home is going to be very different. You will be walking, me rolling right beside you, all the way through town. Get it?"

Joseph rolled his eyes. "When are you going to let me drive this thing anyway? Someone should be teaching me so that I can get my license, buy a car and get out of this place as soon as I turn sixteen."

"Right. Because it's that simple to buy a car, one that starts and goes and stops like it's supposed to." Luke parked in the driveway and clamped a hand on Joseph's backpack to halt his ejection from the car. "I worked for a full year before Dad said this car was safe to go out on the road, and that was with him helping me every Sunday. You think you're going to write a check for a new model with all the bells and whistles?" Luke watched his face. "Where's that money going to come from, J?"

If the kid was dealing drugs, money might seem like no big deal. But that was impossible. In a place like this, everyone would know and after everyone else in town knew, the police were sure to catch on.

The fact that Joseph might not be as disconnected from his old friends as his mother hoped was a concern. Should he tell her?

"I'll get a job," Joseph said slowly. "Can't be that hard. Renita's got about twenty, all at the same time."

"Yeah, and you've seen the fancy car she bought with all that cash. Seems like I put away the two-wheeled model lying on the driveway. You were there." Luke let go of Joseph's backpack. "Go do your homework without forcing Mom to raise her voice and I might show you how to change the oil on this car…in case you ever get one of your own."

Joseph studied his face, to weigh whether or not he thought Luke was making a promise he'd keep.

He shrugged again to show he couldn't care less, but still nodded as he slid out of the car.

Luke watched him go inside and then turned to stare at the house across the street. The shiny SUV he'd seen the tiny redhead in was parked at the end of the driveway. Jen was home.

He should go in and reassure his mother that Joseph was fine. Instead, he headed across the silent street and down her long driveway. A large porch stretched across the front of the house. It had no furniture, no plants, no nothing to indicate anyone lived there.

"Not the type for clutter, I guess." Since his house was all clutter, all the time, this was refreshing. Bare bones, a little sterile, but spacious. Luke stood in the spot where a welcome mat should live and pressed the doorbell.

A split second later, there was barking loud enough to cause a burglar to bolt in the dark of night. He could hear her say, "Good, Hopey. Good dog" in such a goofy voice that he wondered if maybe she had a twin. There was the bad twin he'd always met in person and the good twin who sounded sweet enough to welcome a man home every night with a happy smile and a sweet kiss.

When the dog immediately quieted, Luke was impressed.

When the door swung open, he realized there was no twin. The familiar frown was in place, even if her hair was sleek and stylish to match the ruffled skirt and denim jacket. He was no fashion icon, but her Texas chic was sharp, right down to her cowboy boots.

"What do you want?" she snapped. "I'm making Hope's dinner."

The dog tilted her head at him and sat on

top of one expensive cowboy boot. In her bandanna, the dog was the perfect accessory for Jen's millionaire cowgirl look.

He had a feeling this wasn't going to go well, but he'd come this far. "I have a favor to ask. Can I come in?"

Maybe she wore a frown more often than not, but there was no denying Jen's face was expressive. She must be a horrible poker player. Surprise melted into curiosity before the hard mask of cynical disbelief settled again on her face. Then she held the door open wider and stepped back.

She was never going to win an award for hospitality, but he needed her help. This had to work.

CHAPTER NINE

THE THING ABOUT being caught off guard was that it was hard to regain your balance. She'd never expected to see Luke Hollister standing on her front porch. The element of surprise, added to his complete and total hero vibe in that police uniform, was enough to force Jen to step back.

That was the only reason she'd allowed him inside. Obviously.

"This won't be a long visit, right?" Jen asked, frozen in front of him. *No weakness. He's not a nice guy. Let him make his case and show him how the door works.*

"Probably not, but I'd love to have the full tour." He met her stare directly, a patient curl of his lips the only clue that he was prepared to wait her out.

His careful study, all directed at her, filled her with a restless energy and sent a pleasant but unfamiliar awareness through her. That was a very good reason to get him out of there quickly.

"The favor. Hit me with it." She paused next to Hope's couch. Jen hadn't quite decided if the thing would have a permanent home here or not, but her dog seemed to like it.

"Nice place. I like what you've done with it." Luke turned in a small circle. "Are you planning on renting it out for weddings and proms? Because I'm not sure we're zoned correctly for that."

If she'd been a friend of his, that might have been amusing, the little jab at her complete lack of decoration. But they weren't friends. They weren't going to *be* friends.

And the feeling of being two steps behind all the cool kids swamped her. This was why she'd wanted the best, so she'd never have to feel this creeping inferiority.

What does he know? Nothing. You don't have to make nice with him.

"Funny. This is temporary, of course. The most popular decorator in Austin was working me into his schedule. We've parted ways." Jen pointed at the couch. "He left this and Hope has claimed it. She might let you sit next to her but you will be shedding for days." *Proceed at your own risk, buddy.*

Watching Luke perch on the seat she'd vacated was funny. He wiggled this way and that until Hope jumped up beside him. The fact that her dog had found the couch completely sleepable was no good measurement of its comfort. Hope could sleep standing on her head if she had to.

Luke wrapped one arm around the big dog and then leaned back, easing a bit of the tension in the room. That made it easier to unclench her fists.

"I'm not sure how happy the couch is to be here, but I don't think you should plan on a long-term relationship." Luke bounced forward and back in the cushions. "This is the least comfortable couch I've ever sat on."

Hearing her own opinion from his lips made it harder to keep her distance. She eased down next to him and was reminded all over again how it felt to sit on a board. "And it's scratchy, too. What idiot picked this fabric?"

Luke frowned. "Was it the idiot you were paying to choose these things?"

Yes. But she wasn't going to admit that.

"Sarah and I are going to team up, make

this place fabulous. The next time you see it, you'll be amazed," Jen said and then realized she'd suggested he was going to be visiting again.

He was not going to be making a habit of dropping in. No way.

"The favor? Your chances are dwindling and they weren't that strong to start with." Jen patted the cushion next to her to try to lure her dog to her side, but Hope was paying zero attention at this point. She'd dropped to rest her head on Luke's uniformed knee and her lips were already whistling in and out in ladylike snores. So much for her protection.

"My brother. He's flunking prealgebra. I hear through the grapevine that you used to be a tutor for the middle school kids." Luke ran a hand down Hope's back and it was hard to look away. When her dog sighed sweetly, Jen almost knew how she felt.

"I was, but not anymore. I don't have any trouble paying my bills, so now I have hobbies and…things." Jen stared hard at her hands. The manicure her mother had talked her into getting still distracted her now and then. The fact that she'd already scraped away the white tip of her pointer finger would have normally enraged her by now, but she was trying to come to terms with the fact that the things that came second nature to some people would always be too much trouble for her. The time it took versus how long it lasted? No, thanks.

"Spare time to do what you want. Must be nice." Distracted by Hollister's quiet voice, Jen glanced over to study his face. He looked even more tired than when he'd crashed Rebecca's party. Not that it mattered. He was currently enemy number one.

If his tone and the expression on his face suggested he could understand her dream like no one else she knew, what did it matter? She'd rather be the odd man in the group than share something with Hollister.

Wouldn't she?

"It is. I worked every job I could find for years to pay off student loans. Now I can afford dumb, uncomfortable couches and the idiots that choose them." Jen sighed. "Everything is perfect." Why was she having to force the words past her lips?

"I don't believe you." Luke's smile was quiet, like he didn't use it much and when it appeared, it surprised everyone.

"I think I'll keep it this way. This one

couch. People won't stay for long." Jen crossed one leg over the other. "I have room to stretch out. Before, this place was wall-to-wall leather and dark wood. This airiness suits me. I like my space."

Luke glanced around. "Space, you've got. And quiet. I may never leave. Toys. Loud music. Even this uncomfortable seat could be overlooked for a while." He squeezed his eyes shut.

"Sounds terrible." She'd hate being always surrounded by noise and clutter and people. She had hated it.

But that wasn't something to make her bond with the enemy.

"Pretty much inevitable with kids, as I understand it." He blinked slowly. "They should warn a man about that."

Jen's reluctant laugh surprised them both. "Yeah, they come out screaming and then they get loud, huh?" She'd never decided what she thought about babies. Her students? At least with them, she could use her words. They might not listen, but she had a shot at communication.

"Could you make an exception to your plan for one needy case? That's me, in case you were wondering. I know your friends are not fans of mine, but my brother… I need to get him some help."

"Listen, Hollister," Jen said, determined to send him on his way, no matter how uncomfortable he seemed with asking for her help. "I'll give you a list of names, students who can do the job and who desperately need the cash, as long as you keep this our little secret. I don't want to be caught fraternizing with the enemy."

"Please, call me Luke. When we're alone like this, at least." He shook his head. "Shouldn't happen often enough to get too comfortable."

Jen crossed her arms over her chest and refused to answer his smile. If he was planning on being charming, she was going to have to turn up the volume on her disapproval. They weren't going to be buddies.

"My sister Renita's already tried to help. She's a senior at Holly Heights and smart enough to do anything, but not quite firm enough to tackle Joseph," Luke said. "He needs someone like you."

"They call me the General behind my back." Jen sniffed. "Did you know that?"

"I did not." He frowned as he considered that. "You don't have to sell me on hiring you, you know. You've got the job. Joseph needs someone to give him his marching orders. You could do it."

"Math isn't your strong suit? It seems you've got experience in trying to force people to follow your direction." When her resolve weakened, the only hope Jen had of wiggling free in situations like this was a solid counterattack. Was she going to crumple under the suggestion of a needy kid? That had been enough in the past to convince her to do things she'd never do, like write checks to give away money she didn't have and spend time doing things she didn't want to. Was it going to work this time? With Hollister?

"No. I'm not sure I have a strong suit, other than investigation." He rubbed his forehead, realizing he shouldn't be bringing that up again. "Joseph is new to the family. His old life was rough, so he's never had anyone to hound him over homework so his grades reflect that, but the kid's smart enough to work everything to his advantage, so he can do this, too."

Jen hesitated. "Tell me more about him."

She was totally going to do this. Sarah would hit the roof when she found out that a friend was abetting an enemy and she deserved to. In Sarah's shoes, Jen would plot a clever and terrible revenge. Luckily, Sarah couldn't keep a secret, so any plots could be foiled quickly.

Sarah would get over it, too. Helping kids made a good exception to any rule, even the one that said best friends automatically hated each other's enemies.

"He wants to go home, back to the old neighborhood, but he had friends there who'd get him into trouble. My father died less than a year ago and my mother… She wouldn't be able to handle losing Joseph."

Jen studied his face. There was something he wasn't telling her, but it didn't matter. Understanding the danger to Joseph was easy enough.

"Moving here seems to be a big change, Hollister. You made it to help him?" Jen wanted to say she couldn't understand the sacrifice. But she could. She'd have done the same to help a friend or family member. She would never have suspected Hollister would have similar feelings.

Maybe he wasn't part bridge troll after all.

"Not just him. There's my mother, too. I was afraid the grief would kill her. My mother always dreamed of a place with a nice yard. I could get that for her." Luke smiled down at Hope, who'd snuggled up against him. "I never believed a place like this existed until tracking Sarah Hillman forced me to spend a few hours here and there downtown. It's like the set in all those old television shows."

He was juggling so hard right now. She didn't want to feel this strange empathy, but it was impossible not to.

Jen rested her head against the couch cushion until the sharp corner hurt the back of her head, then she straightened in her seat. "Sure, if you're from the right side, it's pretty awesome."

She didn't meet his stare but could feel the weight of his eyes on her.

"You weren't from the right side?" he asked.

"Nope." And she had nothing more to say about that. "So maybe I can be persuaded to lend a hand to a kid from the wrong side. One last time." She narrowed her eyes at him. "You don't have any other math-challenged kids lurking, do you? Rebecca's already mentioned your sister and her path straight to the top."

"Renita is going to do awesome things." Luke wagged his head from side to side. "Joseph could, too. He's got the right parents. If my father was still around, this problem would have been solved in a heartbeat."

Jen could see the grief and loss. He was doing the best he could in a difficult situation.

"It's kind of you and your wife to step back and help out. That can't have been easy."

Very rarely would she have said a frown was cute, but watching him process her words was entertaining. Since he scratched absentmindedly at her ears, Hope enjoyed it, too.

"My wife," he said slowly. Then he shook his head. "Um, no. No wife." The way his lips slowly curled indicated he was as amused by her mistake as she was by his puzzling. "My sister. My niece." It was hard to pin down what made her label that look smug but it was there, whatever it was. "Have you been thinking about me?"

Scoffing was the only answer. It had saved her from worse situations. "Are you kidding? Thinking about you? Thinking of routes to run you out of town, maybe. I thought Mari looked like you when I saw her. That's all." She tried a nonchalant shrug, but she wasn't sure he was buying it.

"We're all adopted." He grinned. "Except for Mari. She's Camila's daughter, but the Hollisters got the rest of us from the foster care system." He tipped his chin up. "I understand about being from the wrong side in a sense I doubt you ever will."

Insulted and embarrassed, Jen narrowed her eyes. "You don't know a thing about me or my life."

"My first family? Was one woman who had me at sixteen and then did her best to forget about me until I was taken out of the ratty apartment at fourteen. Food was a treat and the men she kept around..." Luke scrubbed both hands over his face, disturbing Hope who lifted her head and put it back on his knee. "Never mind. I got lucky with the Hollisters. And my job to study people and form theories, I bet I understand you better than you think."

Jen rolled her eyes. "I'm a teacher. I get that." They were quiet for a long while. "She's getting hair on your uniform." Which might be the only thing that could improve how he looked in it. Luke Hollister in the Holly Heights police uniform made her think of truth, justice, the American way and being able to sleep soundly at night. A little of Hope's hair made him a man, too. "She can shed every color of the rainbow."

"Pink hair to match her bandanna?" he asked and bent to study Hope closer. The dog seized the chance to press her nose against his cheek, Hope's sweet manner of kissing without getting into trouble.

"Every color of the dog fur rainbow, then." Jen was surprised at how well they were getting along. Like this, he seemed easy, not uptight, and that he cared for his brother was completely human. "Hope's not a big fan of men. She's a rescue and I don't know much about her past. She sure seems to like you."

"Dogs and kids. I can't keep 'em away." Luke didn't look up, but wrinkled his nose at Hope. who chanced a lick this time. "Not even when I'd like to."

"Should I take her out?" Jen asked, ready to escort him to the door. The thing about sitting down with Luke Hollister was that bridge troll was quickly receding and all she could see was handsome man, one who knew how to make her dog sigh with happiness. Since she was head over heels for this dog, that made him so very dangerous. She and Sarah were friends now. If there was one thing Jen knew, it was that friends came before anything else. The ones who'd stick with a person through hard times were priceless. Sarah hadn't had that chance yet, not for Jen, but she'd stuck by Rebecca when the Cole storm had threatened.

Seeing that loyalty in action had cemented their shaky friendship, at least for Jen.

And friends didn't daydream about enemy number one.

"Nah, I should be going." Luke made no move to get up.

Jen tangled her fingers together and bit her lip to keep from asking anything that would make him seem more like a human being.

"But I don't want to." Luke shifted on the couch again. "With one comfortable seat, this place could be my idea of heaven. No light-sabers or plastic blocks to step on. No surly teenager shouting at the television and his imaginary friends in a faraway universe. Even Renita, who is as perfect as any kid should be, listens to music that blasts our eardrums. My mother... She's just... I worry." He dropped his head back and then immediately lifted it. The improbably hard edge of a cushion convinced him to sit up straight, too. The couch had to go.

And he seemed like a man with the weight of the world on his shoulders again.

The urge to offer to help him with whatever she could was on the tip of her tongue, but he slowly stood, saving them both from an awkward attempt that would catch her right between being neighborly and being loyal.

"Do you want to talk about a schedule or what I charge or…anything." She wanted to know more about Joseph's background. Being aware of something about a kid before she had him in class could help. Then she remembered a couple of times where it did more harm than good. She had a long history here in Holly Heights. Realizing one of her students was related to a kid who used to torment her was enough to color her judgment until she'd gotten a firm hold on it. No one should be held responsible for something someone else did and certainly not children.

The fact that her students were taller than she was and half a second from being launched into the world helped. Most of the time, she could see the people they were going to become. And most of the time, that was a nice thing.

It was easy to spot trouble in her class. If she had any way to contain those kids, she did it.

Maybe she and Luke had something else in common. She wanted to make sure her classroom was safe for everyone.

"You charge whatever's fair. I'll pay it. As far as the schedule, why don't I bring him over tomorrow after my shift? You can talk with him and decide how often you need to meet with him. I'd choose every day because the kid needs as much help as we can give him, but you have a life, too." His silent glance around the nearly empty house seemed to say he wasn't sure where she kept that life because it didn't happen at home, but he didn't say it aloud.

"Fine. That will work." Jen stood in order to give him the message that it was time to go. When he laughed at Hope's big wide yawn, some little chunk of her hard heart melted.

"I know exactly how you feel, Miss Hope." He rolled his shoulders and the audible crack of bones as he stretched made Jen wince.

"Have you ever had to sleep next to a four-year-old? She travels. All the way across the bed, until her feet are planted in the small of my back."

Jen didn't laugh but it was a cute picture. "Maybe I'm not the only one who needs to buy more furniture."

"The place is crammed with beds and comfy seats. She had a nightmare." He shook his head. "That was all it took."

Instead of going to her mother, she'd gone to her uncle? Jen didn't say it, but that little girl had a good sense of who'd keep her safe from the monsters and wrapping him around her finger was smart, smart, smart.

Before he opened the door, he sighed. "Thank you for helping me. I'm very aware you didn't have to. Are you going to tell Sarah?" He shrugged. "Just so I have my story straight."

"Probably not yet." Jen tapped her cowboy boot against the gorgeous hardwood. "Not that she'd have any trouble with me helping Joseph because she's a good person with a good heart who will help anyone she can. Now." Jen grunted. "But if you tell her I said that, I'll have to kill you and that's going to make us both unhappy, so don't. I don't want to hurt her feelings if this is a quick fix and I can avoid it."

She watched him process that. When his eyes met hers, he reached out to squeeze her hand. The gesture caught her off guard and only wrapping her hand around his stopped the falling sensation. "I have a feeling she's not the only good-hearted person around. You didn't have to help. I will remember that."

Unsettled but determined to keep everything on track, Jen rolled her eyes. "I'm a teacher, Hollister. It's what we do."

His smile was a curl of the corners of his lips but he seemed younger, more approachable as he stepped onto her empty porch.

"I don't know if anyone told you this, but Halloween's coming. Maybe you could pick up a pumpkin or two. Surely designers can't object to that." He waved a hand at the long, empty expanse. "It's a seasonal thing. What normal people do."

Jen pursed her lips. "I don't see any witches or ghosts over on the Hollister house, either."

Luke nodded. "You have a point. Now that we live with a little kid, we'll have to fix that." Then he frowned. "I'm guessing we won't get many trick-or-treaters this far out. Mari will be disappointed."

"Most of the party happens around the town square on Halloween. That will make up for some of the disappointment." *Don't do it. Drop the conversation and let him go.* "Also there's a tour of decorated homes. You could get yours on the map. Then you'd have more traffic than you can handle."

He braced his hand on the iron railing. "No, thanks. I hate traffic."

She pursed her lips. "Then you aren't going to be happy. Maybe you should take a look at settling in Piney. That town has nothing to celebrate. Should be very quiet. This year, this place is going to be lit up like... Well, I haven't decided yet, but I'm going to enter and win the contest." She shrugged. "There's no other option, Hollister."

He laughed. "Just like that. You decided it so that's how it's going to be?"

"Pretty much. It's always worked for me in the past." She stepped back, anxious to end the conversation before they got any closer.

"I'll see you tomorrow. Maybe then you'll call me Luke." He winked. "Now that we know my wife won't mind." Whatever was weighing him down had lightened as he turned to walk away. Luke Hollister whistled a cheerful tune that she couldn't quite recognize.

Which was a gift. She hated whistlers.

It might not be enough in his case.

Jen shut the door and leaned against it. "Handsome. Single. Enemy number one. This could be a problem, Hopey."

CHAPTER TEN

"GUESS YOU'LL BE GLAD to see your buddies again," Davy Adams said as he unbuttoned his uniform with quick, precise snaps that seemed to indicate his true feelings on the matter.

"They aren't buddies," Luke murmured and wished he'd headed straight home instead of taking advantage of the world's smallest locker room to change into street clothes. The boys from Austin were going to take the lead, as he'd expected. Some things didn't change. They were the ones with the intel. They had a previous warrant out for Red. They'd be the ones making the arrest and taking the credit and if his piddly case happened to be solved at the same time, so much the better. Both departments would pay lip service to cooperation but only one would count the win.

He used to be on that team.

"Still, it will be more like old times, won't it," Davy said.

"I was thinking I'd skip it…unless you want me to be there." Luke didn't want to stand on the outside and peer in the window as someone else did his job.

"Got plans?" Davy asked, a confused frown on his face.

"Sort of. My kid brother is being tutored, starting tonight." Based on Joseph's immediate and angry reaction that he spend more time with a teacher than he absolutely had to, Luke felt like the adult again. And since his mother seemed perfectly content to let him take the lead… He had no choice. It was time to be that adult.

"With Jen Neil?" Davy let out a long, low whistle. "Wow. You aren't scared of anything, are you?"

Right now? So many things.

Luke slammed his short locker closed and grabbed the duffel at his feet. "I'm going to go pick the kid up at school." Thus, the leaving early. Davy had agreed, and the chief had given his approval. Looked like he was about to actually take time off work. All over a kid.

"You know she's tight with Sarah Hillman." Davy shook his head. "Of course you know. She's also one of the hardest and yet popular teachers at the high school. Never would have believed it when she was a little girl."

Curious, Luke paused in the doorway. "Why? What does that mean?"

Davy wagged his head. "Some kids, they get a mixed bag when it comes to parents. Her mom? She's solid, been waiting tables over at Sue Lynn's since I can remember, but that girl's daddy? He climbed out of the crib with a natural talent for trouble. Soon as he found out he was going to be a daddy, he lit out for parts unknown." Davy sighed. "And they struggled. It's not easy to be one of those families in Holly Heights, the ones that need help now and again. But she was a scrapper. Glad to see a piece of good luck come her way. It ain't that often you see someone start with nothing and pull themselves up through hard work, but she did it."

"And then she hit the lottery." Luke stared hard at the cinder block wall as he considered Davy's history lesson. Maybe she did understand where Joseph was coming from, where he'd started out. His lottery had been Connie and Walt Hollister. She was lucky enough to have a good mother, but sometimes only a gift from fate could make a difference.

"And it doesn't seem like she's let it affect her. Not too much." Davy wrinkled his nose. "Although she sometimes seems like she could be on a government watch list. It's the glare. It's powerful."

Luke nodded. He knew exactly what Davy meant.

"Defense. We all learn to do as much with body language as we can. Saves some bruising," Luke recalled. "And eventually some of us grow big enough to take over the bruising." She never had. That expression was all she had to work with.

And a big old gated compound.

And friends that would back her up in a bar fight should she ever need it.

She was doing all right.

All he had was the family and the job.

Most of the time that was enough.

"Can't even imagine how she and Sarah bonded. My niece went to school with them, talked about how Sarah was the bully who ruled the school. But as long as Jen was around, people weren't too worried. The poorest kid always wore a target." Davy frowned. "Guess none of us know what's happening at home. Bobby Hillman surprised us all, too."

"You heard anything about him?" Luke asked as he checked his watch. Joseph would be wondering if he had a ride or not. A little uncertainty might be good for him.

"Better ask your buddies from Austin." Every *S* Davy used had a long, drawn-out hiss.

On that note, Luke held up his hand and headed out the door to the parking lot. Why didn't leaving work early feel like a cause for celebration?

Because he was good at work.

Joseph was sitting on the curb, fiddling with his phone when Luke drove up.

"Thought you'd forgotten me," Joseph muttered as he fastened his seat belt.

"Nope, no way to forget you," Luke said as he turned out onto the main street through Holly Heights. "Having to take off work makes you stick out in my mind."

"Hey," Joseph said, "you're the one forcing this stupid tutor on me. I didn't ask for more math work. I didn't ask for more time in school. Drop me off at the house and go back to the station."

Clenching his jaw made it easier for Luke to bite back his immediate response. If the little jerk could be grateful for anything he'd done to keep the family together, this might not seem like such an unfair development. But no. And he was a kid so Luke had to be the bigger man. In a second, he'd manage that. Right now, he concentrated on breathing in through his nose slowly and then back out. Slowly.

"And when you flunk math and fail eighth grade, what would you like me to do then?" Luke shot a quick look at Joseph and noticed he'd wrapped one arm around his ribs.

"Send me back to my old neighborhood." Joseph turned his head to stare out the passenger window. "We all know it's only a matter of time until you give up anyway."

Luke thought about pulling the car over to make his point crystal clear.

"Flunking eighth grade doesn't have to be a foregone conclusion," Luke snapped. "All you gotta do is pass. No one expects you to lead the school the day you walk in, but Mom wants you to be happy and successful. To do that, you need to be planning to move on to ninth grade. That's how it goes."

"Renita did. Take over the day she walked in," Joseph muttered.

The kid had a point, but very few people could live up to Renita's success.

"She's one in a million. I got you the best tutor we could find," Luke said as he tightened his grip on the steering wheel, "and she might even be able to help with other subjects." What did he know? Weren't teachers good at everything? A math teacher might also be able to tutor a kid in English.

Joseph didn't reply. That was enough confirmation that Luke couldn't drop the kid off at the curb. He was going to have to go in.

Instead of pulling into his own driveway, he turned into Jen's and scanned the outside of the house. It looked like the fencing company had completed setting all the posts. Soon, she'd be locked up safely behind a fancy fence.

It was hard to understand what she thought the danger might be in Holly Heights, but he couldn't argue with the fact that she'd gotten the very best she could buy. Would the same company that built this showpiece also do the mundane-wood privacy fence?

The sound of the dog barking as they got out froze Joseph in his tracks. Mari ran toward dogs. Was Joseph afraid?

"I do not like the sound of that," he said softly and hitched up his backpack. "Junkyard I used to run past to get to church on Sunday had German shepherds outside. They took fences as suggestions."

Luke studied the kid and tried an encouraging pat on the back. Too hard. Joseph lurched a step closer to the door and then scrambled two steps back.

"I've met this dog. So has Mari. She passed the little kid test." Luke waited for Joseph to step forward. "You're a grown man. The dog won't bother you." Would Alex's trick work again?

Joseph tipped his chin up and then marched up to the door.

Grown men didn't tremble at barking dogs, apparently, and neither did kids who thought they were already adults.

When they stopped in front of the door, he noticed two rocking chairs painted a light turqouisey blue. Apparently she'd either gotten tired of waiting or planned to prove she had what it took to do her own thing.

This time he knocked instead of ringing the doorbell. That decision paid off because Hope was a grinning welcome when Jen opened the door.

"You must be Joseph." Jen glanced in his direction. "Hollister."

"Martinez. Joseph Martinez." The kid hit his last name hard enough that Luke felt it like an insult. He didn't think of himself as one of them, clearly. How long would it take for that to change? If something didn't happen soon, his mother would see that, too.

"Great. It'll be easier for us to study at the bar." Jen held her hand out and Joseph slipped past her. When Luke tried to do the same, she stopped him with a hand right in the center of his chest. "Where do you think you're going?"

The urge to brush her hand away and then tangle his fingers through hers was strong. He bent his head. "J's not too happy about this little arrangement. He might act better if I hang around, give him threatening glares. Besides, I have to make sure you're competent." Why was he antagonizing her? Mainly because it was fun. Her chin jutted out. Her eyes narrowed, and she swept one lock of shiny red hair behind her ear. Whatever she fired back with, he expected it to be a direct hit.

Instead, she muttered, "Fine. You aren't

the first overbearing parent I've worked with. Doubt you'll be the last."

Luke immediately wanted to argue that he wasn't a parent at all. He wasn't. He was a concerned son and brother doing his best. He didn't want the responsibility of parenthood. He only wanted to be a cop. But she was paying zero attention to him.

Jen had stepped behind the bar and smiled down at Joseph, who was staring around the empty room. "Next time you visit, I'll have real furniture. Until then, I definitely have real cookies. I did not make them. I cannot guarantee them every time because Rebecca has found a new hobby herself and when Cole is around... Anyway. I don't cook. We have to rely on the kindness of friends to get these, but they are the best cookies in town."

Joseph snorted but he didn't hesitate to take one. "You never had dinner at the Hollisters. Bet I've had a better cookie." Luke was glad he didn't have to say it out loud, but he'd be shocked, too, if anyone made tastier cookies than his mother. It had been a while. Luke was glad Joseph could remember.

Joseph bit into the chocolate chip cookie and tilted his head to the side as he taste tested. Luke was trying to inch closer to the plate, but Jen shot him a mean look and scooted it farther away. "Unless you're here to do homework, hands off the cookies."

That was enough to thaw Joseph. His smug grin would have made Luke laugh but he was the one left with no cookie. "They are good. Maybe even better than Connie's."

Connie? Like this runt was an adult or something. "I'll be sure to tell Mom you said so. You'll be getting coconut cream pie for dessert for the rest of the year." Joseph hated pie. Most of them did, but it made a good threat. "Pull out your books. You've got plenty to learn."

Jen opened her mouth to argue but closed it with a snap before she turned away to grab a treat for Hope. When the dog sat up on her hind legs in a perfect begging position, Joseph's mouth dropped open. "How did you teach her that?"

Jen leaned down to rest her elbows on the counter. "I'm a very good teacher. Trust me."

"Stop stalling. It's time for math." Luke tipped his chin up and grabbed a cookie from the plate. The imaginary steam that came out her ears was entertaining. He'd expect a redhead to blush. Instead, her eyes narrowed and she turned her back on him.

"Math is so easy," she said. "Show me where we're starting." From his spot at the end of the island, it was nice to watch her slowly convince Joseph that whatever he learned, he'd enjoy it. Luke could imagine her in front of a class full of belligerent teenagers. She'd take control with measured steps until every person in the room had forgotten a time when they didn't obey and like it. She was impressive.

Joseph thought so, too. "I might be too dumb to learn, even from a very good teacher."

"Just keep your mouth closed and your ears open, kid." Luke crossed his arms over his chest and caught the scowl Jen directed his way.

"No one is too dumb to learn." Considering some of the people he'd had the misfortune to question over the years, Luke snorted.

Jen tilted her head at Luke. "Some are so dumb they refuse to take the lesson but that's about hardheadedness, not intelligence."

Joseph looked from her to Luke and back before he bent down to pull out his notebook.

The urge to take serious issue with her tone and her pronouncement was hard to fight. When she wrapped her hand around his biceps and tugged him toward the door, Luke was too surprised to do much more than follow her.

"Open the book up to today's assignment, Joseph. I want to see how far along you are," Jen said as she opened the door, pushed him out on the porch with insufficient but convincing force and then closed the door behind them.

"We definitely should have discussed my terms," Jen said as she urged him away from the door. "This isn't going to work. I never try to teach with parents hanging over my shoulder. Kids hate that and I'm not a big fan of it myself." She stopped next to the steps. "You have to go. Give us an hour to talk and look over his current assignments. We're going to have to move back before we can go forward but the kid's got to do some homework, too."

"He'll listen with me there." That had to be the truth. It would have been for him at the same age. A pretty schoolteacher who smelled like chocolate chip cookies? He'd have been half in love and totally zoned out before she opened the textbook up to the correct page. "Joseph needs an order to get moving."

Even scowling at him, Jen Neil was…beautiful. Not in the peaceful, sweet sense, but in the same sense a near brush with death made everything in the world seem brighter and better. She was glaring daggers, but standing this close to her, he wanted to…

Kiss her? That made no sense. She had the soft approachability of a wounded badger. Kissing her would lead to stitches.

"Have you gone away somewhere?" she said with a cautious note, as if she was worried about his mental capacity. "What are you staring at?"

"Your lips." Luke shook his head. "I'm staring at your lips."

Her head jerked back, almost as if he'd jabbed her in the nose. After blinking a couple of times, she asked, "Why would you do that?"

"Because I was thinking about kissing you." Luke waved away the comment. "Don't worry. I'm not going to do it. I can't kiss a woman who refuses to use my first name."

Jen grinned. "You have got to be kidding me. In no universe would that ever work on me, either to get a kiss or to call you by your first name. Get out of here. I'll help with the math. Go find someone else to pucker up with."

She crossed both arms over her chest and muttered, "Kissing. We are not kissing people."

Luke leaned in to say in a low voice, "I definitely am and I think you could be, too."

The quiet thump of her head against the door blocked her retreat. "You are the enemy of my best friend, an annoying neighbor, and if I have to judge by the way you talk to your brother, you're also a bully, at least in attitude if not in behavior. I hate bullies. Worse than anything. Get off my porch. Or I'll call the police on the police."

Luke rubbed the ache in the center of his chest. However wrong she might be, she firmly believed he was capable of bullying Joseph. Maybe he was. "If it gets the right results, what do you care if I force him to be respectful and pay attention?"

"Maybe it gets results. I can't argue with the fact that the biggest and strongest one in the room can make all the rules, but when you're dealing with a kid, you have to think about the lesson he's learning. Do you want him to go through life looking to push people around?" Jen shook her head wildly. "I don't. I'm the smallest one on the end of the line most of the time. That means everyone wants to push me around and it's been like that since I had to run home, afraid, every day after school. There was no one bigger or stronger or scarier for me to hide behind. I won't ever let you teach that it's okay to push someone around because you can, not in my own house for sure."

Caught off guard by her words, Luke stepped away from her and watched as she got control over the emotion making her cheeks red. She thought he was pushing Joseph around? The tension in his gut was upsetting. Maybe she had a point.

He could remember fear like she described, but he'd eventually grown big enough to make other people move out of his way. She never had. He wanted to promise he'd never let anyone make her feel that way again. That was his job.

How could she believe him, though?

"I'm sorry." Luke couldn't relate to the feelings she'd described.

"Don't apologize. Do better." She stepped inside and slammed the door in his face.

Since that was the perfect punctuation to the sentence, he wouldn't have had anything else to say. Luke slowly walked down the steps, faced with a long night of...wishing his life was different.

He could hang out at home, do chores and Mr. Mom stuff until he wanted to throw himself into Holly Creek.

Or he could contact the Austin team coming to find Red. Davy was still at his desk. They could give support, make sure the kid left Holly Heights in cuffs.

As he eased into his car, Luke studied the front of Jen's house the way he might if he were planning the security. From here, he could see the posts for the fence, a nice garage that was lined with lights that must be timer activated. The front of the house was lit all through the night. He'd noticed that the second time Mari had kicked him in the kidneys after her nightmare.

Jen Neil was a woman who took security seriously. On one level, he appreciated that. Eventually, if she ever got the house set up, she'd have lots of good stuff to secure. Even then, she'd be the most valuable thing inside.

Watching her defend a boy she didn't even know against even the threat of bullying was impressive. She would make a dangerous enemy for anyone who threatened someone she loved.

And he still wanted to kiss her. She'd been half a second from shoving him off the porch, but he might have considered it worth it if he'd managed the kiss first.

He backed down the driveway, pulled out his phone and left his mother a message to make sure Joseph made it home in an hour because he'd been kicked out and he was going back to work.

If she wasn't home, that could be a good sign. If she was asleep again, that was a bad sign. At this point, he didn't want to know. He wanted good news. Jen would help Joseph. His mother would be out getting dinner with Camila, Mari and Renita. There would be a note on the table telling him where to join them after Joseph's lesson, and things were going to return to normal so that he could go back to doing the work that he loved. Soon.

Meanwhile, he was going to find Davy,

find some police work and see if he could find some answers that would comfort Sarah Hillman.

He didn't want to be her enemy anymore. Something about Jen made it hard to turn away from her, even though she was in no way his type. All he could imagine was how sweet a kiss she gave would be. He couldn't steal a kiss. She'd never speak to him again. Whatever she gave would need permission. Maybe he could do that. It was a challenge he wanted to take on. Unlike everything else that had landed on his shoulders after his father's death, convincing Jen Neil that he was more than a bully, more than an enemy, sounded like fun.

Like a little exciting police work on a Friday night could be.

As long as everything in the world was turning the way it should, he could take a little time out for himself.

CHAPTER ELEVEN

JEN REFUSED TO WATCH him exit the end of the street like a lovesick teenager desperate to hold on to the last glimpse of her one true love. She was proud of herself for getting her feet in motion after he'd threatened her with a kiss.

She did take a second to stare hard at the door after she'd closed it by pretending to be preoccupied with the long line of locks.

The memory of his face as he'd stared at her lips would keep her up past her bedtime, but for now she couldn't dissect every word Luke Hollister had said. She had an audience. And there was very little chance she'd forget the way he'd watched or how she'd felt that close to him. If he'd bent to press his lips to hers, she would have returned the kiss. As disappointing as that was, she wasn't able to deny that her pulse had kicked up when he'd leaned closer.

Unless she got her head screwed on straight, the teenage boy waiting on her for her help was going to think she'd lost her mind.

"All right. Let's see what you've got." She scanned the pages and studied the homework assignment. "Have you tried any of these yet?" She flipped open the book to see if this one provided any answers. Nope. She and Joseph were on their own. Luckily, she had a solid handle on teaching rational numbers. She loved numbers. All of them.

Instead of beginning with that lesson, though, she flipped back three chapters and tapped a sample problem. "Do you know how to solve this one?" Finding out where Joseph was starting from was going to be the trickiest part. If they had to go all the way back to the beginning, she'd do that, but she didn't want to bore him. Math could be fun, but not if you were stuck swimming in laps when you wanted to strike out for unknown territory.

He frowned. "Maybe. I think we did something like that on the test." He hunched over his notebook and started copying down the problem. His concentration was cute, but she'd never say that to him. She enjoyed working with older kids, mainly because she could have real conversations with them. Little kids like Mari made her nervous. She had nothing in common with them. With Joseph, she had an integer joke that would kill, as soon as he understood what they were and what they could do. Mari was years away from getting Jen's humor.

Mari was still at the age where any wrong remark could scar her for life. Jen could remember a nice enough neighbor commenting on the haircut her mother had given her, an unfortunate combination of a bowl cut in the front combined with a mullet in the back. When she'd burst into tears, the old guy had looked like she'd run over his foot with her bicycle. She'd been seven, old enough to control those tears, but the heartbreak of understanding that she looked funny and had no way to make herself fit in ever was more than she could handle. Her mother had never quite understood why his comment had provoked such a reaction. Brenda still cut her own hair with the help of a handy mirror and sharp scissors she'd picked up on special at the Shop-on-in downtown. As soon as she'd started earning a regular paycheck, Jen had picked a style and a stylist who could help her get it and she'd gratefully written a check, even when she couldn't quite afford the luxury, every two months.

Maybe she dressed from the secondhand stores. Her hair rocked.

Get your head in the game.

"Let me see what you've got." Jen watched Joseph straighten, the tip of his tongue poking out between his lips in solid proof of his concentration.

She ran a finger down the problem. "All right. You nailed this one." She pointed to an underlined term in the book. "What do you know about rational numbers?"

Joseph shrugged.

"Maybe that's unfair. Point out the one on this list that isn't rational," Jen said as she gestured to the page. When Joseph picked up his pencil to write the answer down, Jen wrinkled her nose. "Just talk to me."

Joseph frowned down at the page and pointed at the correct answer. "Did I get it?"

"Were you guessing?" Jen asked as she crossed her arms over her chest. He was so serious. This was not a kid who was failing because he didn't care. This was why she'd gotten into teaching, to help kids like him.

She owed Luke a thank-you for that reminder. Was she going to tell him that? Still anybody's guess.

"No," Joseph said as he ran a hand through his dark curls, "but it helps me to trace the numbers before I answer. I can see them better."

"See them? Do they move around, maybe switch places?" Jen asked as she considered the idea that a kid his age might be dyslexic without a diagnosis.

If he'd never been lucky enough to have involved parents and teachers who'd been trained to identify dyscalculia, Joseph had to fight this battle on his own.

"Sometimes I get them backward, that's all. Deciding which one is bigger or smaller in a list takes me too long." Joseph shook his head. "No big deal."

It wasn't a big deal as long as they addressed it.

"What about letters? Any trouble with those?" Jen made a note to do some research before Monday.

"I can read," Joseph said in the perfectly aggrieved tones of a teenager annoyed with the conversation. "Let's stick to math, teach."

If Luke had been here, there would have been a shouting match. Joseph's completely normal tone was reassuring. She believed he was telling the truth.

"Why don't you try this problem?" Jen said as she flipped the page to the end of the problems assigned. Normally they escalated in difficulty, building on concepts. If Joseph could work this, she'd move on to the next lesson. If not, they'd start right here and move forward. "Trace the numbers if that helps. Use your finger or even write them down. It doesn't matter how long it takes you to work it. I've got plenty to do right here." She tapped her leaning tower of homework that would have to be graded at some point. She had no intention of doing it on Friday night, but there was no way anxiously watching Joseph work could help him.

Once the tip of his tongue was caught between his lips, she could see the working of his brain. He was doing his best to filter what he knew against this problem. He was trying so hard.

"How long have you been a Hollister, Joseph?" If she needed to go back to his school records from his first home, she could request them, but it would be great if there was enough of a history with the Hollisters to evaluate his learning. It was clear that they wanted good things for him. Luke would help her get him a therapist if he needed it.

"Year, year and a half, something like that." He didn't look up. Jen noticed he'd decided to try the last problem on the page. He had a streak of the overachiever in him. Nice. That she could work with. "But I'm not a Hollister."

Jen noticed his wrinkled brow. Was that concentration or something deeper? Then he leaned back to raise both hands in the air and immediately hunched back over, his lips a white line of pain.

When he shot her a quick glance to see if she'd caught his wince, Jen tilted her chin down. Whatever was going on with Joseph at school, it was about more than math. And this was more important than anything else. "Tell me. What happened?" If he was being abused, her whole life was about to get turned upside down. Going to battle with the Hollisters wouldn't be easy, but she'd do it. "Did it happen at home?"

Joseph's wide eyes convinced her immediately that she was on the wrong track. "You think my…family hits me?" He shook his head wildly. "No way. That's why I'm with Connie and Walt in the first place. I was in a bad spot, but not now."

"You said you weren't a Hollister. Do they treat you differently? Are you afraid to tell Luke that… I don't know what happened to you, but are you afraid to tell them?" Jen asked. She wasn't sure what she'd do if this was a case of neglect. She could hardly buy that, either. Mari had dressed like a little girl who made up her own mind. Surely people who could love a little girl that much could treat this kid kindly.

"I meant, Connie Hollister. Camila Hollister. Renita *Hollister*. I'm still a Martinez." Joseph ducked his head as if that mattered less than the line of numbers he was trying to put into order. "And nothing happened. I hit the handlebars of my bike. Please don't tell Luke. He won't let me help him change the oil in his car." He dropped his pencil. "I did the last problem, too."

Jen studied his pleading eyes. "Please. I'm already in enough trouble. I was clumsy, but no one has to bother Luke with this."

To buy herself some time to figure out what

to ask next, Jen studied his answers. Nearly perfect but… "Can you count back from one hundred for me? By tens?"

Jen smiled as Joseph frowned suspiciously. "Can I write the numbers down first?"

After she nodded, Joseph carefully wrote the numbers down, studied his list and made a correction before he read it off. Counting backward gave him some trouble, but he'd already worked out his own way around that.

"Who's your teacher?" Jen asked softly. She knew the answer but it wasn't going to do any good to get angry at this point. When she marched into the middle school on Monday and demanded to speak with Principal McKelvy that was soon enough to get irate.

"Miss Lee," Joseph shrugged and managed to do it without wincing, "but I do my best to miss her class so she might not even be sure I'm her student. When she gets my homework, she's like *Who is this?* and grades it because you guys can't *not* grade a paper." His drawl was so typically teenager that it was hard not to smile at him.

"She should have noticed the trouble you're having," Jen said and then tapped his notebook. "But the good news is that you've got this ordering numbers thing down. Let's move on to some word problems." She sang it over his groan. If she'd ever met a kid who loved a good word problem as much as she did, she'd know that kindred spirits were a real thing. Until then, she was out all alone in the world.

Joseph turned the page and waited patiently. "How do we start?"

Jen smiled down at him. "We still have twenty minutes or so…" She pretended to think. "Why don't we go sit outside and talk over this sample problem? But before we do, show me your ribs. to reassure me that I don't need to call an ambulance, a fire truck and your big brother."

Joseph rolled his eyes but he seemed convinced she'd do it when she moved to pick up her phone. "Fine." He yanked up his T-shirt. The bruising along his ribs was already turning green around the edges. And instead of a sharp point like a handlebar or even a long line as if he'd hit the edge, what Joseph had was fist-shaped and clearly he knew it. "I fell off, too. Such a klutz."

Jen motioned for him to drop the shirt. "Nobody's buying it. Is somebody giving you a hard time?"

She crossed her arms over her chest and wondered if she was going to have to get someone to cover her classes on Monday. Rooting out a real bully would take priority over handing back homework.

Joseph shook his head. "Nothing I can't handle. Don't tell Luke. I don't want the Hollisters involved. Connie's got enough to handle. She's always so tired. Since Walt died, she hasn't been the same. I don't want her to think I'm too much trouble. And Luke… Well, you've seen that guy and how supportive and nurturing he is. I'll take care of this."

"You're handling it by skipping class?" Jen asked. "How is that working out for you? Landed you in a tutoring session on a Friday night. You want to keep that up?" She wrinkled her nose, determined to pretend that this was no big deal.

"It's easier to do this when I can concentrate. Hard to do that in class." Joseph bent over his notebook again. If his head dipped any lower, his nose might come up with a gray pencil smudge.

"Shouldn't be. Is your bully making it hard to concentrate?" Jen wrestled his pencil away. "Doesn't matter. *You* need to tell Luke and your mother and the principal. I'll meet you at school and go with you, but you can't be a quiet punching bag."

His lips were a tight line when he held out his hand for the pencil. "I ain't a punching bag. I'm handling it. Let's do some word problems and get me out of here, okay?"

Jen let him have the pencil. "Have you hit them back?"

Joseph ran a finger down the page as if he was trying to find his place.

"I never did, my bullies. I never hit back. I ran." Jen waited for him to look up. "And I'll tell you it never worked out that well for me."

"So you're saying I should try to hurt them?" Joseph cleared his throat. "I mean..."

Yeah, she knew what he meant. He'd never intended to confirm her suspicions and now that he had, he was sorry.

"I took some self-defense classes in college, too late to do me any good against the people who made me miserable, but I learned a hard chop against the throat will take anyone down." Jen bent closer. "And if it's words, you square off and you give them right back. That's the only way to deal with a bully. It isn't easy, but you don't want to be afraid for the rest of your school career."

The memory of confronting Sarah in the hallways of Holly Heights reminded her of the fear and bravery it had taken to defend herself. Until she'd been pushed to the limit, she'd handled things like Joseph. By hiding the hurt and fear and doing her best to keep it a secret from her own mother, who was stretched beyond her own limits.

No kid should have to live that way.

"Won't matter if I'm no longer here in Holly Heights." Joseph shook his head. "And I won't be here for much longer."

"Where are you headed?" Jen asked. "Someplace with a beach? I've always wanted to live on the beach." The tension in the room made it hard to breathe. Her joke didn't lighten it much but Joseph's rolled eyes made her feel better.

"Seems a shame to live your life afraid for however long you are staying," Jen said slowly. "Why are you planning on making this a short stay? Got a better offer somewhere else?" The more they talked, the more concerned Jen got about what she was going to have to tell Luke. If this kid was being bullied, his family deserved to know. If he was planning to run away, she couldn't keep quiet about that, either.

"I figure…" Joseph bent closer to his notebook. "With foster kids, when things get rough, sometimes families send them back. And Connie's had it rough. Luke will be the first to support that decision, so I hate to get too attached to anyone or anything. When I go back to Austin, things will be that much harder."

Jen tugged his notebook away, anxious to give them both some time to think. "You got both of those right, too. Have you been faking in school? Pretending you don't get it?" She'd seen crazier things happen than a smart kid pretend to be dumb to avoid some heat. She'd tried it herself at least once.

"It's hard to make good grades when you're hardly ever in class." Joseph smiled brightly. "Not that I would know about that."

Jen frowned. "You have to go to math class, Joseph Martinez. Your teacher can't help you if you don't show up."

Was that it? She'd missed the first three days of her homeroom because Sarah and Cece had blocked the doorway until the bell rang when she was in tenth grade. After her mother found out, she'd had to buck up and barge through. With one hard swipe of her crammed backpack, Cece had left crying and the teacher had given Jen the stink eye but they never tried keeping her out of class again. Making her wish she could hide under the desk. Sure, but they'd backed up considerably.

"Take a stand. Tell your teacher what's going on. Get your education." Jen wrote a large red smiley face on top of his paper. "This is the work of a kid who can beat eighth grade math. And I'll tell you what… I can't say what will happen in the future, Joseph. Maybe the Hollisters won't be home forever, but a kid who can conquer math? That kid can make it all the way to Mars. There's no stopping you." She held out her arms to gesture at the mostly empty kitchen. "See what math has done for me?"

"Winning the lottery did this for you." Joseph rolled his eyes again, clearly too world-weary to fall for any hijinks.

"Careful. Your face will freeze that way. What do you think makes up the lottery, Mr. Martinez?" Jen leaned closer and slipped the cookie plate in front of his nose. "Numbers.

Odds. Math. It's what makes this world go around and I can show you in a million different ways how the kid who controls the math can rule the world. When you get to my class and we're studying how trigonometry is used in every science, and engineering and all the things that make this world run, you will be a believer."

Joseph took a small bite of the cookie while he studied her face. It was easy to be confident. She believed every single word she said.

"Where did you get the dog from?" he asked while he motioned with his chin at Hope who was stretched out on the couch, all four feet in the air. "Not much of a guard dog, is she?"

Jen rattled the top of the treat jar and laughed as Hope sprang into action. "She knows how to work hard and play hard, followed by sleeping hard." She waited for Hope to sit and then handed her the biscuit. "She is wise beyond her years. Like you."

He frowned, but the pink covering his cheeks suggested he wasn't as confident as he was trying to pretend. "Wise?"

"It takes a smart man to gather his resources and even to make the best with what he has." Jen crossed her arms. "But it takes some bravery to stand your ground and go after what you want. If you want to learn math, stand your ground. And if you want to make the Hollisters home, you go after that, too."

Joseph knelt to carefully pet Hope who was having none of that. She flopped down on the kitchen tile and showed him where to scratch by waving both front paws in the air. His smile was beautiful. "Not sure how to do that."

"I get that. Like I said, a hard chop across the throat is simple yet effective. And with the Hollisters…" Jen wasn't quite as sure where to go with that.

"If only Mr. Hollister hadn't died. Everything is different now. Connie is so…weak. And Luke, he tries to make it all right, but half the time, I think he'd like to put us all on a boat and ship us out. Except for Mari. Everyone loves Mari." Joseph rubbed Hope's stomach and it was hard to tell how he felt about that. Jen imagined it might be hard to fit himself in around the kid everyone loved.

"I could bring my grades up. Stop meeting with the principal." He glanced at her briefly. "Help out more. Make it easier to have me there, I guess. Maybe. What do you think?"

Jen pursed her lips. "For a long time, I tried to make myself invisible, Joseph. I swear, for most of ninth grade I walked with my back against the wall and ghosted any chance I got when people looked my way. You can't live your life like that. But you can learn to love what you have. I believe that."

She did. It had taken some time to accept Will and his father when her mother remarried. And she'd be forever grateful to her mother for holding on to that connection to Will even after the divorce, even if sometimes his perfection was completely annoying. Even Sarah, the girl who'd made her some of the mess she was, was easy to enjoy now. They shared so much in common. All she'd had to do was stop fighting that and turn to embrace it. Joseph would make this work and she could help.

"What we're going to do is meet on Sunday to look over your homework. I have no doubts you can make a solid start. I will tell Luke I'm impressed with how far you've come, and you are going to tell him about what's going on at school." The kid's urge to argue was apparent but he bit his tongue when she held up her hand. Whatever Luke thought, Joseph was respectful enough with people he could tell cared. "Then next week, we're going to talk about what we can do to cheer up your foster mom. That's what caring people do, Joseph. You're already there. You need a little help. If you want to be a Hollister, you can make it happen. I believe that."

She did. Nothing she'd seen from Luke made her think he didn't have a good heart. So did his mother, she was certain of it. So many adopted kids? Connie Hollister loved them. Mari's words about adoption filtered through her brain. Whatever the situation was now, it had very little to do with whether or not Connie wanted Joseph. He was finding his way. Jen was a teacher. Helping kids find their way right on out the door was what she did. She offered him her hand for a low five, which he reluctantly slapped.

"In the meantime, I might have a job for you." She waggled her eyebrows.

"What does it pay?" He waggled his eyebrows right back. And that was when she fell for Joseph Martinez. He was going to be one of those kids who did great things. She had no doubt.

"Cookies at this stage." She leaned down. "I

need you to do some asking around at school, find out what you can about who's planning to decorate for the Halloween contest and just… keep me in the know."

His jaw was hanging open as he studied her face. "Seriously? A dumb contest."

Jen tilted her head to the side. "Ain't nothing dumb about winning, son. I will win and I only work with winners. Are you in?"

He snorted a laugh. "I guess so, crazy lady. That's what my mom calls you. Crazy lady. Little does she know."

Crazy lady? Was this about her beloved fence? Again? Still?

Then Jen realized she was about to show her neighbors some full-on crazy decoration and nodded. "Little does she know."

When he laughed, she was glad she'd agreed to tutor him. She was made for this. Nothing could change that.

CHAPTER TWELVE

LUKE HAD NEVER been good at standing on the sidelines. Even as a wild kid, he'd wanted to be in the lead, not waiting at a safe distance while all the action took place in front of him.

That made Friday night a long night.

"It's never quite as interesting as you think it will be, police work," Davy murmured from his spot in the driver's seat of the squad car. Luke had managed to catch up with him before the Austin team of detectives and gang task force members had shown up. Then they'd led the way to the trailer park and stood back as they watched the Austin team take the initiative. When Red's girlfriend had answered the door, Luke wondered if they'd blown their best shot.

Then she refused to let them in to take a look around, a classic sign that whatever they might be searching for was in plain sight.

She'd tried to slam the door closed, but

Luis Perez, the guy he'd contacted to find out about Red, was prepared for that. One hard boot jammed the door open and half a second later, the police were inside. He and Davy had waited tensely while the shouting went on, but in a blink, Red was on the front porch, his arms in cuffs, and the officers were leading the girl to the car.

"We should be glad it went down without a fuss," Davy added. He didn't sound glad. He sounded like a man who'd missed the party.

"Yeah," Hollister said as Perez headed slowly toward their cruiser. He slid out to meet him in front of the hood. "Everything secure?"

"We're going to let you guys make sure the trailer is locked down. We've done a preliminary scan, scooped up a couple of handguns, what looks like the animal shelter's cashbox and enough meth to make a solid case against him." He propped his hands on his hips. "We'll notify the schools, as a courtesy, that we've made this arrest. They'll need to be on the lookout for lower-level guys who might be carrying Red's stuff. Wouldn't do to let them get a toehold in a nice town like this."

Perez offered Luke his hand. "Thanks for

the tip. We'll make sure you get full reports on the stolen goods from the pawnshop and anything else inside the trailer so you can close this case."

In an effort to pretend to be the bigger man, Luke shook his hand easily. "Sounds good."

Perez nodded. "Heard you might be planning to move back soon. Could use a good detective on the task force. I'd be happy to put in a good word whenever it's time to come back to the real world. Austin misses you."

The insinuation that Holly Heights was less than Austin was nothing he hadn't thought himself a few times every day since he'd moved here, but out of Perez's mouth it was an insult he didn't want to let slide. But now was not the time to rock the boat. "Just keep us updated on this case. And if you hear any rumblings about the schools here, I'd like to know. I have a brother and sister to watch over."

Perez walked away.

One glance at Davy convinced Luke that the conversation wasn't over.

"You're planning to go back? Doesn't surprise me." Dave marched back to the car and slid inside.

Twice as irritated now, thanks to his partner's moodiness, Luke wanted to go home or with the Austin cops or anywhere except back inside the squadie. But he didn't have much of a choice.

He quietly closed the door and propped his elbow on the armrest. "I haven't been looking or applying or anything, but I told my old chief I was going to want my spot back. You know how departments are. Every cop is a gossip. Every single one. That's all Perez was referring to. Nothing's changed for me."

Davy raised an eyebrow. "You think I haven't been able to tell ever since you walked in that you were anxious to step right back out?" He shook his head. "If I put my mind to it, I can list a few advantages to being a cop in a big city, especially for a man with a chip on his shoulder who wants to be a hero." Adams all but sneered as he spoke. It was easy to see he didn't think much of those men.

"Real cops are heroes just by being real cops. Kids see them and trust them and need them, Hollister. And you, you've got enough hero work to do. Those brothers and sisters need you more than ever. You could be a hero here if that was what you wanted. No,

you want *glory*. That's a different thing altogether. That's what gets good cops killed, too.
If you don't learn a single thing while you're
in Holly Heights, think on that. Whatever happens next, watch the chasing-glory bit. That
family would be devastated to lose you, no
matter how impressive the headlines that accompanied your death might be."

"Want to tell me why we're being so serious and forward thinking, Davy? I haven't
changed a single thing since this morning."
Luke relaxed his jaw and tried to get comfortable in the passenger seat. He hated taking second chair, but more than that, he hated
being talked to like a kid. Like he was Joseph
and needed to be told how to live his life.

The lightbulb that came on was upsetting.
He'd lectured Joseph the same way Davy was
lecturing him. The kid had absorbed what he
was saying, as well.

"I'd hate to see you get hurt chasing the
wrong thing, that's all," Davy said and then
waved as the Austin contingent rolled out of
the trailer park. "Let's go in and lock up."
Their job was to secure the scene. The end.
After the five minutes that took, checking

windows and door locks, and closing up the place, he and Davy headed back to the car.

"Now that the excitement's over, you want to stop over at Piney and grab a drink?" Davy asked as he started the engine.

"I would, but I've got to get home." He hadn't stopped speculating about how well Joseph and Jen had gotten along since he'd backed out of her driveway. He was worried about the kid. That took some getting used to. The woman? Yeah, the amount of time he spent thinking about her would never seem normal. He wasn't sure where the urge to kiss her had come from, but something about standing next to such a vibrant, feisty woman ready to haul him to the carpet in defense of his brother was too attractive. Like, a woman you'd grab and hold on to attractive. Since he'd never thought that about any other woman, it made perfect sense he'd need some time to work it through.

"You sound like a family man," Davy said with a laugh and after the quick trip through town, they went their separate ways. Driving into his neighborhood immediately turned up his energy level. That would also take some getting used to. Her house was dark, except for the floodlights that lit the front. Almost eleven. That whole thing with Red had taken longer than he'd expected. He might be in trouble.

Luke closed his car door quietly and headed up the walk. His own house was dark except for the kitchen. He could try to pretend he didn't see that his mother was waiting up for him like she always used to do when he was a kid and sneak off to bed. But avoiding whatever conversation she wanted to have with him tonight meant he wasn't going to sleep well.

When he turned the corner and saw his mother and his sister Camila both there, cups of coffee cradled in their hands, almost like matching bookends with one chair right in the middle, the dread he'd been ignoring solidified in his stomach. "You're up late."

"Have a seat, Luke," his mother said as she straightened her shoulders.

He turned to Camila. Her tight expression matched his mom's scowl perfectly.

"I told you I was going to work late tonight." He waved his phone and set it on the table between them in no-man's-land. "You got my text, right? I dropped Joseph off and went back to work." He picked up his phone to check whether he'd missed an emergency.

"Yes, Camila and I came back from setting up for the dance rehearsal to pick him up." His mother slowly sipped her coffee to give him a chance to process her words.

"The dance recital? That was tonight?" Mari had been taking tap dance ever since they'd moved to Holly Heights. Tonight was the first show. He'd promised solemnly not to miss it.

And then he'd missed it.

"Yeah. Tonight." Camila didn't sip. She slurped. Since that was an angrier sound, it matched her expression better. "Mari was heartbroken."

From the ache in his chest, Luke thought he might know something about how that felt. He'd missed the first one. For what? A job no one needed him to do.

"I'm sorry. We had a chance to catch the kid involved in the shelter break-in, so I went to help out." That sounded almost like the truth. Telling them that his part had been to stand in the background and clap when it was all over would not help his case.

Camila sighed. "Yes. Your job. It is important, but that little girl is, too, Luke. It's okay if you can't make it to her events, just don't make her promises that you can't keep. I want her to trust family above all else. You and I were lucky to have that. I want the same for her."

The bitter taste in his mouth was impossible to ignore. "I'm not good with kids. I get that."

Camila laughed, her mouth dangling open. "Are you kidding me? With her, you're magic. She loves you, idolizes you, wants you above all else. I hope that someday there will be another man to stand in where her father should be, but until then, you are it. And you are good at it. You forgot. It's okay. But you have to decide whether you're going to be the guy who forgets all the time and let that be who you are to Mari or…not. She will love you either way, but what she learns about people from you will be a factor."

Camila stood up and punched his arm before she hugged her mother's neck. "Thank you for making it, Mom. It meant so much that you were there to help her with her hair. You know I'm a disaster." Camila stretched. "Now, I'm off to bed. I'm headed in early to work. I'm guessing this job might stick."

Whatever he'd done in his life, he'd faced the consequences head-on. This time, he wanted to slink away. Hurting someone he loved was unacceptable. "I'm sorry, Mom. I won't forget again."

One side of her mouth curled up. "Oh, you will. We all do, Luke. No parent is perfect." She held up her hand. "You don't have to remind me that you aren't her parent. I get it. And you don't need to be. Camila is doing fine on her own. No one is perfect, I should have said. If I know Mari, you'll be even sorrier before you're forgiven. People will disappoint her. And she will pick herself up and move on, stronger than she was." She sighed. "Even good men who love her more than life will make a mistake. Sometimes they even die entirely too soon. But we go on. That's all we can do." Her tight grip on her coffee cup made her knuckles white. Luke wiggled the cup out of her hand and wrapped his hand around hers. He didn't know the right words. Someday he'd get used to that.

"I've messed up, too, Luke. I've let this grief keep me down for too long." His mother stood and placed a hand on his shoulder. "You should have seen Mari's face when she saw me with my curling iron. It was like the thing she'd been afraid to wish for had come true. All it takes is showing up. Tomorrow we do better." She smiled. "I'll do better for all my kids. I promise. It's time. You've been too patient with me."

Luke wanted to argue, but he was so grateful to hear her sounding more like the woman he knew, he couldn't. Maybe he had been too patient.

That would be the first time he'd ever been accused of that.

And possibly the last.

The thing about Mari was that she didn't have to make a sound for the air in the room to change. Luke glanced at the doorway and saw his tiny niece standing there, tears still drying on her cheeks. On any other night, she would have launched herself into his arms. Tonight, she clung to the doorway and glanced from his mother to him and back. Camila stepped up behind her. "Another nightmare." She squeezed Mari's shoulders. "She insisted on making sure you were both okay."

Luke felt the pinch in his chest again. When he'd imagined nightmares, he'd thought she had to be running from silly monsters that eventually disappeared and that was a good thing.

Now he understood that disappearing was what Mari feared the most. She'd already taken that step outside childhood. "You miss Papa?" he asked and held out his arms.

"We all do, *cielo*," his mother murmured and ran a hand down Mari's tangled hair. When Mari traced the edge of the doorway and watched him with big brown eyes, Luke sighed. "I'm sorry, Mari. I didn't mean to miss your dance recital. I will watch the video with you twice tomorrow. Okay?"

She pursed her lips and then checked over her shoulder at her mother who shrugged. Then she narrowed her eyes at him and held up three fingers.

"Okay, three times." He waved his arms. "May I please have a hug now? I have missed you so."

In the manner of a queen who is condescending to forgive a peasant, Mari sailed around the dining room table, her button nose raised in disdain. Luke carefully wrapped his arms around her and kissed the tip of her nose. "Thank you, Mari. I am very, very sorry." She rested her head on his shoulder and nodded. "I'm sorry you had a nightmare, too."

As if that was exactly what she was waiting for, she blinked slowly up at him. "Snuggle?" That was her code word meaning *I'd like to take over your bed and kick you all night long. You're okay with that, right?* And he was.

Luke squeezed her tightly. "Definitely."

Camila was laughing as she stretched her arms luxuriously. He thought she muttered, "Bed all to myself" as she wandered off, but he was going to give her the benefit of the doubt.

"I don't know what we'd do without you, Luke," his mother said softly as she squeezed his hand.

That was one of the questions that would keep him awake all night. That and Mari's foot. "Maybe we should make a call about the fence. I think it's time."

His mother dipped her chin. "You think a p-u-p-p-y will get you out of the d-o—" She clapped a hand over her mouth. "Out of trouble. You are a smart man."

He shrugged the shoulder Mari hadn't collapsed against. "More than one of those houses, probably." He stood and lifted his niece, who sighed happily, content and back in control.

"Could be. We could go to the shelter in the morning, take a look around." His mother tried for innocent but there was no way he was buying it.

"If we go, you know how it will end." They'd be lucky if they were able to pick only one dog. "Do you think Camila will approve?" Didn't matter much, but as long as she was camping out with their mother, she would complain loudly if they didn't check.

"That's what we were discussing before you got here. What sort of p-u-p-p-y would work best and how we could take care of it until the men I hired today get the fence put it." She waggled both eyebrows at him. She was so sweet in her satisfaction and it had been so long since they'd seen any of her spark that Luke couldn't even be mad that they'd made the plans without him.

"What did the kid have to say about his tutor?" Luke said in a quiet voice as he and his mother walked down the dark hallway.

"Not much, but he was smiling when he got in the car to go to the recital." His mother sighed happily. "If the crazy lady can do that,

I will overlook the fence. I mean, I worried he would never settle in."

"Do you ever think about going back to work?" Luke asked and shifted Mari, who got heavier as she grew drowsier. "When I was at the school with Joseph, it was clear they needed help. A secretary."

His mother tsked. "I have no experience. Surely they have more qualified applicants."

Maybe. Luke wondered if anyone needed another reason to get out of bed as much as his mother did. "You should at least consider it. You have so much experience working with kids. I bet it would be a good fit. The principal was going to advertise soon."

"Perhaps. If we get Joey settled." His mother grimaced. "Joseph. He doesn't like nicknames."

Luke grinned. "He's a smart kid. Once he sees how awesome it is to be a Hollister, he'll be like the rest of us. You haven't been able to get rid of one of us yet."

She ducked her head and he wanted to kick himself. Had he made her think of Alex?

"You know, you all think you're so smart. The truth is, you were mine all along. I just had to find you." She squeezed his shoulder.

"Now that your father is on the job, looking for more of our kids, in his own special way, there's no telling what we can do."

Did she mean more kids? The weight that had eased off his shoulders immediately returned.

That must have shown on his face. He'd never once given the idea of adoption or having his own family much thought. His purpose was police work. He shifted Mari closer and smiled as she muttered in her sleep.

"Not to worry, son. This generation of Hollisters is set, but your generation, now there is where we could do some good things. Find the woman meant to be by your side and then we'll start growing this family." She was humming as she stepped inside her bedroom and closed the door.

Mari didn't move after he set her in the pile of blankets that she claimed as her own. The rest of his room was in dark plaid. Her fleece was purple and pink and it had dogs wearing crowns on it.

Whatever happened tomorrow, he was satisfied at how the night had turned out. He'd made some mistakes. Trying to force Joseph to be the kind of kid he wanted was at the top of the list and he still had to straighten that out. Convincing Jen to help was a good move. And he and Mari were okay. Tomorrow he'd be her favorite person in the world again.

As for tonight? He had plenty of time to decide what to do with the rest of his life. Although his mother was already planning the next generation of Hollister fosters.

Now he could picture what his family might look like. Babies were too much for him. Every future kid in the Hollister clan would have to pass the sarcastic teenager threshold. Those kids were easy to picture in his head. Then he glanced down at Mari, who'd already kicked one leg wide across the bed.

Well, he didn't have to figure it all out tonight.

That would give him some time to investigate why, in his imagination, all those future sarcastic kids were gathered around a mean redhead.

CHAPTER THIRTEEN

"WOULD YOU COME ON?" Jen snapped as Sarah held up one finger and trotted down the hallway of Paws for Love, the shelter she'd turned around through hard work and charm. "Your right hand, Shelly, is here. Her beau, the handsome vet, Les, is here. Cole is down the road and will come running if anyone pages him."

Jen paced in front of the bulletin board advertising the shelter's current strays and forced herself not to look. She loved volunteering at the shelter, but it was always a test of wills to make sure she didn't bring home a dog. The photo of a cardboard box filled with puppies had only sneaked in at the corner of her eye and she was already doing the mental lecture about how puppies were so much work.

She couldn't stand here any longer than she had to.

"Chloe has already texted to find out why

we're so late," she yelled through the hands she'd cupped over her mouth. It wasn't strictly true but Sarah would do whatever she could not to disappoint the kid. "Twice, Sarah. She's already texted twice."

"That's funny," Sarah said as she marched back toward Jen, "since I texted her that we were getting ready to leave."

"You wouldn't want to lie to your kid, would you?" Jen said and waved toward the door.

"My kid," Sarah muttered as she hustled into her office. "You do know how to push my buttons."

Jen was grinning as she heard a car pull up in the parking lot outside. If she didn't grab Sarah fast, they'd never get out of the shelter before noon. And she desperately needed a comfortable couch. The papers she toted home were stacking up.

Jen strode to the cat room. "Shelly, incoming!" She was out of breath as she slid to a stop behind the long counter in the lobby but she made it before the door swung open. Then Mari, perched on her uncle's hip, entered and breathing was forgotten completely.

Luke held the door for an older woman

with faded red hair and closed it softly after she stopped inside. Her curious stare swept over the room until it landed on Jen. Then she glanced at Luke, one eyebrow raised.

He cleared his throat. "Good morning."

Her first attempt at an answer was garbled. Staring at his lips was going to short-circuit her brain so she turned to Mari. "Good morning. What may I help you with, Princess Mari?"

"We were thinking about adopting a p-u-p…" Luke shook his head.

"I guess the cat's out of the bag, so to speak. We were interested in adopting a dog."

Mari clasped her hands together in a soundless laugh. Jen could easily imagine how that felt.

"That child might be the only way to get me to help you," Sarah said, stepping away from her office. "But it won't be as simple as that."

"Yes, it will, because we are leaving." Jen glanced over her shoulder. "But Shelly…" She wrapped her arm around the older woman who worked with the shelter's volunteers. "Shelly will be happy to help out."

Jen held her hand out to Luke's mother. "Hi, I'm Jen. The crazy lady across the street."

Instead of blushing with embarrassment, his mother genteelly shook her hand. "Connie Hollister. That is quite an…impressive fence you have going in. We will all sleep better when it is complete."

Jen felt a direct hit. She could have been a little more considerate with her fence, but she had gotten what she wanted. "Shouldn't be much longer. The gate and a few fixes here or there, and the fence will be done."

"We will enjoy the quiet." Connie smiled but it was watchful as if she was waiting for Jen's next volley.

"Well, there's this Halloween contest. I'm going to win it, and it's going to mean some traffic." Jen shrugged. "I have to defeat my mortal enemy. You get how that is, right?"

Luke's mother narrowed her eyes as she studied Jen's face. It was obvious where Luke got his powers of observation. "I do. Mortal enemies cannot be allowed victory. If we can help, I will consider it." Then she sailed down the hallway behind Shelly. If this was the woman who was destroyed by grief, she was coming out of it. That was nice to see. A trip to the animal shelter would fix her right up.

Luke let Mari slide to the floor. "Go with *abuela* to see the dogs, Mari. I'll be right there."

He stepped aside and waited for Mari to grab her grandmother's hand. On her way past, Mari held out her hand so that Jen could give her a low five and then she marched away, purple high-tops flashing.

"My mom likes you," he said, raising his eyebrows to make it clear that he knew it was the world's biggest white lie.

"Uh-huh, like she likes ants in her kitchen and littering, probably," Jen said under her breath. "I get that reaction a lot."

"You know, we have a long questionnaire, Mr. Hollister. You should fill it out before that kid gets her heart set on a dog that we won't be able to give to you." Sarah slapped down a clipboard and crossed her arms over her chest. "I would have discouraged this if you'd called before you came."

Jen understood Sarah's feelings. Really, she did, but the guy was here with his family, an adorable little girl who wanted a dog. Sarah was on very shaky ground.

"I'm not sure whether Mari's ready. This is a test." Luke sighed. "But we'll have a

large fenced yard at the end of next week."
He glanced at Jen. "Wood. Privacy. A normal
fence. And my mother is home most days, so
house-training shouldn't be a problem."

"And what happens when your dog chews
something up?" Sarah demanded. "Do you
hit it? Yell? What do you do to make sure it
doesn't happen again?"

Luke glanced at Jen, almost as if he was
looking for support. From her? Why would
he think she'd help him out?

"We already have three kids and one who
thinks her entire floor is a shoe closet. If the
dog destroys something, we'll throw the shoe
or whatever away and learn a lesson about
keeping things tidy. I'll buy chew toys. We'll
give the dog plenty of exercise. Mari will
sleep next to the dog at night, as long as he
or she doesn't mind a wild foot now and then."
He rubbed a spot over his eyebrow. Had Mari
been doing high steps in her sleep?

"Listen, your daughter is adorable. And she
should have a dog. I'm going to approve your
adoption." Sarah snorted. "Then we quit all
this being friendly stuff."

Luke pursed his lips and then winked at
Jen. She almost gasped out loud.

"Not my daughter. My niece. I'm plenty single, but I've heard that same misconception from someone else. Have you ladies been talking about me?" Luke asked.

Sarah blinked slowly, the pink in her cheeks making her even more beautiful, which was a hard thing to watch. "Only as we dreamed up horrible punishments for you."

He nodded once, even though it was clear he knew better. Luke Hollister did not need to hear about how she approved of the way he looked in his uniform.

"Right." He picked up a pen and started to fill out the adoption form. "I would have called, but you'll be glad to know the Austin police picked up Red last night. They've already connected him with the pawnshop that turned in your laptop—we'll have what we need to make sure he faces jail time. He's got other charges to face and is in Austin right now." *With your father.* No one said it, but it hung in the air between Hollister and Sarah.

"Also, I feel like I should…apologize." Whatever he thought, the word didn't come naturally to Luke Hollister. His voice was gravelly, almost as if his words were coming out against his best effort to contain them. "I pushed too hard. With you. I see you were doing everything you could and I thank you for all the help you gave us in closing your father's case. I hope his trial starts quickly and you get some comfort from having him close to home." Luke shoved his hands in his jeans pockets and rocked back on his heels.

Sarah's smile was brief. "Fine. You apologized. I'll accept it, but don't think I'll forget who you are. Or that Eric will or however many other people you've investigated and treated like criminals instead of people in need of your protection."

The urge to step between them was hard to fight and unusual. When it came to confrontations like this, Jen's first response was usually to evade, to scurry away before the cannons turned in her direction. But Luke had the grim lips and tense posture of a man braced to take whatever hits he had coming. He wasn't defending. He knew he'd made a mistake.

But Sarah deserved to say what she had to say. It would help someone in the future.

"How is your father?" Luke asked quietly.

"Don't you know?" Sarah asked. "I'd expect you to get regular updates from your friends. It was a big case, right?"

Luke rubbed a hand over his jaw and waited.

Sarah huffed out a sigh. "Thanks to Will, we have a lawyer we both agree on. He'll remain in custody until his trial, because apparently a man who has to be hauled back from the edge of the country is a flight risk." Sarah's shoulders relaxed. "But I got to see him yesterday. I know he's well and safe. The lawyer believes he'll get a minimum security sentence since he's cooperating." Sarah glanced away from Luke. "Considering how dumb his scheme was, stealing money from his employees and running, this is going to turn out as well as could be expected." Jen wondered if any of that was due to Hollister's persistence.

"He has you to thank for most of that," Luke said. "All of it could have happened very differently. I'm glad he's safe."

Jen studied Sarah. Her friend was so surprised her mouth was dangling open.

"This side of you..." Eventually, Sarah closed her mouth with a snap. "I'm not sure what to say."

Luke shrugged. "I get that. I became a cop after my brother's murder. I want justice for innocent people above all else. I should have taken a minute to consider whether or not you were one of those innocent people, Sarah, instead of jumping to conclusions. I have to do better at that."

Was this a trick? Jen couldn't imagine why he'd be luring them in with humility. It didn't seem to sit naturally on his shoulders, either. It must be the real deal.

"You did it with Cole. You gave the neighborhood ex-convict the benefit of the doubt when the shelter was robbed." Sarah's voice was soft but serious. "He's important here and he needed that." Then she turned on her heel and retreated into her office.

Luke went back to the clipboard. "I hate paperwork." He was carefully printing his address when Jen leaned on the counter.

"I'm not sure what's gotten into you this morning," she said, "but I like it."

He didn't meet her stare. "I messed up yesterday. Big time. Then I had a long sleepless night to consider what I could do to make sure it never happened again."

The scratch of the pen was loud in the silence between them. When she couldn't stand the suspense any longer, Jen said, "And?"

"The only conclusion I was able to make

without a doubt was…" Luke set his pen down and bent close enough that she could see bright flecks in his brown eyes. "I shouldn't have hesitated last night. I should have kissed you." His lips curled into a wicked grin and Jen had a split second of asking herself why he didn't do it now. "But this isn't the place. Or the time." He raised an eyebrow and eased back. "Is it?"

That was enough to snap her out of the trance he'd put her in. "Get real. I meant about your life…and stuff."

Luke nodded. "Yeah, but as far as life goes, maybe I need to stop working so hard to get things back to where they were." He shrugged. "That's as far as I made it. I love being a cop, but that's not all I love. That little girl's pretty awesome, too, and this job gives me a chance to do things like adopt a puppy so it's not all bad."

"All bad? You've been thinking about this move to Holly Heights as all bad?" Jen frowned. She couldn't understand that. She had some issues with her hometown, no doubt, and the people in it but she wouldn't trade it for anything.

"I was hung up on needing to serve and

defend justice and stand as a shield," Luke said, "or whatever, but a wise cop explained the difference between men who are heroes and those who are obsessed with glory. I only want to be one of the former."

Jen tangled her fingers together and tried to listen to the lecture that she was giving herself about not falling any harder for Luke Hollister.

But herself wasn't listening. "Glory? Is that something you thought about?" What sort of jerk decided he was going after glory? Gross.

"No, not really, but deciding one kind of police work mattered more than another because of the kind of attention it received? Sort of the same thing." He rolled his eyes. "If my older brother, Alex, could hear this conversation, he'd shut me up quick, always could and I usually ended up dying of embarrassment."

Luke slid the clipboard across to her. "I miss that guy."

"That must have been hard on you. His death."

"Yeah, when I was seventeen, he was killed by a stray shot at a fight." Luke was serious as he met her stare. "Changed everything for me."

Jen clenched a hand to her stomach where a tight ball of emotion formed. Will was the brother she'd never asked for. If she'd lost him at seventeen, how different would her world be? It was impossible to imagine no Will, no Chloe. Her mother would have been devastated. Life would be changed forever.

She'd fought plenty of battles. Losing someone like that, there was no one to fight, only the grief to get through.

If she'd lost someone like that…the drive to make sure other people got justice made total sense to her. She might have become as hard-edged and committed to a truth-at-all-costs attitude like Hollister.

If she could understand his goals though, where did that leave her with the standoff between Luke and her friend?

Jen studied the questionnaire and tried to corral her thoughts. "I can't do anything with this." She had to clear her throat to make sure yelling for Sarah would work. The lump there wouldn't go away. "Hey, Sarah, Luke's finished the adoption paperwork."

Sarah's glower as she stuck her head around

the door was intense. She normally worked with charm, but he was going to receive none of that. "Send him back to Shelly. You and I are going shopping." She quickly stepped back inside her office.

"Shelly's the lady who led Mari back to see the dogs?" Luke asked and nodded as Jen did. "Right. That lady's ready to be rescued at this point."

"Shelly's tough. She can handle one more minute or two with Mari." Jen set down the clipboard. "Have you had a chance to talk to Joseph lately?"

"He was still sleeping when we left. Up too late playing whatever game he's on right now," Luke said dryly. "Why? Did he give you a hard time?"

"No," Jen said slowly as she tried to come up with a way to address her concerns for Joseph and his safety without breaking her promise, "but you should talk to him. His trouble in school is about more than just… not wanting to be there." She studied his eyes and tried to decide whether or not he was getting her message.

"Okay," he said in the same tone, "like…" He raised his eyebrows.

"I'm wondering if he might not have a learning challenge. I'm not sure it's dyslexia. He did do very well with the homework problems we looked at last night. I'll review his homework on Sunday, but there might be something there." She shrugged. "He's doing pretty well, but you could get him someone who could make sure he's got all the coping strategies he needs. That would help."

Luke crossed his arms over his chest. "I'll definitely check into it." He didn't move to leave, remained solidly planted and curious, as if he knew if he waited long enough, she'd tell him what she was concerned about.

Jen had promised not to reveal Joseph's secrets. She'd go to Principal McKelvy and call his math teacher. Otherwise, she'd do what she'd said she would and give Joseph enough time to address his own problems. "He's excited to have the chance to work on your car with you. He told me about his plans and how you were going to help him." The way Luke's eyebrows rose suggested she was overplaying her hand here, but the gamble would be worth it if it paid off. "Please don't disappoint him." That was all she was going to say, meanwhile, she'd keep a very close eye on Joseph. If things escalated or he showed up with more bruises, she couldn't live with her promise one more day, she'd tell Luke. She would. She wanted to, standing right there in the middle of the shelter with him...watching her with keen eyes.

Eventually, Luke sighed. "All right. This is where I'm going to take advantage of my recent learning and step back. That doesn't mean you've convinced me. I can tell there's something else you want to tell me and I want to hear it, but I'm going to let you do it in your own time. I can learn." His mouth curled again and Jen did her very best not to act like a goofy teenager. It was a good look for him.

"We should be going," Sarah said firmly from the doorway, her face expressionless. "Shelly will be glad to help you, Mr. Hollister. Be sure you're ready to take on everything a puppy means. You don't strike me as a guy ready for a lot of mess." She slid her purse over one arm. "Come on, Jen. We have money to spend."

Jen couldn't help watching Luke walk away. "A dog is always the right choice, Luke."

He slammed to a stop and the smile he

gave her told her he'd noticed she'd used his first name.

He tipped his chin up and Jen refused to look back over her shoulder at him as she left. Since Sarah had her caught in a narrow-eyed stare of suspicion, Jen found many fascinating things to look at before she slipped behind the steering wheel of her SUV. "If I drive, we can haul home a few things. Chloe's prepared to brainstorm the Halloween decor, too. I like her idea of twisted fairy tales. We could do one and go all out, or do you think it would be better to do a series of vignettes? And what about the interactive piece? We'll definitely need to get Rebecca and my mom baking." Jen was trying for chipper. That was a mistake. She was never naturally chipper and trying to pretend was only going to expose her.

Sarah's indifferent shrug confirmed that suspicion. Jen shot her a quick glance to see the frown that usually indicated Sarah was thinking through some big plan. She was the queen of big plans. That was fabulous for the shelter. Jen was in no way fooled into believing that had anything to do with…

"Did you just call him *Luke*? Like you're *friends*?" Sarah said sharply. If that was the part she was getting hung up on, she'd missed the near kiss at the front desk. That was a good thing, even if Jen was getting pretty tired of narrowly missing his kiss herself.

"I'm tutoring his brother." Jen had already planned how she'd handle this. Sarah had a good reason not to like Hollister but his brother was an innocent, completely unconnected to the feud. "He's having some trouble in math. I'm thinking he might have a learning challenge, nothing big, but I want to make sure the Hollisters check it out."

"Sure, but why does that demand a Luke instead of a Hollister?" Sarah asked. This wasn't going to get any easier, so Jen might as well admit the truth.

"It doesn't. There's something about him that makes me want him to be a Luke instead of a Hollister." Jen blew out a frustrated breath. Nerves made her hands shake so she tightened her grip on the steering wheel. Talking about her past with Sarah filled her with anxiety, but their friendship mattered. "That makes no sense, except there's something about *you* that makes me want to make you a friend instead of an old memory that I burn in effigy. I must not be thinking clearly. What else could it be?"

Sarah sneered but she didn't immediately answer. Jen loved peace and quiet. Growing up, she'd never felt like she had enough space to breathe. Now that she was on her own and she'd found this cool new house, she had plenty of room and loads of serenity. In the close confines of this car ride? Not so much of either.

"Maybe..." Sarah drawled. "We've found the guy who tempts you from behind the walls you've put up." Sarah tipped her head to the side. "That guy would be a Luke."

Caught off guard, Jen snapped, "Sure, the walls that I built... Let's see. When was that? Oh, yeah, high school, when I needed to protect myself." She then added, "Not that we're fighting about that again. Because we aren't. Because we are friends. I've already made the apology I'm going to, so don't even bring it up again."

Sarah laughed. "Oh, I'll be bringing it up again. You know how amazing I think you are because you've gotten us this far. I was terrible. Mean. The worst. But you're an awesome, kind, forgiving sort. Not that anyone would believe me if I said it because you want to make sure no one else sees that because..."

Jen rolled her eyes. She wasn't going to dignify any of this mess with an answer.

"Because they might take advantage of you. They might hurt you. And I don't blame you one bit." Sarah nodded. "You're also smart. We've all seen the kind of man Hollister is. Hard. Too hard. Tough when he doesn't have to be. Pushy." She paused. "But, as one of those people who've managed to learn to act better, I can say his apology sounded genuine."

Jen blinked as she realized how much anxiety she'd been carrying about this conversation. Rebecca and Stephanie were the kind of friends that would stand beside her for the rest of her life. They'd been through so much together. Sarah was different, one who seemed to know her better than so many others in such a short time because they had a lot in common.

"Think you could give him a chance?" Jen asked. Why? She wasn't sure. It didn't matter. If Luke Hollister was headed out of Holly Heights as quickly as he'd entered, he'd be better off alone. That was the best way to go fast. There was all of that family mess with him, too, and she'd gotten her life the way she liked it.

It was a good thing he hadn't kissed her. She was sure that a kiss from him could change everything.

Sarah's low chuckle sent a chill down her spine.

"Oh, man, if you're asking that, you're already so far gone and I can tell you don't even know it yet." Sarah laughed again. "This is going to be so good. The grief you've given me over dating your brother? Yeah, you ain't seen nothing yet. You want to date my enemy. You go ahead. Get ready to deal with heavy trash talking."

Jen scoffed. "Is that supposed to scare me? Your trash is weak."

They were both laughing when Jen steered them off the interstate at the exit that led to Will's ex-wife's house.

"I've always thought women like you—" Sarah held her hand low across her lap to make sure Jen was getting the reference to her lack of height "—who drive SUVs this size are compensating. Want to tell the doctor all about it?" Sarah mimed picking up her pen and notebook to take notes.

Ah. And now, it is on. This was familiar, safe ground.

"Women like me, smart, independent women, spend time studying crash test ratings, gas mileage and money back offers and they make the right decisions. We don't all have convertibles given to us by our daddies."

Sarah's smile twitched around the edges and Jen could have kicked herself. How could she have brought up Bobby Hillman and wrecked what could have been a fun day?

"Which brings me back to apologies. For that dumb thing, I owe you a huge one. I'm sorry, Sarah. I get on a roll and I go for the kill. And I don't want to hurt you." Jen hated how her voice shook whenever things got like this, so serious and emotional.

Sarah waved a hand. "No problem. I know how you meant it." She stared out the window and took a deep breath. "I've got a list of stores to hit and ranked them in order. Adding Chloe into the mix was a great idea. She can be the tie breaker for a few of them."

Jen wanted to follow the conversational exit

Sarah was offering her. But she didn't want to feel like an idiot for the rest of the day.

Jen pulled over and jerked the car to a stop. She covered her face with both hands. Somehow that made it easier. "I'm sorry. Please forgive me."

Sarah tugged down her hands. "Don't be silly. There's nothing to forgive." She smiled but it didn't seem right. Some of the Sarah sparkle was missing.

"Nope. Let me do this." Jen opened the console. "I know you're putting everything into building the shelter and your life and you're so worried about your father and finding the money to pay for a top-notch lawyer. The shelter needs you. Will needs you. And your father needs you. The only thing I can help with is the lawyer. Take this. Please." Jen shoved the folded-up paper at Sarah and forced her to hold it.

"This better not be what I think it is. I don't need your charity." Sarah unfolded the paper. "Yep. Five thousand dollars." She ripped the check into tiny pieces and rolled her window down, about to toss it out. She cursed and closed the window. "I will dispose of this safely and without littering but imagine this blowing in the breeze."

Sarah pulled out her phone. "I'm texting Chloe that we're turning the corner into her neighborhood. You better get this thing moving."

Jen produced another check. "Nope. We're going to sit here until we straighten this out. Please. You know how I am. I need to help you. That's what makes me believe you could be my friend, that I've done something nice for you." She held out the next folded slip of paper. "And I will sit here all day until Chloe is forced to call out the police unless you take this from me."

It was a sign of how well they knew each other that Sarah believed Jen wasn't bluffing. This was important.

Sarah's lips were a tight line as she stared hard at the paper. "I'm going to get a loan. Will's already taken a look at things my father might have that we can sell. And I will make payments regularly. I don't need charity."

Jen waved the check at her friend. "I know you don't. You built that business plan to save the shelter. It's not charity—everyone needs a gift once in a while. What are we even living for without presents?"

Sarah reached up to snatch the check but Jen tightened her grip. "Just so you know, if you rip this up, the next one's even bigger." Then she let go and placed both hands on the wheel. "You gotta do you."

Sarah's chuckle sounded reluctant, but she opened the check. "Ten thousand dollars. Like that. I don't even have to ask."

"Are you kidding me? The day that you have to ask me for money is the day we give up. And that's never gonna happen." Jen put the car in Drive and merged into traffic. "I want to shop and have fun with two of my favorite people in the world. I don't want to worry about how tired you are and what I can do to help fix that. I don't want to feel like a heel because I can buy anything I want, while you're worrying about how to pay for your father's defense."

Sarah grunted. "Consider it a loan. And when I hand you the last payment, when we're both in our eighties, I want a real apology."

Relieved, Jen pursed her lips. "You drive a hard bargain, but I accept your terms."

"You're so small. How are you so feisty?"

Sarah murmured as if she couldn't wrap her head around it.

Jen tried to ignore the shot of pleasure at the term. Luke had called her feisty, too. Like it was something he admired. That was the kind of compliment she could get used to.

CHAPTER FOURTEEN

IF THERE'D BEEN any more of a typical family man kind of day invented, Luke had never seen it. He'd gotten up early and gone to church because his mother had insisted. Then they'd gone to Sue Lynn's diner for lunch because Camila wanted to celebrate her job.

Later, Renita had needed a ride to the Monroes' for more babysitting before he'd even changed out of his suit and tie. Joseph had been finishing up his homework when hc returned, expectation clear on his face, so making good on his promise to show the kid how to change the oil was a must. The only peace he'd gotten had been for the few moments he was actually under his own car while Joseph was tracking down some tool he'd asked for. Had he needed those tools? Sometimes. Now the kid was putting them away one at a time.

"Can I borrow this?" Joseph asked and bent to show him the battery-operated drill.

"What for?" What could the kid be needing power tools for?

Joseph stepped away from the car and disappeared back inside the garage. Luke closed his eyes until he heard return footsteps on the driveway.

As soon as he was done here, he'd run off to the woods and contemplate the bad life choices that had led him to the busiest family-focused Sunday he'd ever spent.

Expecting Joseph's ratty sneakers, he was surprised to see a pair of gold slippers like a princess might wear. There were bows on the toes and from what he could spy, the legs were pretty nice, too.

"You aren't Joseph." Luke rolled out from under the car and peered up at Jen. She was wearing a heavy sweater and jeans and looked more fashion plate than Sunday afternoon social. "Taking a break from all the deliveries?"

There'd been a steady stream of trucks in and out since they'd been home. Apparently she was taking care of furniture for her house and in a big way.

"We had a very good time yesterday." She smoothed her hair behind one ear. "I was hoping to catch up with Joseph. We were going to look over his homework. Did you guys have a chance to talk?"

He'd been under a car with the kid for long stretches of time. They hadn't done much talking, but that was how it went, right? He'd made himself available. Luke rubbed a hand over his forehead and then regretted the streak of grime he must have left there. "In the spirit of my new leaf, I'm letting him decide." He grunted as he got up to stand next to her. "I'm not a fan. It's much easier to loom and point and demand to know what's going on." Luke wiped his hands on the rag he should have used before he messed up his face. "So why don't you tell me what you want me to know."

The answer was trembling on her lips. Luke leaned closer. "Just whisper it. He'll never know." That sometimes worked, putting himself on the same side as whoever he was investigating.

This time? The door opened before his careful waiting yielded fruit. Mari hopped out onto the porch behind the largest Chihuahua the world had ever seen. Since Archie had been in the world for quite a while, too, he'd held the championship belt for years. "Walk," Mari practically shouted and then tugged on

Connie's hand. Whatever they'd planned when they went into the shelter, Mari had derailed everything by falling for a geriatric dog who was blind in one eye. Since he'd never seen her happier, he hoped they had plenty of time left together. The crash, when it came, was going to hurt them all.

Joseph cleared his throat. "Luke, I've got all the stuff put away." He stared anxiously under the car. "Did you finish?"

"Nah, I was waiting to show you how to put everything back together." The way the kid glanced from Jen to Archie and back indicated he was torn by too many great choices. "There's no hurry."

"And I see you have a previous engagement." Jen bent to introduce herself to Archie. The dog immediately barked and jumped up and down. It wasn't that Archie had no energy. It came and went quickly. "You better take this gentleman for his walk, Joseph. I can... hang out for a bit." She glanced up at Luke. "Luke will keep me company."

Luke, again, was it? That seemed like real progress.

Joseph didn't jump up and down like Mari and Archie, but his grin was rare and watching his mother blink back tears at the way her family was coming together made Luke feel like the whole day was a success. He was as tired as two men could be, but for one brief second, everyone in the Hollister house was happy. That was nice.

"Walk," Mari said firmly and the whole contingent headed down the driveway. In an empty subdivision this size, Archie had plenty of land to explore.

"If you need to go with them or even finish up your...dirty work, you can," Jen said. "I wouldn't want to take you away from your family time."

"It's okay. I've already had a lot of family time. It's an all-day thing with them." Luke tossed the rag on the pavement next to the car and checked his watch. "In less than two hours, I have to go pick up Renita. Then there's dinner. Mari's bath time. Arguing over who will do what chore. It's enough to make me want to go sleep in a cave, just to find some silence."

Jen tried to stifle a laugh but it slipped out around the edges. "You're handling it well."

Luke paused as he tried to determine whether there was a chance she meant that.

"No, you are." She shrugged. "I would have snapped at someone, made someone else cry and been hiding in my room under my bed at this point."

Luke pointed at the car. "Kind of the same thing."

Their eyes locked and the way it felt to smile along with her hit him at the knees. "Take a walk with me. A long, silent walk where I don't have to explain or referee or anything but...walk."

Jen pointed at the path that ran between their houses. "To the creek?"

"Yeah." Luke turned and they started off together through the grass. "Are those shoes approved for hikes?" He pointed down at her feet, amused all over again at how a warrior like Jen could rock such girly footwear.

"Only in subdivisions like this one." She took the lead and they moved slowly through the growing underbrush and taller trees until they'd made it to the creek. "You might have to carry me out. I was only thinking of terrain, not the elevation."

"I'll happily carry you out." He watched the smooth wash of pink cover her cheeks. Flirting. They were flirting. He was flirting. She was...he wasn't sure exactly what she was up to, but he was content to sit on the chairs that someone had dragged down the hill. He needed to determine which Hollister was responsible for that. Encouraging those kids to hang out around this spot was a bad idea. But now? He eased down in the lawn chair with a sigh. He was happy to have the chair. Seats made flirting easier.

Then he tilted his head back and saw the rough outline of what appeared to be a tree house. "I'm going to kill him."

Jen's head tipped up to match his. "Who? Joseph?"

"Yeah," Luke said with a grunt, "the kid who started in on me about five minutes after we moved in to come down here to build Mari a castle. When he stopped hounding me, I thought he understood and agreed. Instead, he decided to do what he wanted to do." And he'd get Mari killed if he wasn't careful. He was a kid. Why didn't he listen?

Jen studied the platform closely. "It sort of looks like solid work." Her voice was a little shakier than he'd heard before. What did she know about construction? "And it's only, what...five feet off the ground?" She propped

a foot against the ladder leading up to the platform. "Could use steps if it's supposed to be
a castle."

"That's it? That's all you have to say?"
Luke stood up to peer into the rough platform. There was nothing in it. Maybe Joseph
hadn't been stupid enough to bring Mari down
to it. "In this day and age, when bad people are under every single rock, you think a
four-year-old ought to be spending time down
here with a teenage kid who doesn't know
enough to keep her from breaking her neck?"
He could hear the anger in his voice. There
was no sense in that. Neither one of them was
a parent. All he had to do was tell his mother.
She would hit the roof and forbid any more
creek visits.

Mari would be heartbroken.

"You could help him build it." Jen crossed
one leg over the other. "That's all Joseph
wants, is to feel included." Then she bit her
lip and stared hard at the trickling water. Was
that what she'd been trying to tell him? Joseph
didn't feel included.

Luke sank down beside her and followed
her gaze. "My older brother would have done
something cool like this, built us a fort in the

woods and kept it a secret only the two of us could share." He closed his eyes. "Joseph's got a better handle on this brother business than I do."

Jen leaned over to bump her shoulder into his. "You've got more than the brother hat on. That's the difference. Brothers can forget the consequences. Father figures can't." She didn't look at him and that made it easier to consider her words.

"Tell me about your brother." Jen folded her hands in her lap. "That fighter you got from the shelter, I bet, will need a long walk." Then she sighed and closed her eyes.

"He was a foster like me." Luke licked his lips. "Like us. And he was so cool. I dogged his every step until I was seventeen. Then, like idiots do, I decided to become a man. In my neighborhood, that only led to trouble."

He wasn't going to tell her everything, was he? He didn't talk about this, not to anyone.

"Alex was the guy who people looked up to. He always had the right way to convince people to cooperate. I could intimidate, but he could charm." Luke listened to the trickle and the breeze in the trees. Somehow, sitting next to her, it was easy enough to say things he didn't want to. "I was in the wrong place at the wrong time. My mother sent Alex after me. And that's when he was shot. No one was aiming at him or me. It was a stupid accident." That would have never involved either one of them if he'd been home doing his chores like he was supposed to.

Somehow, he expected that confession to change the air between them. Maybe she'd look at him like she blamed him or even give him the pitying look his ex-fiancée had when he'd told her about it. Instead, she shifted in her seat, her shoulder brushing along his arm again, that connection solid. "And then you decided to become a policeman?"

Luke rubbed a hand over his forehead. He was tired. That was the only explanation. "Then, I wanted answers. Only the police had anything resembling information on what happened, who was responsible and what could be done to make sure it never happened again." It had seemed noble, important. Maybe even important enough to explain how he could go on living without Alex in the world. He had a job to do.

"You know, you're lucky to have had Alex. I have a brother that I look up to. Will is good at everything and when we were in the same house, I hated every single second." She turned to stare into his eyes. "Because I could never measure up. Worse, he wanted to fight my battles for me, like I wasn't…as good as he was. That wasn't about him. That was about me." She blinked and went back to watching the water. "That's what I've had to learn. I can't make things about Will. This life has to be about me."

Confused, Luke studied her face and replayed her words in his head. "Are you saying…I shouldn't have made the decision I did?"

"Nope. I'm saying, at this point, you can decide something else. That's all."

"I'm not following you." And he was irritated the conversation had taken this turn. He'd been enjoying himself when they'd arrived here. Now he was thinking too hard.

"If you ever win the lottery, you are going to have to do some serious thinking. The job you love? Should you keep it? Where will you live? Will you make the world better or go out in a flourish of spending like you dreamed of when you were six?" Jen's lips were twitching. "I had this one life, where I worked every job

I could to pay bills because I thought I had to. Now, I have this other life, and I'm not sure what to make of it. You can probably understand that."

"I never intended to be the guy dropping off for babysitting or cleaning up after a geriatric dog, that's for sure." He sighed. "I guess it's a little bit like hitting the lottery, but not in the exciting way."

Jen laughed. "I get that. I'm saying, you still get to decide what you're going to do about it."

He was going to leave Holly Heights as soon as he had the chance.

Wasn't he? What if he decided something different? Something crazy. Like the next generation of Hollister fosters? His heart rate sped up at the idea. Luke didn't want to consider that too closely. The rest of his life would be nothing but Sundays like this.

"You're pretty good at talking and listening. I never would have guessed you'd have the patience for it." Deciding to take a chance, Luke ran his hand through the sleek hair tucked behind her ear.

"I do work with kids." Jen didn't move away from him. He did an internal victory dance.

"What about you? The house must be coming along now. What will your next project be?"

Jen shrugged. "Besides decorating for Halloween, that is the question."

"Maybe you should find a guy, settle down, fill that house with kids." If she indicated she'd like to have him be that guy, what would he do?

"I have no plans like that, especially the kids. I like being on my own. I like independence." She crossed her arms over her chest. "That's the decision I've made."

"You sound a little defensive." He wasn't sure why. He'd admitted basically the same thing.

"Try being a woman my age who doesn't want to be first to hold the new baby when a teacher comes to visit while she's on maternity leave. My mother will be so sad if I only keep giving her grandpuppies, you know?" She smiled but it didn't reach her eyes.

"You're a teacher. You're great with kids. I've seen it." He didn't want to go further with the conversation because it was clearly loaded with trouble.

"I like teens. I like to see young minds, ones that sit right on the edge of it all, learn and grow. Teenagers are already strong enough to dream big dreams and still soft enough to shape into good people." She grinned. "I guess I'm meant to be a grandmother? That sounds even stranger."

Luke bent forward to brace his hands on his knees. "Nope, I get it. That's why we have Archie instead of a puppy. We could see who he was going to be."

"Whatever bad habits he has, you know them already. Little kids like Mari? They're so fragile, particularly if they don't have two parents ready to protect them. It's hard." She shifted in her chair and Luke had the idea that this was where the conversation needed to go.

"It is." Luke stretched his legs. "Growing up without a dad, that's never easy." He didn't look at her, but he could feel the weight of her stare. This was something they had in common. "I was Joseph's age before I had one." And it had made all the difference in how his life had turned out. How could he leave Renita, Joseph and Mari, knowing that?

"I had a stepfather, never a dad." Jen stared off in the other direction. Luke could only see her sleek hair and hear the hard tone of her voice. "Eventually it doesn't matter much."

That was a lie. Surely she knew that now.

"Think you'll ever take the plunge? Picture life with four or five mean redheads running around your big house?" he asked, even though he had no idea why.

Jen snorted and crossed her arms over her chest. "Hey, I came down here to talk about Joseph. You're tricky."

"Unless you're going to tell me what it is the two of you are hiding, I'll pick a new topic." Luke wanted to know what she knew. He was almost desperate to force her to confess. "Maybe kissing."

She blinked at him twice. "You think I can't handle a kiss without spilling the beans?" She leaned over the arm of her chair. "Test me."

Before he'd decided he was going to do it, Luke had his lips pressed on hers. Instead of spice and heat, Jen's kiss was sweet and perfect. Like a dream.

He could picture starting each day with one just like it.

She'd reached up to brush her fingers through the hair at his nape when the sound of laughter drifted down the hill. Luke leaned back. "I believe that is Connie Hollister's laugh. Archie and his crew must have made it back home."

The satisfaction of watching her eyes slowly open was nearly as nice as the kiss itself. "Tell me what I need to know, Jen."

Her lips firmed and the faint wrinkle on her brow warned him, but he didn't move fast enough to avoid a shove on his shoulder. Soon she was marching up the hill.

"I didn't want to carry you anyway," he called out to her and then laughed as she made a rude gesture behind her back, like he'd expected her to.

Whatever the rest of the day held and however long it would take to get Joseph settled, he'd look back on this trip to the creek as a real highlight of moving to Holly Heights. If only he could believe Jen felt the same way.

CHAPTER FIFTEEN

ON MONDAY, Jen had done her best to put the ill-advised visit to the creek behind her. After the kiss, she'd stormed up the hill, helped the kid, Joseph, with his homework, which had been close to perfect, and then marched right across the street where she slammed her front door, locked every lock and settled in with her dog to grade papers on the brand new plush couch that folded up around her like an expensive hug.

Typical Sunday afternoon, then.

After the kiss.

For all of Monday, it was like the Hollisters had followed her to school. First, the old windbag Mr. Wilson had been complaining about the student who'd ruined the curve of his diabolically hard trigonometry test. Since Rebecca had seemed ready to launch herself at him over one of the tables in the teachers' break room, Jen had intruded in their conversation. Renita Hollister was making the ego-mad teacher look bad.

She'd never even met this Hollister and she was already very close to being her favorite. She'd been plotting against the rotten Mr. Wilson and his rotten methods of teaching trig ever since she'd gotten the job at the high school. Someday, an empowered feminist would make the blood vessel in his forehead burst and she'd step right into his spot.

Renita Hollister might have been the one she'd been waiting for all along.

Her look must have combined ghoulish watchfulness and simmering anger because he'd grabbed his coffee to go.

"That guy is a caveman," Rebecca had muttered. "And not in a good way."

Before Jen could demand to know how many good cavemen there were, Rebecca had added, "Chloe's been sending me spooky-gross food links." She shuddered. "Technically, the gunk will taste great, if you can get past the gruesome visual. I take it we're going with a twisted fairy tale or something? So far, I've seen Cinderella's bloody toe and a wormy pudding thing that I guess has something to do with Snow White…" Rebecca stuck her tongue out and made a barfing noise.

"That kid. You should have seen her at the party supply place. She took control the second we stepped into the warehouse. She found more than enough creepy trees and critters to build her scary forest. She makes me so proud." Satisfied her Halloween plans were moving forward, Jen grinned. "You're in, right? With the treats? To help us defeat Cece?"

Rebecca crossed her hand over her heart. "Until my last breath."

Jen had been laughing when she realized she should have tried to call Joseph's math teacher at the middle school before first period. At her break, she did try, but was forced to leave a message.

Which had worried her all day long. She'd wanted to make sure his teacher was watching for Joseph. If they could get him inside the classroom, nothing would stop the kid. When she hadn't heard anything by the end of the day, Jen packed up all her work and headed for the middle school.

That explained what she was doing in the

principal's office, but not Connie Hollister, who was leaving.

The tears on Connie's face robbed Jen of words for a minute. Then she hurried forward to put one hand on her arm. "What's happened? Is Joseph okay?"

"What are you doing here?" Connie Hollister stepped back, breaking Jen's hold. Her suspicious stare matched her son's perfectly.

"I…" Jen glanced at Principal McKelvy and then around the messy office before she said, "I wanted to try to catch Joseph's math teacher before she left for the day. To talk about his difficulty in her class." Jen smoothed her hair down behind one ear. "To see if I could help."

"He got in a fight." Connie narrowed her eyes. "Seems like you might know something about that? No one I know would tell him to throw the first punch."

Off-balance, Jen reached out to brace herself against the doorway. The office was deadly quiet as everyone listened to this conversation.

"Could we go into the principal's office to talk about this?" Jen asked. "Is Joseph okay?"

"What do you think?" Connie snapped. "He's in trouble now at school." She hitched her purse higher on her shoulder and seemed determined to make Jen sorry, so very sorry.

"But did he get hurt?" Jen checked with the principal.

"No, not badly, but we can't have this behavior," Principal McKelvy said as she held both hands out. "Fighting in the bathroom, that's something we can't overlook and hope Joseph figures his way out."

She'd watched Joseph labor over his math homework for no other reason than he wanted to get it right. Anxious to make sure the boy was safe, Jen said, "Where is Joseph?"

"Luke took him home." Connie brushed Jen's shoulder hard as she headed for the door. "Principal McKelvy, I would like to talk further, but right now, I want to check on my son. Tomorrow, I will explain how I can help you with this office." Her gaze was hard as she faced Jen. "We won't be needing any more tutoring, not from you. Stay away from my kids. *All* of my kids." She spun on one heel and marched off, but not before Jen heard her mutter "crazy lady" as if it was the worst curse.

Suddenly weak in the knees, Jen sat down in a vacant chair with a thud. "I came by to help. That's all. What happened?"

Principal McKelvy gestured to her. "Let's talk in my office." With her careful urging, Jen managed to stand and lurch into the office where she plopped down in the nearest seat.

"At some point, Joseph got some advice that he should stand up to his bullies." Principal McKelvy sighed as she leaned back in her chair. "All eyes are on you for that."

Jen nodded. "I did say that. I also said that he should tell his brother, his teacher and you about what was happening. It's not like I'm some vigilante who's given up on justice and have to go my own way. I was bullied. Standing up to them was the only means to change anything."

Principal McKelvy looked skeptical. "Because you tried telling your mother, your teacher or your principal what was going on and they failed you?"

Jen licked her lips nervously. "Well... No. I wanted to take care of it myself." Independence. It was a good thing, right?

"Yeah, Joseph picked up on that. His decision was to meet the kids in the bathroom and give each one a hard chop to the throat. It was almost effective, but there were three of them and he only had the one surprise hit.

Officer Huertas heard the shouting and responded quickly, but when he got there Joseph was on the floor, two kids standing over him, while the third gasped for air."

Jen covered her face with her hands. This couldn't be happening. It should have been simple enough. Tell the bullies to back off. Back up words with actions *only if necessary*.

"He's a little bruised, but okay." Principal McKelvy braced her elbows on the desk. "The older Hollisters? Mad as mad gets. *You should have seen how he was being treated. You should have stopped this before it went this far. You should do a better job of keeping every student safe. You should be ashamed of punishing a boy who was only defending himself.*" She tipped her head to the side. "We had a nice long loud conversation on the difference between defending yourself and leaving one kid struggling to breathe."

The horror of her own stupid mistake made it impossible to sit still. Jen stood to pace in front of the desk. "I never had to hit anyone like that. I never saw the effects, what happened in my self-defense course." She couldn't believe she'd been this foolish. He was a kid. Who did she think she was, giving him advice?

"Well, it's pretty effective, if you ever need to use it," Principal McKelvy said with a twist of her lips. "The other kid's okay, too, but his parents... They know curse words I've never heard before and I work in a school."

The argument about how ashamed they should be about their kid attacking Joseph Martinez in the first place bubbled on her lips, but one look at Principal McKelvy's sympathetic face forced her to bite her tongue.

"Very rarely is a parent going to accept any of the blame for something like this, Jen. You know that. They believe they've taught their kids right and wrong. Most of the time, bullying is a 'harmless' prank, kids being kids." She sighed. "I don't understand how anyone can think that anymore. These gray hairs? Not caused by harmless pranks." She smoothed a hand over her hair and leaned back.

"What can I do? I need to do something." Jen's hands were tight fists and her brain refused to concentrate on anything else. All she could think of was how badly Joseph's acting on her words might have turned out for him.

Math. That's what she knew and she should stay in her own lane.

But this kid, this family… She had to do something to make it up to them.

"Why don't you tell me whatever you came to speak to Ms. Lee about?" Principal McKelvy picked up a pen and a file that must belong to Joseph Martinez. "If we can ever get him in class, she'll be glad to have a heads-up."

Miserable, uncomfortable in her own skin, with a pounding headache and a sweaty flush of heat, Jen sat back down. "I'm fairly sure he's dyslexic. Or more accurately, that he struggles with dyscalculia. He has trouble with numbers, traces them to see them better." She hung her head and wished for an arctic bath, three ibuprofen and a complete do-over on her last few days. "With me, in the quiet of my kitchen and even on his own, Joseph understands the concepts being taught. He had no trouble with the lessons they've recently covered. He could put the numbers in order with concentration. The stress of the classroom though, and this bully…it's enough to make it too difficult for him to focus. For anyone, really."

Her mouth was dusty dry as she met Principal McKelvy's stare. "I wanted to help."

"Why didn't you tell the Hollisters?" The principal squeezed her eyes shut. "I don't know how this would have played out, but neither one of us would be sitting here, sick to our stomachs at what's happened."

Jen hung her head. "I was him. At one point, I knew exactly how he felt. I didn't want to worry my mother, who had more than enough to work through. I could handle it, so I did. He begged me for the same consideration. Demanded that I promise he could tell them on his own." Jen took a deep breath. "I thought it was the right decision."

"Really?" Principal McKelvy shook her head. "It's never the right decision to keep something from the parents. Years of working with kids has taught me that."

Jen wanted to argue, but as a teacher, she felt the same way. So why hadn't she ignored Joseph's request? Bullying was serious.

When was the scared little girl inside finally going to grow up? At some point, Jen had to let her go.

Jen groaned. "I'm so sorry."

"Ms. Lee and I will take a look at Joseph's

homework and tests more closely," the principal said. "If she's missed that he's needed help, that's something else that we'll address immediately. Once Joseph returns to school."

"He's been suspended?" Jen asked, and then realized how truly terrible the situation was.

"We have zero tolerance for fighting." The principal stood. "I'll make sure that Joseph's mother understands that you identified a learning challenge and recommended evaluation. Someday she'll remember that and be thankful." The finger she pointed at the door was impossible to ignore.

Jen trudged slowly toward the door, the hallway and freedom.

If she could get it this wrong, was she even doing her job well?

And if she wasn't doing her job well, what was she accomplishing with her life?

She needed to talk to Luke, but she had no idea what she'd say. What apology would be good enough? He'd asked her down at the creek. All she'd had to do was tell him, force Joseph to talk to his family.

That kiss. His wicked laugh as she'd marched away. She needed to see him, but his anger, that might be the heaviest blow.

The urge to cry was strong enough that it required an application of her best friends, their encouragement and possibly a tub of ice cream. Stat.

Since the shelter was closed, only Rebecca's and Sarah's cars remained in the parking lot, when Jen arrived.

She could hear the women laughing from the other side of the door and wanted to pretend that she had everything under control, but the vision of Connie Hollister's face was impossible to ignore. She swung the door open.

"Hey, there! We can finally talk..." Sarah's voice trailed off as she got a better look at Jen's face. "Or it could wait."

Rebecca turned away from the computer and Chloe's image there and mouthed, "What's wrong?"

Determined not to drag Chloe into her bad day, Jen cleared her throat. "Did you guys start the meeting without me?"

She took a deep breath and straightened her shoulders before Sarah turned the laptop so that Chloe could see them all.

"Rebecca was complaining about the gross pictures I was sending her." Chloe held up what looked like a severed finger. "Hot dogs. These are awesome! I made this one myself!" She chomped through it with enough relish that Jen felt a lurch in her stomach. The hot dog finger looked real.

"And it goes perfectly with my vision." Chloe held up both hands. "Picture this. The front of Jen's house is covered in creepy-looking trees, all black and gnarled and stuff. There are two paths. One leads to Cinderella's ball and the other to the dwarves' little hut in the forest. Sounds innocent enough, right?" Chloe's evil grin was impressive enough to shake Jen out of her funk for half a second.

"One side is for the little kids, where we'll torment the ugly stepsisters with green goo and the prince can be Bub dressed up." Bub, Sarah's big brown dog, stirred on the couch at the sound of his name, but he didn't get up. He was used to their shenanigans and always completely on board. Chloe continued to explain. "Nothing too spooky. We'll do white lights and have critter-themed treats. The mouse tails made of licorice will work there." She flipped through some papers. "But on the other side, the very innocent-looking cottage? The dwarves have lost it. There'll be axes. Bloody gems for treats." She squealed in pleasure. "We'll have Rebecca as Snow White seated on a gnarled bench we found, crying her eyes out. Then, when your visitor reaches her, she'll raise an ax and force them to eat a severed finger. It will be awesome."

Sarah and Rebecca exchanged a look. "You've nailed interactive. Why Rebecca?" Jen asked, curious.

"She looks so innocent," Chloe shouted. "No one would suspect her. Then she grins, shows those bloody fingers and insane dwarves melt out of the shadows to force other treats disguised as tricks on people as they run shrieking down the path. This is where the smoke machine comes in. We'll play creepy noises and it will be amazing." She tightened her ponytail so that the purple streak showed clearly. "What do you think?"

Sarah and Rebecca turned to Jen who was too tired to evaluate it and too soft not to love everything Chloe did. "I think I'm going to be hiring a lot of actors. How will we pull this off?"

"I'll definitely be there. I want to be a gate-keeper." Chloe frowned. "You do have the gate up, don't you?"

"Yes, they finished it Saturday while we were gone. I'm going to use it for the first time when I get home." Jen sighed. If she ever got home. Why didn't she feel as excited as she'd imagined she would? "So all of this happens *inside* my gate." She wasn't sure she was up for that.

"Just on the night of." Chloe cackled. "Before that, it will look like a creepy forest. We can put up glowing eyes, some spooky scarecrows. That will attract some attention, then on Halloween, bam! The show. Sarah can be a ghost in a costume, the specter of Cinderella or something. You'll need a couple of assistant scarers and a few more partiers at the ball. Could kids from the high school help out?"

In the future, this kid was going to make a terrific stage manager or director or dictator. She had a clear vision and knew what it would take to get it done.

"I sent you links for the stage dressing, cobwebs for the trees and such. You could order most of what you need to finish decorating. I'll help you set up." Chloe was losing steam. Apparently Jen's hesitation was robbing the whole conversation of the excitement it had when she walked in.

She could do better for this kid. "Fine. I'll get to ordering tonight. Make sure your father knows he's participating. I'll get Mom, too. She'll want to be on the good side, though, with the little kids. Rebecca and Sarah and Cole…" Jen counted on her fingers. "A few more people would be good." She'd have to do some thinking.

"Next weekend?" Chloe asked. "Can I visit next weekend? I already cleared it with my mom. I want to experiment with the fog machine before the big night."

Jen smiled. "Of course. That would be smart. I'm labor. You're the visionary."

Chloe nodded. "Okay. It's a plan. I should get started on my homework." Pausing, she wrinkled her nose. "Do you really like the idea, Aunt Jen? I could come up with something else. We have a day or two left and…" She stopped and waited.

"I love it, kid. I *love* you and your brain. We're totally going to win and that's going to rock." Jen smiled brightly at her niece via the computer screen. "We couldn't have done all the shopping we managed this weekend without you, either. Sarah would have stolen my car and left me to walk home."

"You bet I would." Sarah's sigh was loud and long. "I can't believe you aren't going to put a dining table in that monster house."

"Don't need it," she and Chloe said at the same time.

"See you this weekend, Aunt Jen." Chloe was waving as she ended the call.

Sarah closed the laptop and crossed her arms over her chest. "Now. Tell us what's wrong."

"I messed up." Jen never cried. She'd learned it was a weakness. Had no value. But the burning pressure in her chest and behind her eyes wanted out. Rebecca wrapped an arm around her shoulders and it took everything Jen had not to shake it off. "With Joseph Martinez. I told him to stand up to his bullies and he got in a fight and now the Hollisters hate me." She covered her face and willed tears but they wouldn't come. "Luke hates me."

"And somehow, Luke Hollister has transitioned from a troll who looks good in a uniform to someone whose opinion matters," Rebecca said softly. Jen could only nod her head. "Oh, boy."

Jen expected some reassuring words or helpful advice. Sarah and Rebecca could be relied on to have one or the other or both. The silence confirmed her worst fears. "There's no way to fix this, is there?"

She'd fixed her problems with Sarah, but she couldn't even come up with an answer for this one. The first stinging tear was no surprise, but Sarah whispered, "Oh, man, this is serious." Rebecca squeezed Jen closer.

"I have to do something." Jen crumpled her skirt in her hands and wished someone else would say something.

Rebecca bumped her shoulder. "Listen to me. You made a mistake. Everyone does. For years, I've wished I'd done more to help you when you needed it. For Sarah, I should have stepped up when the whole town was ready to kick her out over her father's decisions, but I didn't. I made mistakes. Do *you* hate *me*?" Rebecca grabbed her hand. "Seriously. How big does the mistake have to be for you to hate me? Does knowing you were bullied every day and not telling your mother count?"

"I begged you not to, just like Joseph begged me." Jen waved it off. "You were being my friend."

"No, I was being young. A friend would have told one person after another until something changed." Rebecca sighed. "At some point, I learned that promises can't last forever. There are limits and personal safety is one of them."

Jen rolled her eyes. "Your promises to me? Those go to the grave."

Sarah snorted. "Okay, then how about me? You have every reason to hate me still, but..." She gulped. "You're generous when you don't have to be." She didn't bring up the money, but it was easy to understand.

But these points had nothing to do with her situation.

"None of this applies to my problem," Jen said, frustrated and determined to do what she could immediately and then she'd find a deep, dark hole to hide in.

"Everyone makes mistakes. You don't stop loving people because of that." Rebecca smiled. "If Cole were here, he could do better with this explanation. We know I messed up plenty with him and he still grins like I'm the sunrise when he sees me." She ducked and dodged until Jen was forced to meet her stare. "Nothing is forever. No mistake will last forever. Joseph is okay?"

Jen nodded.

"Then you do the first thing you can, an apology. And you keep chipping away." Rebecca rolled her eyes. "We all know you never take no for an answer. Why would this be the first time?"

"Because I screwed up so big I just…" Jen had to take slow breaths to get air around the lump in her chest.

"And because it matters what he thinks." Sarah's soft voice was annoying mainly because she was right. "Luke matters. So does Joseph. Those students are the reason you get up in the morning. I matter. Rebecca matters. You care about us, and hurting us doesn't feel good. I get that. I've lived that." Sarah paced back and forth. "Face it, Jen. You're as human, soft on the inside, as the rest of us, even if you hate it."

"I do. I hate it," Jen said in a garbled groan that made the other two women laugh. Rebecca squeezed her close, intensifying the ache in Jen's chest. "What else can I do?"

"You're going to have to wait and see. Welcome to the hard part," Sarah said sadly. "We'll keep you company."

As if the shelter was bugged, Rebecca's cell phone rang on cue and Sarah's phone chimed.

When they both glanced and shoved their phones away, Jen had no doubt who was on the other end. Her friends had happy lives to get back to. "I'm going to go home and apologize to the Hollisters. I'll check on Joseph. Then I will eat every single thing in my refrigerator and watch dumb sitcoms. That's the only way." She tried a brave smile. "I'll let you both know how it goes."

"We can postpone the board meeting until next week. We need Cole anyway to talk about the new kennels he's planning along the back fence line." Sarah stood. "Are you sure you're okay?"

Jen nodded, determined to make them think she was okay. Eventually, she would be.

She did as she'd done a thousand other times when she wanted people to believe she was fine. She marched to her car, started it up and drove away without hesitation. Hesitation would tip her hand, and anyone looking for a weakness could exploit that.

Her hands were clenched so tightly around the steering wheel as she turned into the subdivision that they ached. It was appropriate. The dull pain matched the one in her chest.

When she spotted Luke standing in front

of her mailbox, she zoomed up and then slammed on the brakes, blocking his exit back to his own driveway. "I'm so glad to see you. I need to—"

"I'm dropping off a check for the tutoring session." Luke pointed at the mailbox. Then he crossed his arms over his chest.

Jen wanted to touch him, to wrap her arms around him, but the cold expression was enough to stop her in her tracks. "I tried to get you to talk to him."

Luke didn't answer immediately. "And I let you get away with…holding on to something like that, something that could have gotten the kid hurt because I was afraid you wouldn't like me. The bully." He grimaced. "I would have kept him safe."

"I'm sorry he got hurt. That wasn't what I intended, Luke," Jen said as she followed his retreat around her SUV, "but you've got to know you won't always be there to fight his battles. Then what?" That was how she'd gotten through every single day. Maybe her mother could have helped or the right teacher, but there would always be someone else waiting to catch her off guard. The only sure way to protect herself was to do it *herself*.

"I will always be there to fight his battles," Luke responded. "You don't get it. We're family. That's what we do." He held up a hand and marched up his driveway. Jen watched him until he stepped inside the house. Then she saw Joseph, his eye a purple shadow, and Mari in the front window watching them.

Until Luke pulled them away.

Angry at herself for forgetting her plan to drive them out of Holly Heights in the first place and letting them sneak under her skin somehow, Jen climbed up into the driver's seat and parked in her garage. As soon as she was safely inside with the garage door down, Jen rested her head against the seat and tried to chase away the memory of Luke's cold eyes.

Before she could decide whether the tears would come, Jen slid out of the car and made it inside, where Hope's happy dance to welcome her home lifted her spirits. She stepped out on her front porch, still mostly devoid of decoration in anticipation of Chloe's grand plan, to pick up the box the fence company had left.

She pulled out the remote that worked the gate and watched the beautiful wrought iron swing closed. Instead of the relief she'd expected at having one more layer of protection against the world, she was sad. She couldn't see the Hollister house as well now. If Mari was back, sitting in the window, Jen couldn't see her.

Sad all over again at losing a connection she tried to remind herself she'd never wanted in the first place, Jen closed the door and padded over to slide down next to Hope. Eventually, she had to get up, start shopping for Chloe's grand Halloween production.

But right now, she was going to be sad.

CHAPTER SIXTEEN

LUKE WAS ANGRY all over again when he saw Joseph's bruise two days later over the breakfast table. Joseph's suspension was over and it was a bit easier to breathe in the Hollister house. "I can't believe you didn't tell me what was happening." He jammed his spoon into the large bowl of corn flakes and then shoveled a big bite into his mouth. Chewing would keep him from saying any of the things that had kept him awake all night.

Didn't the kid realize how much danger he was in?

One look at his mother was enough to make it hard to look at Joseph. It was clear she hadn't slept any more than Luke had.

"Because we're so close?" Joseph muttered and then took his own angry bite.

His mother sat between them, a steaming cup of coffee in her hands. "And so much alike." Luke shot her a glare but she sipped slowly and ignored him. He'd watched her do the same with her husband for years. Was she about to take charge?

He hoped so. If she left him with the reins much longer, the whole family could go down in flames.

"I will be taking both Joseph and Renita to school today," his mother said, "because I need to speak to both principals. I have decided it is time to pull myself together. That begins with knowing what my kids are up to." She closed her eyes. "I should have paid better attention."

Joseph hunched his shoulders and stared hard into his cereal bowl.

"I will find us another tutor, one who will come here, where I can monitor your work," she added.

Luke watched Joseph consider arguing, but the kid thought better of it. Whatever Jen had said, she had a solid influence on Joseph. That would have been good news if she'd stuck to tutoring on math. On life advice, though, she'd gotten an F.

"I want Luke to take me to school," Joseph said and tipped his chin up.

Luke was not a fan of that idea, but his

mother pursed her lips as she studied them both. Then she dipped her chin in royal agreement. "Fine. That's what we'll do. I will stop in to see Principal McKelvy after I talk with Principal Sepulveda at the high school."

Luke tried to keep the grimace off his face. "Get in the car, then. I've got to get to work."

Joseph bumped his chair hard as he trotted past to get his backpack. Luke glanced at his mother. "You sure about this? Maybe he should sit out one more day, give his own stupidity time to sink in."

"I'm not sure he's the one who's learning a lesson, son." She waited for him to understand that she included him in that statement, then brushed a hand over the knot of hair at her nape. Instead of worn and frazzled, there was a spark in her eyes of the Connie Hollister who'd once convinced him she would fight off all his enemies. If this drew her out of her grief though, then maybe it was meant to be.

"I believe I will ask about the job, too. That place needs a firm hand." She raised an eyebrow. "That was good advice, son."

Luke didn't let his jaw drop but he wanted to.

"I don't want to be the school nurse, not

anymore. That was my Austin life, the old life. Those days are gone. I want to do something new here because I need the change," Connie said, "but that doesn't mean I don't love the school or the kids. I could be a good secretary."

Of course she could. She'd know every single kid in the school the first week, and have their parents and all their issues classified and labeled by the second. "Good for you, Mom."

Luke stood and rolled his shoulders to try to ease some of the tension. "What do you suppose this ride is all about?"

She shrugged. "You're the big brother. I imagine you have a better clue than I do."

He didn't. That was enough to worry him.

Standing around, wondering what was going on, wouldn't help anyone. "Let's go, kid," he yelled.

Joseph was waiting by the front door, his backpack hanging off one shoulder when Luke got there. The bruising around his eye was changing color, turning the sicker shade of brown and green that bruises went through before they disappeared. At least Joseph hadn't been hurt too badly. Maybe the redhead had given him tolerable fighting advice.

"You sure you're up for this?" Luke asked. He opened the door and watched the kid slink through it. Joseph was moving well, too, but Luke had done enough faking of his own in his early years to understand that not every injury would show.

"Nope. Do I have any choice?" Joseph slipped into the passenger seat and slammed the door.

Fair point. His mother said Joseph was going in, so he was going in.

"Nope." Luke started the car and backed down the driveway. Joseph scanned the neighbor's house as they passed by, but he was quiet until they'd almost made it to the middle school parking lot. Since the line to drop kids off wrapped around the entire block, that left them with plenty of time to solve the world's problems.

While they inched forward in a slow parade.

Traffic jams. Thought I'd be done with those after the move.

"Thanks for bringing me today. The bus is no good." Joseph fiddled with the strap of his backpack and watched the bumper of the car in front of them as if he could will it to move faster.

"You going to tell me what this is about?" Luke was clinging hard to his decision to try a different way in Holly Heights, but the patient act was a strain. Ordering the kid to talk would be easy, but it might not get them one step closer to…wherever this might be headed.

"I want to keep working with the crazy lady. The tutoring. She helped me." Joseph didn't look at him, but the jut of his jaw was determined. "That was the whole point."

Luke braced his elbow on the door and the car rolled one car length forward. The front doors of the school were finally in sight.

"Yeah, but…" Luke sighed. "She should have told us about you and your problems."

"I begged her not to." Joseph licked his lips. "Think back, please, and remember how hard it was to find anyone you trusted. In the early days, before you were one of the family," Joseph stated emphatically. "It's impossible, right?"

Luke didn't have to think too much. The conversation with Jen was fresh on his mind. Then, behind that, there were plenty of memories of how his own mother had failed him and how hard he'd fought the Hollisters because he'd known they were going to let him down eventually, too. "Okay. I know what you're saying but…"

Joseph banged his head against the seat. "Why won't any of you listen to me? She helped me. She didn't make me feel…" Joseph looked on the verge of tears. "So let's get rid of her. That makes sense." Before Luke could try to calmly explain why it was time to take a look at who Joseph had in his life and what would make him happy, the kid shoved open the door and hopped out. He was moving so quickly down the sidewalk that Luke couldn't even order him back in the car. Joseph disappeared in a mass of kids and Luke had to watch helplessly.

By the time he made it into the station, he was almost vibrating with annoyance. Davy noticed immediately. "And good morning to you, too, sunshine. Had a message for you." Luke read the name, his old captain's, and thought about tossing it in the trash. He was stuck in Holly Heights forever. Nothing would change that.

Luke twirled his phone on his desk. Instead of taking another shot in the gut with a reminder of his old life, he called his mother. "Joseph's at school. He wants to keep working with Jen. That's what the ride was about."

"In this, I am certain I know best. We will continue with tutoring, but not with her," his mother said firmly. Luke considered arguing, trying Joseph's tactic of reminding her the kid deserved to make some of his own choices, but he wasn't the parent here.

"I've just come from Principal Sepulveda's office." His mother cleared her throat. "Renita is on course to graduate with honors. I met with her counselor, Miss Lincoln, who was the prettiest, sweetest woman I've ever met. I should have gotten her phone number for you."

Luke thought about telling his mother about the ex-convict who had managed to steal Rebecca's heart and who could pulverize him if he gave her a glance, but she was chipper. Excited. He didn't want to do anything to mess with that.

Learning how tightly Rebecca and Jen were connected would put a damper on her optimism.

"What a nice day. Joseph is on track. Renita is thriving. Even Camila has found a place she likes to work. You go on and do your very important job. Keep the streets safe and all that. I will try to talk to Joey's principal about a job. At the end of the day, we could have everything fixed. Won't that be nice?" He could hear the smile in her voice. That sounded so much like the old Connie Hollister that it was tempting to believe that things could get better. Maybe they were in very slow steps, but any improvement was welcome.

"Call me if you need me."

After Luke hung up, Davy held up the car keys. "Let's patrol, shall we?" When they were in the car, Davy said, "Everything okay?"

Luke studied his face and wondered if the man wanted to have his own advice column or something. Since he was trying to get along with his partner, too, he decided to keep that observation to himself. "Kid got into a fight. Actually, he started it with some boys who were picking on him. That's why he's been skipping class, apparently." Not that Joseph had ever admitted that. Not even through the long, silent dinner had he ever complained about the treatment he'd endured before taking his chance to hit back. "We have the new tutor to thank for that."

Luke still couldn't believe it. That much they'd gotten out of Joseph, that Jen's advice to take the bully by surprise with a hard hit had worked.

"She could tell the kid where to hit, but not tell him who to talk to or take care of it herself." It made no sense.

"Guess she thought she'd learned her own lessons well enough as a kid to pass something along," Davy said with a sigh. "I swear, it's a miracle some kids make it out of high school and have a chance to grow into reasonable adults."

Right. Like Luke had. Camila was getting there. Renita would pass them all. Jen had grown up in this cozy town with best friends who'd...probably seen what she went through and, instead of telling, had kept her secret. Why?

Because she'd asked. Like Joseph had asked Jen to keep his secret.

"Gotta wonder why the kid didn't come running to you." Davy didn't glance his way but since Luke had been working toward the same question, he had the feeling this wasn't idle observation. "It's almost like he doesn't trust you."

And there it was. Trust. They were back to it.

"I've backed off. The kid had plenty of time to tell me while we changed the oil on my car this weekend." Which hadn't needed to be changed at all, but Luke had gone forward with it because that had been the time he'd been most comfortable talking with his foster dad, while they were covered in grime and staring at engine parts.

"Maybe it's hard to seize the first chance. Second or third might gain some results." Davy sighed. "In my albeit limited experience, with some people you have to do or say things more than once before they can hear you." He glanced over at Luke and shrugged a shoulder.

His innocent expression made Luke laugh. Davy had to come up with several different ways to say the same thing before Luke had understood he had to change his methods. "Fine. I get it. I'm expecting too much, too soon."

"It's kind of a problem with you, isn't it?" Davy turned down one of the streets closest to the high school and the sight of Jen's red hair bouncing as she headed across the parking lot snapped him out of his good mood.

"Now then, what to do about the girl?" Davy murmured.

"You sound like a movie villain plotting evil deeds. All you need is the dramatic tone." Luke forced himself to look away from the school. She was late. Was everything okay?

"Nah, more like the faithful sidekick who prefers a happy ending now and then." Davy pointed at him. "You should have seen how you slid to a stop the day I mentioned Jen growing up. That was not idle curiosity. You're into her. And you made a good choice."

Luke grunted. "Sure, until she messed up big time. I have no time for people who keep secrets."

"Well, well, well." Davy pursed his lips. "Aren't we superior?"

He's an old guy, Luke. Respect.

"I guess you've never made a mistake." Davy shrugged and started whistling as he headed out on the highway. The guy loved traffic stops. It was sad.

That left Luke plenty of time to mull over the morning ride to school and how he might have kept Joseph talking.

Which led to the realization that he might have made his own mistakes. Wonderful.

As soon as he got home, he'd talk to Joseph. Maybe Davy had a point. It was very close to the same points his mother and Jen had made so it was getting harder to ignore that Joseph needed time and attention.

Settling into the wait-and-chase mode of traffic stops had never worked for Luke. He wanted to be doing, so when his phone rang in the middle of the afternoon he grabbed it with relief. No matter what kind of emergency his mother had, it was going to get his blood moving again.

"What's wrong?" he said as he answered the phone.

"Joey didn't come home. I had to wait until this afternoon to talk to the principal about a job because she was covering a class. I missed my chance to pick him up from school. And now, he isn't here." His mother sniffed loudly and the threat of her tears was enough to snap Luke to attention. "I made a quick turn through town but I didn't see him. Mari won't leave the front window, like she's watching for him."

More than a little fed up with thinking

about Joseph, worrying about Joseph and taking care of Joseph's emergencies, Luke took a calming breath. "Give him a chance to come home on his own. It's still early. The kid thinks he's an adult. Maybe he needed… some space." He knew the feeling very well. "If he isn't home by the time I get off my shift, I'll…" What would he do? "I'll call in reinforcements, but I'm sure he's fine."

"Should I check with the crazy lady when she gets home?" his mother asked. "He might have gone there?"

If he had and Jen hadn't let them know, Luke would explode. He'd told her Joseph wouldn't be coming over. That should have made it crystal clear that he didn't want Jen and Joseph together.

"If he isn't home by dinner, I will do that myself, Mom. Don't worry. I'm sure he'll be okay." Luke rubbed the ache in his temple and did his best to ignore Davy's curious stare.

"He's a little boy." The bright, alert tone of the morning was bleeding back into fatigue and worry. The little boy who thought he was a man had better be safe and sound; they couldn't keep doing this.

"He's smart, Mom. I'm sure he's on his

way. He thought walking was better than the bus last week. Maybe he wanted to prove his point. Give him a couple of hours and then we'll decide what to do."

She didn't argue but the tension on the line as she hung up told Luke that she was not a fan of his plan.

"Trouble?" Davy asked as he turned off the highway and steered back toward the high school.

"My brother skipped the bus again. Drop me off at the door. I'll make sure McKelvy's on the lookout in all the bathrooms." The runt better not be hiding again. If he'd skipped class, that was one thing, but there was no reason not to go straight to the principal if he was having more trouble with bullies. His secret was out.

The safety officer nodded as Hollister strode inside the school. "Headed for the office?" He held out his hand to indicate the direction, as if he and Luke hadn't met in the same spot.

Instead of waiting for someone to notice him and offer to help, Luke strode into the principal's office without knocking. Principal McKelvy raised an eyebrow. "Apparently it's my day for surprise Hollister visits. Did you mother send you in to sing her praises? She's very convincing, but she has zero administrative experience." The older woman sighed. "But if I don't get some help in here soon, we're all going to be buried under paperwork. Not the way I'd want to go out. Scary."

Distracted, Luke squeezed the chair in front of him and tried to regroup. "No, that's not why I'm here, but if you're considering hiring her, I can tell you why you should."

"She was a nurse, not a secretary. They don't share much in common." Principal McKelvy smoothed the wild gray hairs that had escaped her neat hairdo. "But I need help."

"She's got decades of experience with kids, her own and all the students. Besides that, she loves them. Every one of them. Sick or mad or sweet, she loves them all. She's filled out plenty of forms and knows how to answer the phone. Anything else, you can teach her. You can trust her to do a good job."

Principal McKelvy nodded slowly. "Seems like she's had some…health issues lately. Is she up to the pressure of middle school?" McKelvy squeezed her eyes shut. "Believe me, it's a full-contact sport some days."

That was a good question. He wasn't quite sure of the answer. His mother had seemed more like her old self until today. "She needs this, Principal McKelvy. You won't be sorry if you hire her."

She nodded slowly. "I'm going to give it serious thought." She tapped her pen on the stack of files teetering on her desk. "Why are you here?"

"Checking on Joseph. He didn't take the bus and my mother's worried." Luke braced his hands on his hips. "Thought I'd check to see if you've emptied the bathrooms lately."

"Officer Huertas," Principal McKelvy shouted. She shrugged and pointed at the intercom on her desk. "Stupid thing stopped working and I haven't had time to get it fixed."

When the safety officer stuck his head in her office, McKelvy said, "All the doors checked and locked?"

He nodded. "Yes. Someplace I need to re-check?"

"Better clear the boys' bathrooms, in case." When Huertas turned to follow the order, Principal McKelvy pointed at the seat. "If you'd like to sit and wait, go ahead."

Luke shook his head; there was the first

trickle of unease settling across his shoulder blades. He expected Joseph to act like he always had. What if their argument was enough to force him to change that pattern?

"He showed up for his math class today." Principal McKelvy shifted through the files and tried to make more manageable piles. "Ms. Lee is updating me on the status of Joseph's attendance. Turned in his homework. Even raised his hand to answer a question." She raised her eyebrows. "If you only knew how rare that was, your mouth would drop the way mine did when I heard. Kids do not volunteer to answer questions anymore. No kids. Never happens." She tilted her head to the side. "Made me wonder what you'd said that got through to him."

Since Luke knew the answer to that, it made him wonder if *Jen* had said something that had gotten through to Joseph. And if she had, why should they keep her from doing it again?

They'd be the worst kind of adults to prevent a teacher who could accomplish that from helping Joseph because of one mistake.

"All clear," Huertas said from the doorway.

Luke nodded. "It would have been so much

simpler if he'd been hanging out here for some reason."

Principal McKelvy sighed. "So you haven't actually worked anything out. Maybe the suspension got his attention. Seems to have worked for the other three boys. Ms. Lee said separating them and moving Joseph to the front of the class has improved all four boys' attention." She smiled. "All she needed was a heads-up, I guess. She's young. Eventually, she'll get better at spotting trouble." She eyed her paperwork. "And she's watching Joseph's homework for any signs of struggle. She met with Jennifer Neil beforc first period to get a quick rundown of what she'd observed when she worked with Joseph one-on-one."

Surprised, Luke studied the ugly pattern of the industrial linoleum. "Seems above and beyond the call of tutoring."

McKelvy sighed. "Yes. Jen's been doing this long enough to know the signs. We all have classes in college, but they don't make sense until you see it happening in the classroom. Jen's good. She's an excellent teacher. You're lucky to have her for a tutor, even if she has some strange boxing advice."

Now that he'd checked the school—the one

place he was certain Joseph could hide out—Luke was out of options on where to go next.

"I'll do a circuit myself. If I find him, I'll give you a call." Her forehead wrinkled. "If he isn't home tonight, you give *me* a call." She scribbled her phone number down and handed him the piece of paper. Luke shoved it in his pocket and turned to go.

"It isn't often we see such a stark change in a kid, Officer. He's lucky and seems to know it." She followed him to the door. "Please contact me if there's anything else we can do here at the school."

When he got back out to the car, Davy was on the radio. "Looking for a young male, fourteen, dark hair and eyes. This morning, he was wearing—" Davy glanced his way.

"Jeans. Red T-shirt. White sneakers. Might be headed toward Austin." Luke clutched his phone and considered calling his mother while Davy finished speaking with Dispatch. When he turned out of the parking lot, Luke said, "He hasn't been missing long enough to panic, start an official search."

Davy shrugged a shoulder as he slowed down next to a playground where the rougher crowd liked to hang out after school. It was empty. "More of a courtesy call." He nodded. "You can do that when you've got friends in town who can always be on the lookout. Doesn't hurt to have a few more pairs of eyes looking, does it?" Davy drove behind the shops on the town square and studied each alley as they passed.

"Let's head toward my house. I need to check on my mother."

Davy agreed but he didn't hurry. "Sure thing. As we go, I'll cruise by the usual places. Not my first rodeo, hunting for a mad kid." On the way through each neighborhood, Davy stopped and helped Luke search carefully where a kid might be likely to hide out. It was good to have someone who'd grown up in Holly Heights along for the ride.

Just before they turned into the subdivision, a static call from the dispatcher came through. "Heard from Piney patrol. The guy thought he might have seen a kid matching Joseph's description over by the highway headed out of town. Patrolman did not sound convinced, but you asked for any updates."

"Thanks, Dispatch." Dave shot him a worried look. "You still want to go home? Or should we turn back for Austin?"

Trying to determine the best solution while he was under the gun like this had to get easier, didn't it? Luke wanted just five minutes of quiet and to wrap his arms around Joseph to squeeze until the kid laughed. "Home. Then we split up."

Davy picked up speed. A quick punch of a button and two rings later, and his old partner Marcus answered. "I knew you'd miss me sooner or later." Marcus's East Texas radio disc jockey voice was reassuring.

"I did. I've been having to do my own paperwork." Luke waited for Marcus to laugh before he added, "I need a favor, man. Big one."

"It's yours. Hit me with it." He and Marcus had graduated together, learned everything they knew about police work together. It was good to know he was the kind of friend who had his back no matter how long it had been since they'd talked. Luke wasn't sure he was the same kind of friend, but after this, he would be.

"Kid brother, Joseph Martinez, didn't ride the school bus home. He's probably still close by, but we have a report of a kid headed your way. Could you check the old neighborhood

for me? Maybe around the middle school."
Luke rubbed his forehead as Davy turned into
the subdivision. "My mother brought him to
the department's child safety day last year.
That's a pretty current photo."

"I'll head out now. If I find him…" Marcus
paused. Like wasn't sure what Joseph's situation
was, legal or illegal or a combination of
both, that might have brought the kid back
to Austin, but he'd do what he could to help.

"Grab the troublemaker and hold him down
until I get there," Luke muttered but then an
attack of conscience hit. "Easy, though. He's
bruised up from a fight at school and he… We
want him safe, that's all."

"Got it. Call you in an hour or so for updates."
Marcus signed off and Luke was relieved
to hear the urgency in his voice. This
was another one of those courtesies. No one
owed him a thing, but because they… What?
Respected him? Liked him? They were willing
to help.

What a humbling situation to be in.

He was staring out the window when the
sunshine hit Jen's red hair. She'd stopped at
the mailbox, her pretty dog sniffing the post

very carefully. Luke knew he had to call in one last favor.

"You go on in. Let my mother know I'm checking with the crazy lady and I'll be in soon." Luke slid out of the car before Davy could ask the obvious question hovering on his lips.

As soon as she realized he was headed for her, she tipped her chin up. "My mailbox. I can still get my own mail, can't I?" The combination of frost and fire in her voice was impressive. Instead of challenging him directly, she peered at the Hollisters' window. Only Mari was sitting there.

"Yeah, listen…" He ran a hand through his hair, frustrated with his inability to ask for things the right way. "Can you help me?"

She raised one eyebrow slowly and crossed her arms over her chest.

"It's Joseph. He didn't get on the bus to come home today. Since that's not all that unusual, I didn't panic, but I've been to the school and he isn't there." Luke clasped his hands together to keep from touching her. He wanted to touch her. That would settle him down. "He isn't with you, is he?"

"You trust me to tell the truth?" Jen shook her head.

"Not the time for retaliation." She took a deep breath.

"No, I haven't seen him since this weekend." *Not even when I begged to.* She didn't say it but her eyes were glaring it.

"We heard he might be headed to Austin. Since the kid talks about his old neighborhood as if he's forgotten what a nightmare it was, it kind of makes sense he'd go back there. Life here hasn't been what I promised." Luke rubbed a hand over his jaw as the wave of panic inched a little higher in his chest. Unless he found the kid soon, that panic would be hard to control.

Her wrinkled brow made him think she might refuse. Instead she said, "I'm not sure that does make sense. He was listing ways to be a better Hollister. That's not a kid who's looking for a way out."

"A better Hollister?" Luke snapped. "What does that mean? Is this something else you should have told me but didn't?"

Jen's mouth closed with a snap but she eventually said, "I told you. He only wants to belong. He's not a Hollister. Renita Hollister. Luke *Hollister*. He said it clearly. Then he mentioned how he only wanted to stop causing trouble that upset your mother." Jen shook Hope's leash. "I told you he only wanted to belong. And not to have you skip out on the time you promised him. To *talk* to him."

"I tried," Luke said.

The two of them glared at each other for a long minute.

"But obviously not enough."

"What can I do to help?" she said softly. "I want to help. I can drive through town. I can call everyone I know. What can I do?"

Thinking of his mother, alone with only Mari as he would be out searching, Luke squeezed his eyes shut. "Renita's at the Shop-on-in tonight. Can you come over to sit with my mother? Help her watch Mari? Camila is working, too. I don't want to call her back, but Mari will be a lot."

Jen glanced down at Hope. "Fine. I'll be happy to. As much as your mother dislikes me, I do enjoy Mari. I will make this work." She clenched the leash. "Let's see if Hope and Archie get along. Otherwise, I'll need to bring her home before you head out."

He began to march up the driveway. She

was a silent shadow behind him. Before he reached the door, he turned. "Thank you. You don't have to do this. I appreciate it." The feeling that he was taking advantage somehow of her good heart wouldn't go away.

She narrowed her eyes at him. "I'd do it for anyone. Ask around." Then she brushed past him, leading her happy dog through the now open door.

Instead of the usual racket, all he could hear was silence.

In the Hollister house, that was never a good sign.

As he announced his presence, his mother scooted up in her chair and frowned when she saw Jen lurking in the hallway. "I called Marcus. He's going to take a look around Austin. Davy is going to continue searching here in Holly Heights." The older man's immediate nod made it easier to make his decision. "I'm driving down to Austin now, to make sure."

"What's she doing here? Come to tell us some other bad advice she's given my son?" His mother tipped her chin up. "Sons?" The last *S* was drawn out.

"No, I've come to make sure Mari has company. Since you're too...weak to handle that yourself." Jen immediately led Hope away. Archie jumped up from his bed and followed. He should go and make sure there wasn't a dogfight in the living room, but he had this catfight to settle.

His mother covered her face, the emotion of the afternoon clearly getting to her. "The crazy lady is right. Too weak."

Luke moved forward to reassure her, to do whatever it took to get them back out on the road and searching for Joseph, but she stood up with a snap. "You go. I will handle this house and Mari and your friend." Her lips twisted but she didn't smile. "Bring Joseph home."

Before he could argue, his mother brushed past him, Mari in tow. "We will have dinner waiting when you get back."

Luke wanted to stay and smooth things over.

"Best to get while the gettin's good, Hollister," Davy said and motioned toward the doorway. "We've got our jobs to do."

Davy made the quick trip back to the station to drop Luke at his car. "Keep me updated." Davy assured him he would.

As Luke slid into the driver's seat, he whispered a quick prayer that this would turn into a learning experience for the whole family. If this was another tragedy that they had to live through, he wasn't sure his mother would stand it.

For that matter, he'd have another reason to never forgive himself. How did a man live with that much guilt?

CHAPTER SEVENTEEN

ARCHIE AND HOPE had survived a ten-second standoff before they'd sprawled under the table to snooze. It looked like all was quiet on the canine front. Mari was currently under the table, too, listening carefully to any conversation that might leak out while she and Connie Hollister sat across from each other.

Not that there was any danger of that.

Every now and then, Mari's shoulder would brush Jen's leg, reminding her of why she would endure this frostbite.

Connie Hollister could do a mean scowl when she wanted to and this was the perfect occasion.

"I've apologized to Luke." Jen sorted through all the conversational openers tumbling through her brain in the desperate need to break the silence. "I shouldn't have given Joseph so much leeway. He's a kid. I wanted him to have his chance to talk to you." She cleared her throat. "But I did what I thought was best."

"What had been best for you, not what's best for him." Connie tipped her head back, the overhead light catching on the silver strands of hair at her temple. "Right?"

"I know something about bullies. I told him what worked for me. Standing my ground was the only thing that ever made a difference." Jen crossed her legs slowly and immediately felt Mari lean against her chair.

"Your parents would have done something if you'd told them, this I know." Connie tapped her chest. "I would have. This is what we are here for, to protect our kids."

"While you were filled with grief?" Jen asked softly.

Connie's chin trembled for a second before she straightened in her chair. "Of course. Nothing is more important than my children. Everything I do is for them. If you were a mother, you would understand this." She swiped a hand across the spotless table. "Perhaps I see your point, however."

This was the minute she needed to shut up. Nothing good would come of antagonizing her neighbor further.

Unless she could help her understand Joseph.

"Why isn't his last name Hollister?" Jen asked. This was what was most important.

"I haven't had the time to complete his adoption. My husband was sick and..." Her shoulders slumped. "It's been too many months. That doesn't work as an excuse anymore."

The tense silence stretched between them again and Jen was wishing Mari was a talkative four-year-old girl who wanted to know about her boyfriend and her birthday and her favorite color. This tense waiting was too much.

Jen pulled out her phone and stifled a groan. Barely an hour had passed, but it seemed like a week. A week filled with the joys of standing in lines and waiting rooms and death glares.

If Luke had left immediately, he was already in Austin, but they'd had no updates. Desperate for help, she texted Rebecca. Need company. Bring food to the Hollisters'. ASAP.

That would be the perfect signal. Rebecca always had leftovers and this was a situation that required carbohydrates and soon.

Instead of asking a bunch of questions, Rebecca responded quickly. You okay?

Yes. Joseph didn't come home from school so I'm waiting with Luke's mother and niece. Come fast please.

"Is that Luke you are texting?" his mother asked suspiciously.

Jen wondered how close his mother thought her son had gotten with the woman who'd brought catastrophe down on their house. "No. Rebecca Lincoln. I asked her to bring food. You need to eat and I only cook takeout. Since I can't actually go get it, that leaves plan B." Jen waved her cell phone.

"I will be cooking any minute." His mother sniffed. "A woman who doesn't cook. You would have made a horrible wife."

Jen's head dropped forward. The shock was paralyzing. "Wife? We kissed one time."

His mother's eyebrows lowered ominously. "Oh, really. That was before you ruined Joseph's school career?"

The urge to stomp out of the house was strong. Mari's tiny hand on her knee kept her in her seat.

Instead of grinning like a victor, Luke's mother closed her eyes. "That isn't true. He's been going to class. His teacher is testing him further to check the dyslexia. Principal McKelvy told me I have you to thank for that." But she would fall out of her chair with a croak before any gratitude would pass her lips. That was fair. Jen could completely understand the sentiment.

Before she could reply, her cell rang with a number she didn't recognize. "Hello?"

"Is my mother okay?" Luke asked. Jen could hear the road noise that indicated he was still driving.

"Sure. Yes, she's…um, she's fine. Just as soon as she chews me out a little longer. Then…it'll be my turn." Jen's lip curled and she jerked when she noticed a matching smile on Connie Hollister's face.

"I've looked everywhere here that I could think of, talked to his best friends. No one in Austin has heard from him in months." Luke sighed. "That was what we wanted, but right now, I'm sick. I want to know he's okay. Stupid is fine. Even inconsiderate. I need him to be breathing and safe somewhere."

"Don't give up." Jen stared meaningfully

into Connie Hollister's eyes. "He's a smart kid and he knows this is home." Luke didn't answer and Connie slid away from the table. "Are you headed back to Holly Heights now?"

"Yeah, and Davy, too. We'll regroup at the house." He sighed. "It might be time to panic."

"Drive safely. I'll call everyone I know. My friends will help us look." She had no hesitation there. They would. Maybe she felt like the odd man out sometimes, but she'd stake her life on the fact that her friends would back her up.

"Thanks." The silence between them stretched until Jen thought the call had dropped. "You didn't have to do this. I appreciate it."

Jen cleared her throat. "I like Joseph." She lowered her voice. "And I like you, and I even like your mother but if I disappear mysteriously, I'm going to make sure everyone looks in her direction first. You have a big backyard, but the pile of dirt over my body will be noticeable." A snorted laugh caught her attention. Connie Hollister was shaking her head as she put a large pot on the stove.

"Smart. She likes smart. I do, too." Luke

didn't laugh but something about him sounded different. A little more optimistic.

"She's already tried to wound me by throwing the word *wife* at me, but I dodged it." Jen glanced down under the table at Mari's soundless laugh. She'd covered her mouth with her hand and it was easy to see bright pink nail polish.

"I know what you mean. She told me I'm going to make a great foster dad someday." He took a deep breath and released it. "Worse, when I imagined it, right in the center of the picture was a fiery but kind redhead."

He hung up the phone so quickly that Jen banged hers on the table in her haste to set it down far, far away.

When the doorbell rang, Jen scooted her chair back, but Connie stopped her with a look. "My house. I will answer the door." She hurried away and Jen whistled soundlessly. Whatever happened between her and the Hollisters, it was impossible not to admire Connie's grudge-holding capabilities. She might not be quite as good as Jen, but she had potential.

When Rebecca, Cole, Sarah and Will marched in carrying stacks of containers in both hands, Jen knew dinner was under control. She nodded as Connie Hollister immediately commandeered her troops.

"You okay under there, young Jedi?" Jen asked Mari, who had moved to clutching her leg as the kitchen grew more crowded.

Archie and Hope were both clever dogs. All three of her favorite people were watching the bustle from under the table with wide eyes. When Renita Hollister and Davy Adams arrived, the added conversation elevated the noise level, Mari clung harder, and Jen decided it was time to move her part of the group to a quieter spot.

"Want to show me your room, Mari?" Jen asked. "I need to take a peek at your closet. For inspiration, girlfriend."

Mari scooted out, the dogs followed and Jen formed the end of the line as it trooped down the hallway. Mari's room was overwhelmingly decorated with butterflies and dogs. "You are obviously not a redhead. You would keep pink away from your person at all costs, but I do like your style." The small space was obviously intended to be an office. The lack of a closet meant Mari's dresses were arranged on a hanging rack, her shoes were scattered, and more than anything, the room desperately needed organization.

This was the kind of place that gave Jen anxiety hives. She would not think about it.

Mari walked over to a pile of books. Jen stepped carefully around the other piles of dolls, building blocks and what appeared to be a tool belt. Watching Mari dig diligently through her books was sweet. Jen, Archie and Hope were all waiting for her to make her choice when she pulled three out from the stack. She thrust them at Jen. "Castle."

Jen nodded. Reading a little girl a book was well within her skill set. She could do this and it gave her the perfect excuse to stay here, where it was quiet, and she was surrounded by her people. Ignoring the mess would be easy once she buried her nose in the book. "Good choice, princess."

Jen eased down on the bed and patted the mattress. When Mari frowned instead of climbing up next to her, Jen shrugged. "Okay, if you'd rather stand, that's fine." Weird, but fine.

Mari shook her head and tapped the book. "Castle."

Jen opened the cover. "Right. Here we go."

Mari tugged on the book. "Joey. Castle." She widened her eyes and huffed out a breath. "Joey went to the castle."

The look on her face was enough to convince Jen that this wasn't about the picture book she was holding. "The tree house? Down by the creek? That's where Joseph went?"

Mari nodded. "He had homework." Her forehead wrinkled. "Promised not to tell his hiding spot."

Jen pulled her phone out, found Luke's number and hit Call. As soon as he answered, Jen said, "Are you close? Joseph went down to the tree house to do homework." She wasn't sure what to hope for, that the kid was still there, blissfully unaware of the mess he'd created or… Yes, that was the best option.

"I'm driving through Holly Heights now. I'll be there in less than five." The road noise grew louder as if he'd accelerated. "Is Davy there yet? If we have to search the woods or creek, I might need help."

"Yes, he's here and Cole and my step-brother, Will." Jen took a deep breath. "Do you want me to call…" She stared at Mari, who was watching her closely, her fingers clenched together and covering her mouth.

"Not yet. Maybe. I'm not sure. I'm close. If we need police, we'll know shortly." The road noise got louder. "I'll be there in less than two. See if you can get the others headed to the creek for me."

Jen quit the call and said, "Mari, can you keep the dogs out of the way? It's an important job."

Mari nodded solemnly so Jen jumped up and hustled to the kitchen. "There's a tree house, down by the creek. Mari says Joseph went there to do his homework. Luke is close, but he wants us all to get a head start."

As everyone hurried toward the front door, Jen could hear the sound of a car screeching to a halt outside. She was able to catch sight of his Mustang parked crookedly in the street.

Her eyes met Luke's for a split second before he yelled, "Follow me."

When his mother moved to chase after them, Jen wrapped her arms around Connie's shoulders and offered Renita a small smile. "It's a steep hill, not a lot of clearing. Wait here." No matter what the situation was at the bottom of the hill, they'd know soon.

His mother squeezed Jen's hand tightly. No one said anything. They waited tensely.

Jen whispered a quick prayer that this turned out well and was happy Connie and Renita weren't waiting alone.

This was why everyone needed noisy, messy, troublesome people, so they never had to wait alone.

She ought to remember that.

CHAPTER EIGHTEEN

LUKE HAD BEEN fighting the urge to recklessly rush home ever since he'd left Austin. Every horror story he'd investigated or heard about through the grapevine or watched on the news had run though his head.

He'd known the kid was out of sync. Why hadn't he pushed harder or figured out the right method to coax the kid into talking sooner?

As soon as his car came to a stop, he'd jumped out and spotted Jen. His relief grew when he saw Davy Adams trotting down the driveway and people pouring out of the house. And now he could run, go as fast as he could, so Luke reached the bottom of the hill above the creek before the rest of the group. He anxiously scanned the tree house. That was where the kid should be, hiding out, maybe as a punishment, to show the rest of them. That would be fine. Luke would take every bit of his anger, worry and frustration and swallow it, even if it choked and burned all the way down. He'd very casually say Joseph was late for dinner and life would go on.

He'd have time to fix everything.

Instead, the ladder was missing. That was his first clue. Joseph's backpack was on the ground under the tree house. Luke rushed toward the creek.

When he saw Joseph leaning against a tree, Luke nearly buckled. The tears on the kid's face could be dried. This was a happy ending.

Joseph swallowed hard. "I think it might be broken." He motioned with a limp hand at his leg, stretched out in front of him. "The ladder fell and I knew I'd be in trouble if I missed dinner, so I tried to jump." He shook his head pitifully. "Fell. Heard something crack. Rolled right down the hill." He winced. "Should have kept going, drowned myself in the creek, put us all out of our misery."

Luke braced his hands on his knees and breathed in deep and slow until his heart stopped racing in his chest. The adrenaline was making his hands shake but relief was quickly draining him of energy and strength. "Nope. You should have left a note on the table." Luke straightened slowly as Davy and the others slid to a stop behind him. "He's a little banged up, but okay." Luke glanced over his shoulder and tried to communicate clearly that a low-key rescue was the only way to do this. That's what his gut was telling him.

Yelling at Joseph for scaring them half to death and sending every police official he knew into action would only compound this problem.

And it was all going to be fine. Luke had the time he needed to work this out.

If he had to repay the favors he'd called in for no good reason for the rest of his life, that would be easy enough to do.

Joseph shifted as if he was going to try to move.

"Wait right there." Luke checked on his support team. "Cole, you okay with climbing?"

Cole nodded.

"Davy, grab his backpack. Cole, you join me and we'll carry him back." Luke tipped his chin at Will. "Would you go ahead of us and let everyone know the situation?" He waited until Will nodded, indicating he'd understood Luke's message and had taken off up the hill.

To Joseph, he said, "Let's get you out of here. Dinner will be getting cold."

"Yeah, Mom hates that." Joseph tried a weak laugh and Luke could feel a smile twitching on his lips. The kid was quick. No matter how easily Luke played this, Joseph must have known he was in trouble with Connie Hollister. Big trouble.

"I saw a chili pot and something smelled delicious," Davy said cheerfully. "Dinner is worth climbing up the hill for, I'd say."

When Cole joined him, they both stepped carefully down the last few feet of the crumbling, rocky bank. "You grab his shoulders. I'll take his legs." Luke met Joseph's worried stare. "Carefully. I'm going to be very careful." But it would hurt anyway. Joseph nodded. "On three."

Luke counted softly and they hefted Joseph up. Cole took the lead, reversing up the bank slowly with Luke following. Davy fell in behind Luke. The trip seemed to last a lifetime, and Luke was covered in sweat and breathing hard by the time they reached flat ground, but Joseph endured quietly, his lips a tight, white line.

"Should we call an ambulance?" Davy murmured next to Luke's ear, but Joseph immediately shook his head no.

"Not necessary, I'll take him to the hospital. Let's put him in the car. Davy, you let my mother know we're headed to the ER? I'll call when I know more." His eyes met Joseph's as the kid drew in a deep, relieved breath.

"Sure thing, Luke. Do you want us to hold dinner?" Davy's comically worried face, as if that would be a horrible turn of events, surprised a laugh out of Luke, as it was meant to. Davy clapped a hard hand on Luke's shoulder, and they both enjoyed the feeling of relief and friendship.

"Nah, we'll be back before your second helping." When Joseph was settled in the passenger seat, his leg extended in front of him, Luke strode around to the driver's seat.

Cole had his arms crossed over his chest. "You want me to follow?"

There would be a wheelchair and help at the hospital. Still, Cole's show of support meant a lot. Luke shook his head.

"Later." Cole turned to follow Davy up the sidewalk and Luke started the car.

"Thanks. For not making a bigger deal of this," Joseph said in a low voice. "I was going to try to be less trouble, not more." He thumped his head against the headrest and closed his eyes.

"Accidents happen, man. There's not a whole lot you can do to get around that." Hearing the words come out of his mouth, the same words other kind people had said to him over the years about the loss of Alex, was shocking enough that Luke was distracted from the road for a split second.

He'd meant every word he'd said to Joseph even if he'd always had a hard time letting go of the guilt and grief of losing his brother in such a senseless way. It had been an accident. Luke hadn't pulled that trigger.

When Joseph shifted and gasped in pain, Luke snapped back to attention. He had to fight the urge to press hard on the accelerator again. *Not an emergency. Don't put others in danger.*

The hospital came into view as Luke glanced over at Joseph. "I mean it. Accidents are accidents, J. You hear me?"

His little brother finally met his stare and nodded. Some of the tension in Luke's gut eased. He braked in front of the ER doors, where a man in a suit, a doctor in a lab coat and a nurse with two orderlies and a wheel-chair were waiting.

Before Luke could run around to open the door, the orderlies were helping Joseph out of the passenger seat and into the wheelchair.

He was amazed and truly grateful for Holly Heights. Maybe for the first time. The small community had rallied round and he'd never forget it.

The man in the suit held out his hand. As Luke shook it, the man said, "I'm the hospital administrator. Rebecca Lincoln called me at home to let me know you were coming, so I thought I'd see if I could do anything." He motioned at Joseph. "She's sent us so many young people as volunteers that we are happy to have a chance to repay a small bit of her help. Besides, it's a slow night so far."

The doctor bent down to pull up Joseph's jeans. "We're going to need an X-ray. We'll start there." He stood and pointed at the Mustang.

The administrator nodded and said, "As soon as you move your car." Luke sprinted back to the driver's seat. This time, he pushed hard on the gas and screeched into the closest parking spot. Then he ran back up to the group that was already in motion.

Whatever he'd thought about small towns before, this trip to the hospital made up for a lot. At every step, the nurses were patient, the doctor was calm and the administrator hovered in the background.

While they waited for the technician to complete the X-ray, Luke realized he had a whole lot of people to repay in addition to his fellow police officers. Rebecca had called in favors on his behalf. Cole, Sarah and Will had shown up to help with a search because they were good people.

And Jen was the person who'd started the whole ball rolling. After he'd spoken to her like he had, it was hard to believe that she would have gone so far out of her way to help.

"I don't see anything broken," the doctor murmured as he studied the X-ray. "The swelling and bruising is bad, but no broken bones is good. We'll splint this. Give you crutches. A sprain like this will need some serious recovery. Ice for swelling. Over-the-counter pain killers should be enough, but keep me posted on the pain." The doctor nodded at the nurse, who bent to place the splint on Joseph's leg. "You're lucky your injuries weren't more severe. Unfortunately, now that the ankle's been weakened, you'll be prone to reinjure it. Whatever you did? Don't do that again."

Before he left, Luke offered his sincere thanks.

The nurse expounded on how to ice the ankle to help with swelling, how often and how many ibuprofen to take and what to be watching for. The administrator came back in. "Just got off the phone with your mother, Joseph. We're all set to discharge you."

Luke leaned in and said in a low voice, "What about all the paperwork? Insurance?"

The administrator held out a clipboard. "Sign by the *X*." Luke did that quickly and handed it back. "And we're done."

No way. There was no way it was that easy.

The administrator shrugged. "Rebecca and I handled it with a phone call. You're free to go tonight. Get Joseph home because you've got some very concerned people there."

Luke wasn't quite sure how it all happened so simply and quickly, but he wasn't complaining as he pulled the car back up in front of the ER's doors and helped load Joseph in.

When they were on the road for home, Joseph said, "So, how much trouble am I in?"

Luke sighed. He still wasn't sure how to talk to the kid, but he wasn't going to let that be an excuse anymore. "You know, I don't think you're in any trouble." He shook his head and stared hard at the road. "You were doing your best. This whole time, you've been doing your best. I told you that's all Mom expected."

"It ended in a trip to the hospital, Luke," Joseph said dryly. That made it easier to remember why he liked the kid.

"Accidents happen," Luke repeated. Then he took a deep breath. He was running out of time to make this work. It was now or never. "Do you know why I'm a cop?"

Joseph shook his head.

"You've seen the pictures with Alex, the first foster the Hollisters adopted. Well, when he was shot, I felt like it was my fault. He was in the wrong place at the wrong time. Because of me. The cops were the only ones who could get answers or justice." He glanced at Joseph to see that the kid was staring at him, his eyes wide. "And I could… I don't know, maybe my life would mean enough if I worked hard every day. For Alex."

Luke slowed as he came up on the subdivision.

"I never believed it when people said it was an accident, but I need you to understand that when I say to you that this was all an accident, I mean every word. You have nothing to feel guilty about or...whatever." Luke made the turn in and saw the cars still parked in front of his house. They'd answered the call for help, and no one had left until they learned how everything turned out. Good people. Jen and Sarah had connected his family to some very good folks.

"Think I'll ever be adopted into the family?" Joseph asked in a low voice. "I want to be a Hollister."

Luke stepped hard on the brakes and closed his eyes. The way the kid said it convinced him that this was at the heart of everything, Joseph's trouble fitting in at home and school and... Why hadn't he seen this before?

"Yes." Luke stopped at the curb behind the cars in front of his house. "Yes, of course. Mom's been struggling, but I'll make this happen, Joseph. You are a Hollister. To her, to me, and that's forever. Don't you even think for a second that Mari will let you go." Luke realized he needed to get as close to the house as he could with the patient, so he eased up to block Davy in the driveway and turned off the ignition. "When Alex broke it down for me, this new family thing made sense. I should have done that for you. I'm sorry. This isn't for a minute or a day, or until things change again. The Hollisters are forever, even if things change again. That's been true since I walked in the door, even through my wild times and losing Alex. You can trust that." He offered Joseph his hand. "I'm giving you my word that you'll be a Hollister before school is out."

Joseph grabbed his hand and squeezed. "Guess it's not anyone who would move to this place because they were worried about my safety."

Luke nodded. "Yeah. I know that's right, but after today, small-town living's growing on me."

Joseph sniffed. "Maybe we can go back to Austin soon. To visit."

Luke smiled as he watched Joseph's eyes sharpen. The kid could see his chance to twist the softy into some lucrative agreements. "Definitely," he said, chuckling.

"Maybe I could even drive your car," he said innocently, "because it's time I learned, don't you think?"

"To Austin? No way." Luke cleared his throat, and then added, "But somewhere with wide-open spaces and no traffic, like a parking lot, maybe."

Joseph wrinkled his nose. "Okay, but you're going to have to help me with the tree house. That place is a death trap and little Mari deserves better."

The twist of the trick he'd used to get Joseph to pick up his bicycle wasn't lost on Luke, but the effort was stellar and such a turn in attitude that it was easy to agree. "Okay, but you don't need to take her down there alone. If she clobbers you with her lightsaber, you'll be sorry."

Joseph was laughing as he opened the car door and banged and yanked and cursed under his breath until he managed to liberate the crutches from the backseat. "Deal."

Luke fought the urge to lift the kid up and instead crossed his arms over his chest as Joseph lurched down the driveway. The dark night was darker here on the edge of town. Luke could hear wind blowing in the trees and the faint trickle of water. Then a burst of laughter erupted from behind the front door.

"Sounds like they started the party without me," Joseph muttered. "What are the chances I can slip by and make it to my room unnoticed?"

"Zero. You need to go in and reassure Mom." Luke smiled as Joseph straightened his shoulders, prepared to do his manly duty.

Thank you, Alex.

Luke enjoyed seeing everyone crammed into the kitchen. Dirty dishes lined the counter and his mother dropped her apron near them as soon as Joseph paused in the doorway.

"My baby. I should have gone to the hospital. Those places are so cold, and the waiting..." She wrapped her arms around Joseph and squeezed until the kid squealed.

"Actually, we happen to have friends in high places who smoothed things over for us." Luke watched a pink flush spread across Rebecca's cheeks. Sarah's eyes narrowed but she shrugged a shoulder.

"And Will here has given me the name of

a good lawyer to help me get the adoption proceedings finalized." His mother bent her knees to stare into Joseph's eyes. "I'm sorry, Joseph. I'm too late with this, but we will make up for lost time. Walter would be put out with me so don't tell him, okay?" She blinked rapidly. "Joseph Hollister. That sounds right."

Joseph ducked his head. "You could call me Joey. But only you."

His mother was grinning as she squeezed him tightly again and she wrapped one arm around Luke's neck. "My boys. I'm so proud of you."

The warm glow in the center of his chest should be embarrassing. Luke was a grown man who'd seen and done some hard things.

A mother's pride and unconditional love should never be taken for granted.

"We should be going," Sarah said as she stood and slipped her hand in Will's. "I'm glad everything worked out okay."

Sarah seemed satisfied with that and tugged Will toward the door. Luke followed, determined to wipe his slate clean if he could. He wanted to make a new start in Holly Heights and everything started with Sarah.

Luke caught them at the edge of the yard. "Hey, Sarah."

He knew she was trying to get along when she didn't answer with a snide remark about his lurking or trying to catch her off guard. "I need to say thank you for coming to help."

"Jen asked. I answered. That's what friends do." She stared down at the ground. "But you're welcome. I'd have done the same if you'd asked."

Luke rubbed his chest, right over the spot where the ache was forming. Good people. Was the whole town made up of good people?

"I don't deserve that, but I'll take it."

She wrinkled her nose. "Can't deny that, but I've been on the receiving end of a lot of forgiveness and love that I never deserved. I guess I have a little to spare." She narrowed her eyes. "But if I hear of you doing anything to hurt my friend Jen, I will run you out of town myself." Her smile showed all of her teeth, but no friendliness to match. "Just so we understand how far the line between us has moved."

"I get that." Luke laughed as he glanced at Will, who was shaking his head in despair. "They're exciting, aren't they?"

Will sighed. "Unfortunately. Once you fall for one, you won't ever be the same."

"You're her brother. Don't you have some threatening to do?" Sarah asked.

"Has it gotten that serious?" Will asked as he squared off in front of Luke. There was no chance he was going to attempt to answer that question.

"Jen's going to forgive him for making her cry. It's that serious." Sarah tilted her head. "And this man made her *cry.*"

Luke thought he could take Will in a fair fight, but the ugly scowl on his face didn't seem to promise a fair fight. "Don't do that again. I've spent some time daydreaming about how I would break your nose for the way you treated Sarah. We'll get past that. It was a job. This will be personal." Will didn't back down until Luke nodded.

"My hero." Sarah batted her eyelashes. "Take me home, sweetie."

"Yes, dear," Will said as he held his truck door open. Sarah slid inside and they were laughing together as Will drove off.

They fit. Jen and her friends were smart and strong. Only smart and strong men could keep up with them.

So where did that leave him?

Luke studied the front of Jen's dark house and wondered when she'd left.

He was going to regret not having the opportunity to talk about every single minute of this day with her.

When had that happened?

CHAPTER NINETEEN

As soon as Will had scrambled up the hill to let them know about Joseph's accident and asked them to go back in the house so as not to make a fuss, Jen had retreated to Mari's room. Archie and Hope were watching anxiously as the little girl cried as if her heart was breaking.

Caught unprepared, Jen immediately knelt in front of Mari. "Joseph is okay, Mari. Luke has him and they're going to take him to the doctor for a checkup but he'll be home tonight." She hoped.

Mari swiped a hand across her eyes and shook her head wildly. Mari might not make much noise, but she cried with as much drama as she did everything else. Her hair was tangled, her eyes were red and Jen had to scramble to find a tissue for a runny nose.

This was why little kids were beyond her. She never had a tissue when she needed one.

But this little girl cried herself into a big mess. In this, she and Jen were kindred spirits.

"Tell me what's wrong," Jen said in a low voice. "Archie is worried."

Mari checked to see what the dog thought. Archie wrinkled his brow on cue.

"Joey will be mad. I broke my promise." Mari's lower lip trembled and Jen was desperate to avert continued tears.

"Joey will understand." Jen squeezed Mari's hands. "You are smarter than I am, Princess Mari. Sometimes we have to make hard decisions to keep the ones we love safe. You did that. You were so brave." And because of that, Joseph was going to come home instead of being lost overnight.

The frown on Mari's face suggested she wasn't convinced, so Jen added, "I bet when you see Joseph again, he gives you a huge thank-you kiss." Jen wrinkled her nose as if she agreed with Mari that that might be awful, but made a mental note to make sure that Joseph did exactly that.

Mari ruffled Archie's ears and leaned against the edge of the bed. She wasn't sure, but she was coming around.

Jen eased over to the massive beanbag that

took up the only clear corner of the room and tried not to remember all the clutter surrounding her. "I am going to show you a secret." She waggled her eyebrows. "Did you know books are magic?"

Mari raised one eyebrow in response.

This kid was hilarious, but laughing wasn't the best choice at this point.

"It's true. Find your favorite book—" Jen waved her hand vaguely around the mess "—and let's read it." Then she plopped down, startled when two massive purple wings billowed from the sides of the beanbag. Jen squirmed to get a better look. One gigantic butterfly. That's what the beanbag was. And every shift she made caused a flutter of wings. "That's awesome." Maybe she should have had Mari contribute to the decorating of her house. A chair like this might make grading homework fun.

Mari wandered closer and held out a book. Jen tried not to wince at the stickiness of the cover or the way half of the spine had been... chewed off? "All right. Here's the magic." Jen patted the bag and before she was prepared, Mari launched herself down to land with a thump right next to Jen. She'd rolled over and rested her head on Jen's shoulder before Jen had quite adjusted to the fact that it was happening, but it was…okay.

When Hope and Archie arranged themselves carefully along the edge of the beanbag with their chins hanging over Jen's dangling feet, Jen was pretty sure she'd die in that beanbag without a rescue. There was no way she was going to get herself out, but Mari had stopped crying.

"Now, the magic of a favorite book is that it can make bad days go away," Jen said as she opened the book. "A princess who drives a tow truck? That is even better than this chair." She tried to inch to a more comfortable spot, heard both dogs huff and decided she was fine where she was. "And her dog looks like Archie." The attraction to the dog with one eye made perfect sense. The princess had found her missing piece.

At some point, her entire audience drifted off to sleep and Jen quickly finished the book. It wasn't every day that she got to read about a princess with a job. She appreciated Mari's reading choices.

Then she dropped the book behind her head on the floor and stared up at the ceiling, wondering how Joseph was, how Luke was recovering, and whether anyone would ever come to rescue *her*. Her eyes slowly drifted shut as she realized there were worse things than falling asleep in a magic beanbag under a pile of love.

The sudden absence of Mari's weight took a minute to register in Jen's foggy brain, but she was blinking her eyes slowly open when she saw Luke lean carefully over Mari's bed to deposit her under the covers. Pins and needles in her feet made it impossible to jump up and hit the road before Luke had a chance to corner her, but even if she'd managed to stand, his expression would have frozen her in place.

"Everything okay? How's Joseph?" Jen asked as she tried to fluff her limp hair and pretend that it was perfectly fine that the butterfly beanbag was going to be her final resting place.

"Bad sprain, but I think…" Luke sighed. "That's what it took for us to talk. Like you begged me to do. We talked on the way home and everything is so simple now and so important and for the first time I understand what I'm doing here with him, in this place, and it's just… I had to be scared out of my mind to open my eyes." He braced his hands on his hips. "I shouldn't have spoken to you like I did. You didn't have to do this, help me and comfort Mari and call for reinforcements and… It's all so much."

Jen nodded. She knew what he meant. "Us independent types, we like to be self-sufficient. That means no one can let us down or surprise us." She looked around Mari's room. "I guess we both learned something tonight."

"What did you learn?" Luke asked as he stepped closer.

"That it's nice to have the people who love you by your side." Jen licked her lips. "And that good people deserve more space in my heart than I've given them in the past. Sarah came. Rebecca came. Will and Cole and each one of them could have called on more friends and knowing that I wasn't alone in my worry helped me."

"And my mother. And Mari." Luke stared hard at her. "And the dogs were obviously very worried."

Jen laughed. "They were. I had to read them to sleep, too."

Luke tilted his head. "All that's sweet. Doesn't explain why you're still here."

"I couldn't get out of the beanbag." Jen held out both hands. "Unless you help, you better be ready to feed me four square meals a day."

Luke grunted as he lifted her easily to stand.

"Not a flattering sound," Jen muttered as she yanked her sweater down over her jeans and tried not to grab him as she teetered on top of the leaning tower of toys.

"You could have left all the noise and trouble behind as soon as we carried Joseph back up." Luke was doing it again, cataloging the details of her face and body language. There was no reason to lie.

"I couldn't, not while Mari was upset or until I'd seen for myself that Joseph was okay or while your mother might need me." Jen ran a hand through her hair. All that was true. He would buy it.

"And?" He dipped his chin, the corners of his mouth twitching.

So he wasn't going to buy it.

"I wanted to see you." There. It had taken every bit of the bravado she'd learned to pretend she had in high school but she'd said it aloud. "Crazy, right?"

He pretended to think hard on it. "Not when you take into account that I'm a seriously good kisser."

Jen snorted and then held a finger over her lips as Mari kicked out of the blankets. "So modest, too."

"And bossy and hardheaded and in serious need of some patience and practice talking to kids." Luke squeezed his eyes shut. "This turned out well, but what if it hadn't? My first instinct was to let the kid learn his lesson wherever he was. How would I have lived with myself if I'd done that?"

Jen could hear the guilt and worry in his voice and that was when she realized the key to Luke Hollister. No matter how hard he seemed on the outside, his heart was tender for his family.

If she was a hard shell protecting old soft spots, Luke was, too.

They were doomed.

"You need justice too bad, Officer. You would have rushed after him no matter what." Jen smiled as he frowned at her. "If only to explain to him how wrong he was."

He narrowed his eyes. "That does sound like me."

Jen was still laughing when he pressed his lips against hers. There, in the shadows of Mari's cluttered, cramped bedroom, it was impossible not to lean closer to enjoy every sweet second of their connection.

When he stepped back, the gleam in his gaze was impossible to ignore. "Think you can forgive me for being wrong, wrong, wrong?"

"This time?" Jen pretended to scoff. "Okay, but don't press your luck with me again."

He shrugged a shoulder. "Yeah, we both know that I'll be asking that question again. Soon. Years of experience doesn't fade."

Jen sighed. "Luckily for you, I have as many years' practice putting people in their place. I can show you yours."

His low laugh filled her with the joyful anticipation that she'd wondered if she'd ever find.

"Gotta go home. Tomorrow is the day we Halloween my house up." She raised an eyebrow. "Bring your power tools and your entourage. I'll put you to work."

"Fine, crazy lady. We'll enjoy the show you

put on tomorrow." Luke held her hand as she crossed the cluttered floor, Hope trailing behind them.

When she made it out into the hallway, she found that her friends had bailed without saying goodbye.

"No one wanted to wake you." Connie Hollister was seated on the couch with her arms around Joseph and Renita while Camila, a late arrival, was bustling around to pick up. "You were drooling." Her smile was cute. Jen would never tell her that.

She shot a glance over her shoulder at Luke, who was communicating deeply with Hope and completely skipping the conversation.

"Joseph, I'm glad you're home." Jen gently rested a hand on his shoulder. "Tomorrow, make sure that Mari understands that sometimes promises to keep secrets have to be broken. She's worried."

He nodded. "Sure thing. I should never have asked her not to tell. It was dumb, but I wanted that tree house to be our thing, something I could do for her." He sighed. "Guess I'll have to tear it down."

Everyone turned to look at Luke, who

frowned. "It's dangerous to have two kids down there by the creek."

"Not if they have a sturdy tree house, let people know where they are, always go together and take their favorite adults with them to sit in the chairs that I hauled down there," his mother said. "Really, Luke, isn't it about time you got on board with the project?"

Jen raised her eyebrows at him. It looked like his weekends were booked for the foreseeable future. Luke held his hands up. "Fine, but we've got to help Jen decorate for this contest thing. I already promised."

Jen pursed her lips and considered explaining that it wasn't so much as a promise but a likely excuse now that he needed one.

Joseph straightened in his seat. "Oh, I meant to tell you. I heard some gossip. Some kids were talking about the best house on the map, can't remember the name, but instead of a witch this year, they're doing a twisted fairy tale."

"Oh, no, that's what we were doing," Jen told them. She pulled out her phone, checked the time and decided Chloe would still be up. This was an emergency. Her general needed to start thinking. "All those rentals. We'll have to scramble now."

"We will be happy to help. We are good in a crisis," Connie Hollister said with a knowing grin. "I think you will fit in fine."

Before she could comment, Luke was urging her toward the door. They were silent as they walked up her driveway. "You didn't have to see me home. I've got this dangerous dog for protection." They both looked down at Hope, who was leaning against Jen's leg. Her dog did not like the dark.

"Try not to let fitting in keep you up tonight," Luke said as he pressed another too-brief kiss against her lips. "These Hollisters sneak up on you and before you know it, you can't imagine life without them."

Jen stepped inside and turned to watch Luke slowly walk back home, his head tilted up to study the stars.

"Yeah, they already have." Jen wasn't certain what the future looked like exactly, but it wasn't hard to picture Luke in it.

CHAPTER TWENTY

Halloween

THE SCRAMBLE TO come up with a new theme after Cece had scooped hers had paid off. Chloe's brainchild, an undead picnic, had worked in all the props they'd managed to find at the party rental places and was easy to split into a ghost party for the little kids, complete with famous dead literary types like Dumbledore, and a vampire ambush for the older trick-or-treaters.

As soon as they'd mentioned vampires, Mari had bared her teeth and whispered, in the creepiest voice Jen had ever heard from a real live human, *Blood*.

Renita had confessed she might have spent too much time in Forks with the *Twilight* crew, but Mari promised to be a vegetarian vampire and hand out the hot dog severed fingers that Rebecca had slaved over.

And if the screams and shrieks she could hear coming from the vicinity of her house were any clue, the party was still going strong. Jen stretched out her legs and crossed both arms behind her head as she stared up at the sky through the canopy of the trees. The creek was bubbling and here she could breathe.

Before Luke could say a thing, she sighed. "Did they send you to find me?"

He climbed up on the tree house platform, scooted over to lie next to her, and leaned back. "Nah. I missed you."

She twisted over to stare at him. He was watching her. "Really. In all that noise, you missed me?"

She didn't believe it. "How did you find me, anyway?"

He tapped his chest. "Detective. It's what I do."

Jen laughed. "Right. I'll have to work harder to cover my tracks if I want to stay hidden."

"The judging committee's been and gone. Aren't you anxious to see if you've knocked Cece from her throne?" Luke asked. "The bloodthirst for revenge totally works with this theme, by the way."

When she'd gotten into the contest, it had been about the need for something else to fill her time and a whole lot of bragging rights. Now, the bragging rights would be sweet, but her time had been filled with the family across the road. She and Joseph worked on math. The first time he'd brought home a test with a bright red A marked across the top, Connie Hollister had invited her over to enjoy her famous homemade ice cream.

That ice cream was so good it was much easier to imagine being nice to Connie Hollister in the future.

Mari had decided Chloe hung the moon and stars so both weekends her niece had been over to refine their Halloween concept, Mari had been her tiny, fierce shadow.

"Did we win?" Jen asked lazily. She'd been pretty sure they would, but at this point, things were too good to be bent out of shape if they hadn't. There was always next year.

Luke dangled a blue ribbon close to her face. "First place. Sarah wants you to wear this every day next week, so that everyone, including Cece, can see you do your victory lap."

Jen sat up and accepted the ribbon. "Winning. It feels good."

"So you can imagine how the party has taken on a new celebratory atmosphere. You're missing it." Luke sat up and shifted close enough to slide an arm under her shoulders. Jen rested against him.

"Why do I feel like I'm right where I need to be, then?" she asked, smiling at him.

"You don't like crowds or noise or mess." He sighed. "That's all I bring with me."

Jen wrinkled her nose. "Well, not all." She ran a hand down his chest. "You do look nice in your uniform, too. Besides, I can take control of your noise and mess. Watch me."

Luke bent his head to study her lips. "You think you've got what it takes to whip the Hollister house into shape?"

"I'm a teacher." She tapped her chest the same way he had. "Bring order out of chaos. It's what I do."

His chuckle went all the way through her to settle into her bones. Life was good.

She wouldn't change a thing.

EPILOGUE

Summer, Andes Mountains, Peru

JEN WASN'T SURE agreeing to come to see the villages where Stephanie and Daniel worked and to serve as bridesmaid at their marriage ceremony in the village church was a decision she'd live to regret. Flying was no problem. High, twisty roads like these? She was scared to death they were about to sail right over the side of the cliff, the one with no guardrail.

"Get closer to Daniel." Jen leaned forward in the seat to urge Luke to follow directions. Blackmailing him into coming along? She didn't regret that for a second. She wouldn't trust anyone else behind the wheel.

He replied, "I won't be able to see if we get any closer. The dust. Besides, he's watching us."

"Daniel should be watching the road, not us," Jen muttered.

"We're nearly there," Cole said from the backseat. "It's almost four. That was Daniel's guess on arrival time." He looked over at Rebecca, who'd managed to sleep through the flight and most of the road trip.

Just as they reached a tight bend in the road, Rebecca straightened, rubbed her eyes and said, "Oh, no. No, no, no. We aren't there yet?" Her plaintive wail would have made Jen smile but she was beginning to share the sentiment.

"Almost," Cole said softly and Jen glanced over her shoulder to see Cole wrap his arms around Rebecca.

"You know, I'm going to need that arm again someday. If your fingernails go any deeper, you'll hit bone," Luke said. Jen glanced down to where she'd wrapped her fingers around his wrist. Unclenching them took work.

"Nice civil ceremony at the courthouse. That's what they should have done," Jen grumbled.

The truck crossed a tiny stream and began to climb; Jen could tell they were getting close.

When they finally stopped, Jen was ready

to have her feet on solid ground again. She ignored Luke's frown as he came around to open the door for her. It was one of the tiny power struggles they fought day-to-day. She enjoyed his notion of gentlemanly behavior but it was fun to tweak that sensibility now and then.

Stephanie held her arms out. "Isn't this place gorgeous?"

Jen braced her hands in the small of her back and stretched as she turned in a slow circle. The buildings were cinder block and painted pink or green or gray, but everywhere she looked, she could see mountains. For as far as the eye could see, there were nothing but rolling mountains until in the distance, sunshine beamed between the hilltop range and lit the center of town.

"Amazing," Rebecca said slowly. "I never imagined…"

Jen knew exactly what she meant. No matter how many photos they saw on Steph's Facebook page or the blog she'd set up for HealthyAmericas, nothing could prepare them for this.

"Let's get the bags inside," Daniel said, "before it gets pitch black out here." While the men gathered the few dusty bags they'd brought along, Stephanie waved anxiously. "Come on, I can't wait to show you guys this church."

Without electricity, it was difficult to see the details carved into the wood, but all the candles did the job. A small woman was lighting and humming as she went.

This was going to be the most special place in the world when one of her best friends married the brother of another best friend. How sweet. It touched a corner of Jen's heart she didn't even know she had.

"Beautiful, Steph," Rebecca said in a hushed voice. "I can see why you wanted to start your life together here."

"This is where it all began for me and Daniel," Stephanie said with a sniff. "Or where it began *again*, maybe. Have I ever thanked you for moving that stupid dart, you jerk?" On a dare, Stephanie had put on a blindfold and tossed a dart at a world map to determine where her first trip as a new millionaire would be. In an effort to play matchmaker, Rebecca had moved the dart to the remote village where her brother was working and sworn Jen to secrecy.

Rebecca brushed off her shoulders. "No sweat. A little planning, that's all. I knew it would work out like this."

Sarah had been hanging back but now she said, "Somehow, I can totally believe that you planned to win the lottery, set up your best friend and then force yourself to fly over in a stupor so you could see the fruit of all your labor."

Rebecca shrugged. "Maybe I should have thought about the travel piece a little longer."

Stephanie waved at the woman who was watching them curiously and they stepped back out into the town square.

"We could make it a double wedding," Sarah said in a singsong voice. "Rebecca and Cole could get married here and then go to a justice of the peace like they're threatening to do when we get back home."

Rebecca rebuffed the notion. "Nope. My parents would kill me. I'm pretty sure they're put out because Daniel wouldn't postpone this ceremony so it didn't conflict with their state golf championship for seniors and whatnot." She sighed. "But the party I'm going to throw for my brother and his happy bride when they come to visit is the only thing keeping my brother safe from our parents' wrath. I've been saving recipes for weeks."

Jen focused in on Sarah. "What about you and Will? Seems like that engagement ring entitles you to the step-right-up wedding ceremony, too."

Sarah studied the modest diamond that she and Will had compromised on. "Chloe would never forgive me if I rob her of the event-planning challenge of her lifetime. Besides, she's my maid of honor. The show can't go on without her."

When all three of her friends turned to stare at her, Jen coughed. "Single lady here. Back away from the single lady."

Anxious to get a little space from the giggling and teasing, Jen said, "I'm going to go explore. I'll meet you back here."

"Hey," Rebecca called, "watch your step. It's a long way down."

"Yes, mother," Jen muttered as she navigated the cracked sidewalk. She could go downhill, the easy choice, or she could head up, way, way up to look out over the mountains. Jen was wheezing by the time she stopped climbing and saw Luke leaning against a rock wall, the view of forever, nothing but mountains behind him. "Whew. You are definitely going to get to carry me to where we're staying, hero."

He flexed his arm. "No problem, little lady."

Jen wrinkled her nose, but the view robbed her of any sarcasm. "I never imagined a place like this."

He nodded silently and Jen was so happy to be standing next to him in the silence, while they looked out at the horizon, gorgeous and unforgettable. She slipped her hand in his and relaxed when he squeezed.

"It's amazing what can happen when I say a brave yes instead of a fearful no," she said softly.

Luke glanced down at her. "Funny you should mention that. The big questions in life take some bravery, don't they?"

Jen frowned as she tried to figure out where he was heading. "Uh-huh," she said slowly.

"Like, if I wanted to ask you the *big* question, the one that leads to figuring out what we do with the rest of our lives, how we build on this thing, whether we want to be the next generation of foster Hollisters..." Luke bent his head closer. "What would you say?"

The attack of nerves surprised Jen. This was a question she'd been looking at out of the corner of her eye for weeks, too afraid to stare it head-on, but then she'd come to this place and wouldn't have been happy without him here. "I'd say…" Jen licked her dry lips. "I dare you."

His rough chuckle made the butterflies in her stomach flutter.

"You better not be messing with me," she said in her best, mean teacher's voice.

He stared into the distance. "Well, I'd planned this big deal, at the airport, when we got home, so my mother would be there and the kids. There's a banner. Joseph was going to see about bringing a boom box to play something romantic…"

Jen leaned closer. "You are. You are messing with me."

Luke held out his hand. Even in the shadows, she could see the wink of a diamond.

"What are we going to do with the rest of our lives?"

Jen covered her mouth with one hand and stared hard at the ring. She wanted it. She wanted to figure it all out with Luke.

"Fight a little. Laugh a lot more. The rest,

we'll decide together." He smiled at her. "My mother will drive you nuts with talk of foster kids. Fair warning."

Jen took a deep breath. "I think… I might be the kind of person who was meant to be a foster parent. We'll get the most sarcastic teenagers, and I'll teach them math and all the wisdom I've picked up."

Luke ran a finger over her brow. "I see you do have it figured out. That's good. I was afraid I'd have to do more persuading. I'm getting a handle on being a big brother. Maybe it's time for a new challenge."

Jen held out her hand and closed her fingers around the ring.

"She said yes," Sarah called out, which drew her and Luke's attention to where her three best friends were watching the entire conversation.

"So much for privacy," Jen muttered.

"Better get used to it," Luke said with a smile as he pressed his lips to hers.

* * * * *

LARGER-PRINT BOOKS!

GET 2 FREE
LARGER-PRINT NOVELS
PLUS 2 FREE
MYSTERY GIFTS

Love Inspired®

Larger-print novels are now available...

LARGER-PRINT BOOKS!

GET 2 FREE
LARGER-PRINT NOVELS
PLUS 2 FREE
MYSTERY GIFTS

Love Inspired®

SUSPENSE

RIVETING INSPIRATIONAL ROMANCE

Larger-print novels are now available...

LISLP15

WESTERN WP PROMISES

YES! Please send me **The Western Promises Collection** in Larger Print. This collection begins with 3 FREE books and 2 FREE gifts (gifts valued at approx. $14.00 retail) in the first shipment, along with the other first 4 books from the collection! If I do not cancel, I will receive 8 monthly shipments until I have the entire 51-book Western Promises collection. I will receive 2 or 3 FREE books in each shipment and I will pay just $4.99 US/ $5.89 CDN for each of the other four books in each shipment, plus $2.99 for shipping and handling per shipment. *If I decide to keep the entire collection, I'll have paid for only 32 books, because 19 books are FREE! I understand that accepting the 3 free books and gifts places me under no obligation to buy anything. I can always return a shipment and cancel at any time. My free books and gifts are mine to keep no matter what I decide.

272 HCN 3070 472 HCN 3070

Name _____ (PLEASE PRINT) _____

Address _____ Apt. #

City _____ State/Prov. _____ Zip/Postal Code

Signature (if under 18, a parent or guardian must sign)

Mail to the **Reader Service:**
IN U.S.A.: P.O. Box 1867, Buffalo, NY 14240-1867
IN CANADA: P.O. Box 609, Fort Erie, Ontario L2A 5X3

* Terms and prices subject to change without notice. Prices do not include applicable taxes. Sales tax applicable in N.Y. Canadian residents will be charged applicable taxes. This offer is limited to one order per household. All orders subject to approval. Credit or debit balances in a customer's account(s) may be offset by any other outstanding balance owed by or to the customer. Please allow 4 to 6 weeks for delivery. Offer available while quantities last. Offer not available to Quebec residents.

LARGER-PRINT BOOKS!
GET 2 FREE LARGER-PRINT NOVELS PLUS
2 FREE GIFTS!

HARLEQUIN *super romance*

More Story...More Romance

YES! Please send me 2 FREE LARGER-PRINT Harlequin® Superromance® novels and my 2 FREE gifts (gifts are worth about $10). After receiving them, if I don't wish to receive any more books, I can return the shipping statement marked "cancel." If I don't cancel, I will receive 4 brand-new novels every month and be billed just $5.94 per book in the U.S. or $6.24 per book in Canada. That's a savings of at least 12% off the cover price! It's quite a bargain! Shipping and handling is just 50¢ per book in the U.S. or 75¢ per book in Canada.* I understand that accepting the 2 free books and gifts places me under no obligation to buy anything. I can always return a shipment and cancel at any time. Even if I never buy another book, the two free books and gifts are mine to keep forever.

132/332 HDN GHVC

Name   (PLEASE PRINT)

Address   Apt. #

City   State/Prov.   Zip/Postal Code

Signature (if under 18, a parent or guardian must sign)

Mail to the Reader Service:
IN U.S.A.: P.O. Box 1867, Buffalo, NY 14240-1867
IN CANADA: P.O. Box 609, Fort Erie, Ontario L2A 5X3

Want to try two free books from another line?
Call 1-800-873-8635 today or visit www.ReaderService.com.

* Terms and prices subject to change without notice. Prices do not include applicable taxes. Sales tax applicable in N.Y. Canadian residents will be charged applicable taxes. Offer not valid in Quebec. This offer is limited to one order per household. Not valid for current subscribers to Harlequin Superromance Larger-Print books. All orders subject to credit approval. Credit or debit balances in a customer's account(s) may be offset by any other outstanding balance owed by or to the customer. Please allow 4 to 6 weeks for delivery. Offer available while quantities last.

Your Privacy—The Reader Service is committed to protecting your privacy. Our Privacy Policy is available online at www.ReaderService.com or upon request from the Reader Service.

We make a portion of our mailing list available to reputable third parties that offer products we believe may interest you. If you prefer that we not exchange your name with third parties, or if you wish to clarify or modify your communication preferences, please visit us at www.ReaderService.com/consumerschoice or write to us at Reader Service Preference Service, P.O. Box 9062, Buffalo, NY 14240-9062. Include your complete name and address.

HSRLP15